DEAD
EASY

Phillip DePoy

A DELL BOOK

A Dell Book
Published by
Dell Publishing
A division of Random House, Inc.
1540 Broadway
New York, New York 10036

For information, address Dell Publishing,
New York, New York.

Dell® is a registered trademark of Random House, Inc., and the colophon is a trademark of Random House, Inc.

ISBN: 0-440-23643-6

Printed in the United States of America

Published simultaneously in Canada

October 2000

10 9 8 7 6 5 4 3 2 1
OPM

*For
Heather Heath
with her new life;
Frances Kuffel
with her new attitude;
Tracy Devine
with her new office:*

*No more three A.M. calls,
but you know what Lao-tzu says:
easy come, easy go.*

CONTENTS

DEAD
EASY

1

EASY DOWN PAYMENT

I cut the dirty butcher paper, and a severed hand slapped the sticky floor with a sucking sound. Only a tiny band of gold made it seem remotely human. I was thinking that a shroud ought to be soft and white, not crackling and brown. I was thinking about that ring, too: how the sound of that hand broke the holiness of the night the way death breaks a marriage vow. I just didn't know why I was thinking that—yet. It was four in the midsummer morning at Easy.

Dally caught her breath, then sat on a stool.

I looked up at her. "Is this why you called me?"

"Did I know what was in there? No." She blinked once. "Was I worried about it? Yes."

"Any idea where this came from?" I searched the package.

"Oh, I'm pretty sure it's a package from home." She sounded like a zombie.

"I see." I rubbed my eyes. Why she thought the thing was from home, I didn't want to ask.

I had just fallen asleep when I'd gotten her call, only thirty minutes earlier. She'd been in a weird mood for quite a while, and things between us had been uncharacteristically strained. But I only have three rules to live by, and one of them is that whenever Dalliance Oglethorpe calls, I come. Later for the other rules—but they both involve her too.

Home. Invisible, Georgia. That's where we grew up—what we got out of. The town was so small it didn't make the state maps, and you couldn't even see it from the highway. It's in south Georgia, which is usually flat, but Invisible is surrounded by little hills and old pines—unless you're standing in the middle of it, you can't see it. Hence the name. We'd always tried not to talk too much about it.

So even though I thought better of asking why she thought the package was from *that* place, I heard myself say:

"What makes you think that?"

She only looked away, confirming that I'd been wrong to ask.

"Well," I told her, getting to my feet, trying to change the mood, "it's not your birthday, so I have to wonder what's the occasion. It's got to be something important—must have been a lot of postage."

"No postage." She shook her head. "It came special delivery."

"Yeah"—I glanced back down at the package—"I guess it did, at that. You didn't happen to see who brought it in?"

"God, no."

"You were here all alone?"

She nodded.

"But you hadn't locked up?"

Another nod.

"That means to me that somebody was watching, knew just exactly when to slip in, plop this down, and take off. My guess is that you were back in your office checking the totals for the night?"

She pressed her lips tighter.

"Why wasn't the door locked?"

"Hal was anxious to leave. Had a date. I said I'd lock

up. I was just taking the cash box back to the safe. Before I locked the doors. I heard a noise. I thought it was Hal. I yelled out. No answer. I came in. There it was."

Unusually short sentences for our Ms. Oglethorpe. She was knocked all the way back, it seemed, by her little gift.

"Okay." I took in a deep breath. "Do we open the package the rest of the way?"

"Let's see what we've got." She was breathing funny. I thought I should humor her.

I knelt back down. There was nothing else in the nightmare Christmas package except for an envelope, unaddressed.

"Care to see what this says?" I sat on the floor.

She nodded again. She would not, under ordinary circumstances, have been a woman of so few words.

I ripped open the envelope, pulled the note out, and read it aloud. "Easy payment plan: installment one."

2

LYING AFTER MIDNIGHT

"What the hell does that mean?" I didn't much care for sitting on that sticky barroom floor with a severed hand, so my mood was cranked a little.

"I don't know." But I could tell she was lying.

Which made that night a red-letter occasion. The last time Dalliance Oglethorpe had lied to me, she'd been eleven years old, and Halloween candy had been involved.

What's more, she didn't even seem to know that I'd realized she was lying. She was too preoccupied.

I stood. "I'll start first thing in the morning."

"That's okay, Flap," she said quickly.

"Excuse me? It's *okay*?"

"I'll take care of it, I mean." Her voice was empty.

"Hm." I folded my arms. "And I say 'hm' because in the one hundred and seventy-three years that we've known each other, this would mark the first time I haven't helped you out in a situation of this sort, wouldn't it?"

She flashed a look in my direction. "Tell me when's the last time you unwrapped a human hand in this bar, and I'll buy you a case of that Cantenac-Brown you're always hollering about."

"That's a safe offer," I told her.

"So I guess your similar-situation theory holds no water, then." Her voice could have chipped ice.

I stood my ground. "Lying and touchy both inside of two minutes—this is not at all the woman I know."

"Lying?" Her voice rose a little.

"You know why this little package is here," I told her calmly. "Don't tell me you don't."

She looked away. "Flap, could we cut the coolest-detective-in-the-world show just for tonight. I've got somebody handling a little problem for me. This is connected. I didn't ask you about it because it's no big deal. It's not worth your time, and there's no money in it."

"Hm." I shifted my weight. "First place: I've got more time than I know what to do with. Second: You know I don't care about the money. But, third: It's your world. I just rent. So if you need me out of this, then I'm gone."

"It's nothing, Flap. Really." Her voice was getting tired, and her eyes still wouldn't meet mine.

"All right, kiddo." I glanced down at the package. "You tell me a chopped-off hand doesn't signify, then it doesn't. Want me to do something with that, at least?"

"Just leave it." She wouldn't meet my eyes.

"Okay." If you'd asked me at exactly that moment, I'd have had to tell you I was feeling something very close to jealousy. "Somebody else'll clean up."

She nodded once.

"So why'd you call me?"

"Force of habit. Wish I hadn't."

I buttoned my coat. "Same here, as it turns out."

I took one quick look around the place, I don't know why, and then headed out the door without a bit more ado.

I heard her heavy sigh. But I didn't turn around.

3

SHADOWS

I only took three or four steps in the parking lot before I saw the other guy in the shadows.

I could tell he was watching me. I was also fairly certain he had no idea that I knew he was there. I shoved my hands in my pockets and headed up Ponce. Within half a block I ducked between a couple of buildings and checked to make sure no one was following. Then I beat it back to the Easy parking lot. What the hell. I was up, and not likely to go right back to sleep even if I went straight home. And curiosity is actually one of my better attributes.

The guy was nowhere to be seen. But the front door to Easy was ajar, and I knew that Dally would have locked it tight behind me if something hadn't stopped her. I didn't want to panic, but I was pretty certain that shadow boy was in the club.

I hustled up to the door and peeked in the crack.

I could hear their voices, and I could see the back of the guy's head. It was obvious Dally wasn't in trouble—as obvious as it was that she knew the guy. When he bent over to pick up the Addams Family delivery, I finally caught a good look. I knew him too.

He was none other than Risky Jakes—a cliché right out of a B movie. Jakes was a common enough thug for hire. Nice guy at the end of the day, as far as I knew. I'd heard of him since the old days, when the Yankee musicians' union had tried to strong-arm the Atlanta club scene—with scant success. You had a couple of tough guys from Jersey who thought they could push around some redneck bar owner and get results, only to discover the true meaning of *whup-ass*. Because you have not been stomped at all until you've been stomped by a good ol' boy—drunk, mean, doing it for fun, and somewhere, genetically, still sussing out some kind of revenge for the "War of Northern Aggression" and the utter devastation of "Reconstruction"—the most perversely named historical phenomenon in America. But I digress.

Jakes encountered that particular club scene once, quickly saw the lay of the land, and got out of the music industry altogether. He stayed in Atlanta, though—fell in love with humid air. That's the line of reasoning I always remembered from the guy: "I think I must be some kind of a tropical thing, set down in New Jersey by mistake. Thank God I finally made it to Atlanta—it's much better."

As far as I knew, no one had ever explained to him that Georgia—while hot enough in the summer to drive long-haired dogs mad—was not, strictly speaking, a legal part of the tropics.

His parents had actually given him the name Risky— they'd met at the blackjack tables in Las Vegas. The guy hated his name, and most people knew him as *Jersey*.

And there he was, bad Kmart cloth shoes, loud Hawaiian shirt, too-tight Sansabelt slacks and all, talking to Ms. Oglethorpe.

"It's a hand," he pointed out to Dally.

"Damn it, Jersey, I know it's a hand." I could barely hear the next sentence: "It's not his . . . is it?"

"His?" He seemed to think that was a pretty good joke. "Naw—unless he's lost it in the last couple of hours."

"You were supposed to keep me apprised."

"Of this?"

"Of the situation. I was supposed to know where he was and what he was up to all the time. I shouldn't be surprised like this."

"Jeez, Ms. Oglethorpe"—he took a quick look back at the package—"I think anybody would be surprised to get a thing like this."

"Shut up about the hand."

"It's a pretty hard thing to ignore."

"I mean it, Jakes," she told him tensely. "You should have told me he was around. He did have something to do with this . . ."

"Oh, I'd expect he had everything to do wit this, all right." Jakes's head gave a little involuntary twitch. It was a habit of his when he was perturbed.

He claimed it was only a nervous tic he could get rid of anytime he wanted to, but he'd had it as long as I'd known him. Maybe he'd kept it on purpose. I'd seen him pull his pistol immediately after a twitch like the one he'd just exhibited, and that's the sort of rumor a tough guy likes running around about him: "He's okay until his head jumps, but when it does, brother, take off. That's when he starts shooting."

He did not, however, pull his gun on Dally. Nor did he stoop to the dead hand.

"I'm just as messed up as you are," he continued, "about this thing. I thought he was going back home."

Dally's voice was colder than the chunk that sank the *Titanic*. "He doesn't trust anybody else enough to do a thing like this."

"Yeah. I can see what you're saying: He delivered it here in person. Whose hand is it, do you know?"

"How would I know a thing like that?" Good. She

was finally getting irritated with the guy, which was promising, I thought. "I'm just glad it's not his."

"It don't look familiar?" He was clinical.

"The hand?"

"It's got a ring on it."

"I know it's got a . . . damn it, Jakes. You're the next best thing to worthless."

"But I'm here," he said right away, in his defense.

"Uh-huh." She wasn't, apparently, comforted that much by his presence.

"What I mean to say," he continued, "is that I am here—I am not Flap Tucker."

"You certainly aren't that." And the disgust in her voice made me a lot less angry with her than I had been.

"Who is?" he agreed.

Which made a guy like me proud: to be so well thought of after four in the morning—under the circumstances.

"I'm saying this only makes me think," Jersey needled.

"Is it at all possible that you could be a bigger idiot? That's what I'm thinking." Her voice had grown dangerous. "You steer clear of figuring out anything and you'll be better off."

"I was just wondering," he kept on, ignoring the warning bells. "And when I'm done, my conclusion will be that Mr. Tucker don't know about . . . him."

"Mr. Tucker's been here tonight. He knows all about the hand."

"I know that." His voice was harder too. "I was watching outside. I'm not exactly the sap you take me for. I heard you argue. I saw him leave. I'm not talking about the hand. I'm talking about the guy who brung it to you."

"Oh." That's all. And considerably less gutsy than any of the previous syllables.

"Which is a real switch in my little world," Jersey finished.

"What is?" Back to the zombie delivery.

"I'm surprised to know something that Flap Tucker don't. I think it's one of the seven seals of what you call your apocalypse."

I wouldn't have taken Jersey Jakes to be the sort of person who'd be up on his Bible enough to make a jibe of that sort. It still didn't prepare me for Ms. Oglethorpe's response.

"Well," she said, sitting down on the closest bar-stool, "it certainly signals the end of something in this world."

4

THE SEVENTH SEAL

By two the next afternoon I was up and dressed. There was jasmine something-or-other in the air, and magnolias were opened all the way down Ponce.

I don't usually start my day at Easy, but it's not entirely unknown. The darkness of the place temporarily blinded me when I first opened up the door, but it only took a second or two for my eyes to adjust.

Hal slapped the bar the way he always did when I came in.

"Dr. Tucker."

"Is the boss in?"

Hal looked away, cleaning something that was already spotless. "She . . . she kind of ducked into her office when she saw you come in."

"I see."

"She just came in, Flap," he tried to explain. "She's going through the mail."

"I need food, Hal." I decided to let him off the hook.

"You need the cassoulet." He was relieved. "Marcia made it special."

Ever since I'd started telling Marcia, in the kitchen at Easy, about my French heritage, she'd every-so-often make up something out of some French cookbook she had. Her idea was that it classed up the joint. My idea was that she needed a vacation. But her cooking was getting better.

"You tried it?"

"Me?" Hal responded quickly. "Not on your life. I don't like to eat at all before nightfall. It's bad for the digestion."

"I see."

"But some have had it for lunch. They raved. Marcia!"

She appeared in the window between the bar and the kitchen.

"Flap, here, questions your cassoulet." Hal turned back to me and winked.

"I work," she began in a monotone, "I slave—what do I get? Heartache."

"You know how I care for you personally," I tried. "But the chef at Café de Foy you are not."

"Café the who?" She leaned on one elbow.

"It was a great restaurant of nineteenth-century Paris."

"Well then how the hell could I have been the chef at it?" She slung herself back up to her quasi-erect posture. "I tell you, Flap sweetie, sometimes you don't have the sense God gave a horseradish."

She went directly to the cassoulet, dished it, shoved it into the window, and dinged the little bell to let Hal know there was a food order up.

Without a word, he grabbed it and set it down in front of me in a single motion the envy of Astaire.

"Wine." My one-syllable grace.

He obliged. I had a bottle of the Parallèle "45" Côtes du Rhône stashed behind the register—good enough for lunch and certainly capable of saving a bad bean casserole.

But before Hal could pour a glass, Dally's voice pierced the mild after-luncheon crowd noise.

"Christ!"

Hal moved almost as quickly as I did. Dally never yelled unless something was really up. The last time I could remember a sound like that coming from her office, a rat the size of Richard Nixon had taken control of her desk.

I made it to the doorway first. She was standing at her desk, staring down—so the rat theory was gaining credence.

"You okay?" I tried not to startle her.

Didn't work. "My God!" She looked up, then sunk her shoulders. "Flap."

"What the hell is it?" I asked her, taking a step into the office. "Not another surprise package, is it?"

Hal was right behind me. "Dally?"

"Okay. I'm okay, you guys. I . . ." She trailed off.

I edged my way to the desk. "What is it?"

She didn't want to touch it. I finally saw the envelope on the desk in front of her. No return address, but on the back was a crudely drawn outline of a hand, like the kind of thing a kid might do.

"Another present from your secret admirer." I glanced at Hal. "Should I be jealous?"

"It's okay, Flap. Really." Her voice was very quiet.

I froze. "Again, it's okay, you're telling me?"

"What are you doing here? This time of day?"

"There are rumors about Marcia's cassoulet all around Midtown. I didn't want to come in. I *had* to."

She shook her head. "I'm fine. Just . . . finish your lunch." A quick flash of the eyes to Hal. "Please?"

"Yeah." He nodded. "Let's go on back out there, Flap, what do you say?"

"I say," I told him as amiably as possible, "that this is unusual weather we're having."

Dally sank back into her chair and looked away.

I shot a look to Hal, but he just waved his hands

at me and headed back to the bar. All I could do was follow.

I resumed my seat, sipped my Côtes du Rhône, and stuck a fork into the cassoulet.

"Hal?"

He didn't look. "Flap?"

"She's been getting these notes and packages for a while now."

He hesitated. It's tough trying to decide, in the middle of the afternoon, whether to lie for your boss or not. Especially if your boss is also your friend.

But Hal's the sort of person who fancies he might have a conscience. "Yeah. This is like the fifth thing she's gotten, I think."

"I see."

"Thought you'd already know about all that."

"You'd think." I lifted the fork to my face. My nose tried to tell me that the garlic and parsley had been mixed appropriately. I sampled. "Not bad."

"The beans?" Hal finally gave me a second look. "Good."

"Marcia?" I tried not to yell too loud.

She appeared once more.

"My compliments."

"Uh-huh." She leaned forward in the window. "After one bite?"

"You've been watching me?"

"You're not so bad to look at." She exhibited one of her rare, slow smiles. Her whole face changed, and suddenly even the *Mona Lisa* seemed more ordinary than Marcia's face.

"Takes one to know one, sugar."

"Don't flirt with the help, Flap," Hal underplayed, "we still got to get through the dinner rush, and I don't want Marcia distracted."

"Hu-ah," Marcia blew out. "Take a whole lot more than a sweet mug and a one-sentence compliment about industrial cuisine to turn this head." And she disappeared again.

"I think she's taken with you," Hal commented, still deadpan.

"She's only trying to make you jealous."

He went back to work.

I kept expecting to see Dally come out of her office and stand in the door looking at me—the way Marcia just had.

I finished my meal and the second glass of wine. Hal had already added it to the tab. I dropped a ten on the bar. I knew he'd give Marcia half.

The place was pretty much cleared out. I glanced at my watch. It was three-thirty.

I started back to the office. Just wanted to say good-bye. But I was stopped in my tracks by a rude voice.

"Jesus, this sucks."

A patron at the bar was taking issue with his meal.

"Sorry you didn't like it," Hal was saying in a very unapologetic tone. "We're kind of famous for our food around here. This recipe . . ."

". . . it's too hot," the customer-is-always-right guy explained, "it's got too much garlic, not enough clove, the balance is off. I swear I could make a better cassou-let out of my own pee."

He shoved the bowl toward Hal.

It struck me then that he was the kind of guy who had probably always gotten away with that sort of behavior. He was dark, good-looking, had the kind of cool voice and grand old southern accent that made everything he said sound reasonable and threatening at the same time. People like him, they usually get what they want.

Hal watched the dish for a second, then looked up at the man. "Do you notice how I'm not the least bit curious," he said very slowly and softly, "as to how you'd know a thing like that?"

"I'm not paying for it." He actually smiled. It made his face even more attractive. I hated that, and I didn't even understand exactly why—at the time.

"I understand," Hal told him, still nice as you please. "How about if I just bring you a check for the water."

"Excuse me?"

I couldn't help myself. "Nat 'King' Cole said it—in a song called 'Frim Fram Sauce.' For most of the song he tells the waiter what he doesn't want; just keeps asking for the sauce. At the end of the record, he says, 'Now if you don't have it, just bring me a check for the water.' "

"Who might you be?" the food critic wanted to know. "The bouncer, or just an extra in this little scene?"

"Me?" I sat down with one stool in between us. "I'm a regular, set up here to give the joint a little color, mostly. But I also happen to be the cook's husband, and I know that she worked especially hard on that dish." I leaned toward him a little. "The ingredient you mentioned is not in her particular culinary vocabulary. Maybe you could exchange recipes and she could make a batch special for you the next time you're in town."

Now, ordinarily I wouldn't have butted in at all, let alone spoiled for a confrontation. But for some reason, this guy had rubbed me exactly the wrong way. Couldn't say what it was. Maybe it was that voice, or his tailored blue suit, the wave in his hair. Mostly it was that face, I guess.

"What makes you think I'm from out of town?" That's all he said.

"Most people in this neighborhood aren't as rude as you seem to be," I told him. "Thanks for asking."

"As it happens"—he started to stand, straightening his coat—"I am from out of town. If I have offended your 'wife' in any way, I'm sorry. I'm a stranger and not familiar with the quaint local customs. Where I live, people don't have to eat food they don't care for. And in better establishments, the management generally refuses money in such a case." He took a step toward me. "On the other hand, the 'pee' comment was out of hand, tremendously ungentlemanly, and I am truly sorry I said it. I'm a little high-strung. I sometimes don't know what I'm going to say next."

Then our eyes were locked. Despite the warmth of his accent, his eyes were strangely vacant. I had the sensation of staring into the windows of a house where nobody lived.

"As opposed to me," I told him affably. "I always know *exactly* what I'm going to do. Next."

Even I'm not certain what I meant by that, but it seemed to satisfy the guy on some incomprehensible level, and he backed off.

He buttoned his coat, creased his lips upward in a lifeless smile, and sidestepped the stool.

I turned on mine, and pretended he wasn't watching me anymore. "Hal? Maybe just one more glass."

After I heard his footsteps pass through the door, and I'd taken my first sip, I caught Hal's attention again.

"Any idea who's the charmer?"

"That guy?" Hal looked toward the door where the guy had disappeared. "None whatsoever, but he's been coming in just lately. Daytime only. He's a curious sort."

"You mean he's strange or that he asks a lot of questions?"

"Both." Hal folded his arms and leaned forward onto the bar. "Wants to know about business like he's a tax assessor or some such."

"Hm."

Hal stood for one second more before pushing off the bar with his hips. "He's asked about you."

"About me?" I watched Hal's back as he moved toward the cooler for another keg.

"More than once."

"What's he asked about?"

"Mostly about you and Dally." He tried to sound casual. "He knows Marcia's not your wife. He knows who you are."

"Really. What'd you tell him about me—and Dally?"

That stopped him. He turned. "I told him exactly what *you'd* tell him about you and Dally," he said plainly. "To wit: I don't know."

5

THE SCREAM

I'd already decided I needed to find out exactly what Jersey Jakes was doing for Ms. Oglethorpe. I had reckoned that it wouldn't be hard at all—Jakes is anything but a tough nut to crack.

He usually hung out, as the evening pressed toward the next day, at the Clairmont Lounge, a little east of Easy on Ponce. The Clairmont was a surreal blend of fifties strip bar and nineties post-punk clodhopper chic. Some of the dancers had been bumping the grind since Abraham tried to ice Isaac. Some of the kids who played there of a weekend were born when a grade B actor tried to pull off the role of president. Made for a Tom Waits kind of scene.

I'd spent too much of the afternoon arguing with my so-called friend at Green's liquor store. He had ordered a case of the Château Puy Blanquet and some more of the '86 Simard, but it was taking too long to arrive.

"This is the last time I pay you in advance." I believe that was the line that annoyed him.

"Then this is the last time that I order this kind of crap for you from France. Buy American from now on—like everybody else."

"Bite me, like everybody else."

"Not for one hundred dollars cash would I bite the likes of you."

"Really?" I lifted my chin. "That's not the rumor.

Everybody says you'd bite nearly anything for a quarter."

"Looky, Tucker," he started, "I take only so much from you."

Green's is on Ponce right across from Easy. The fact was that he probably took guff from a hundred people a day, and much worse than what I was dishing out. The place was stacked to the ceiling with cases of every imaginable liquor. There was always a policeman or two inside. And only the week before I'd been in the place when a client, drunk and disorderly, had threatened to rip somebody's liver out if he didn't get a drink inside of a ten count. *Liver* being the operative word, given that the poor guy's own organ was doubtless completely kaput.

But I digress.

"You're right." I backed off. "I'll wait."

He'd been surprised. I just split, like a sudden flash: like a safety pin in a light socket. Pop and gone somewhere else.

Then I walked. When all about you makes scant sense, take a hike—that's one of my mottoes.

The hike had ended up back at my apartment, where I had taken a nap. Naps are good. Einstein took naps. Cats, I am told, do the same. If it's good enough for such a broad spectrum of mammalia, it's good enough for me.

I only mention it because during the nap I dreamed that Dally and I were arguing, in Green's, about, of all things, the proper way to shake hands when you're good friends with somebody and they give you a bottle of wine as a present. I said you should shake firmly, locking eyes with your benefactor. She said you should do it quickly, modestly looking away. I was right, of course.

But the point was that kindly old Dr. Jung was trying to tell me something in my subconscious. I was just too stupid to get it at the time. I woke up, confused by the image and the argument. The streetlights were bright against a black crepe sky.

I hustled out the door to the Clairmont.

In an atmosphere comprised primarily of blinding smoke, the clear-eyed man is king. Alas, no royalty at all that night at the lounge—it was husky with fog. Emerging from and vanishing into same, figures like something from German Expressionism bedeviled my eyes. Churning noise of taped industrial funk, drunken screeching, and forced laughter contributed to the mud in the air.

I sat at the closest table.

"Drink?" The woman, sunken-eyed and slack-shouldered, had appeared out of nothing.

"Screwdriver," I told her over the noise. "Without the vodka."

"Funny. Just the orange juice?"

"That's right."

"You know . . ."

". . . you have to charge me for the full drink." I nodded. "I know. I've been through this before."

"You're Flap Tucker."

"I am."

She looked around. "How about if this one's on me?"

"What for?" Beware Munch paintings bearing gifts.

"Let's just say you got a rep," she told me emotionlessly, "and leave it at that."

"Okay," I agreed, "but you're not going to get all huffy with me if I ask you to taste the drink before I do?"

"Like in the court of the Borgias," she deadpanned. "I understand."

"That's good, but maybe you don't. I've been conked out by gift drinks before."

"Mm. Your line of work." She turned and disappeared back into the smoke.

I had long since ceased to be surprised by the sort of person one could meet at the Clairmont, or the erudition involved. They liked to say that William F. Buckley had come in one night with Annie Sprinkle on his arm. I always doubted that exact pairing had ever paid a visit in the flesh, but it did convey the spirit of the place.

When the ancient kid brought my beverage, she made a great show, without any facial expression whatsoever, of setting down the tray, waving her hand over the drink once like a magician, showing that there were no wires attached, then lifting the glass to her black lips and sipping, like bizarro communion. Then she set the glass down right at the edge of the table.

She let a thin trickle of juice drip out of the corner of her mouth, off her chin, onto the floor. Then she touched the opposite corner of her lips with the tip of her tongue, mostly, I thought, so that I could see she had it pierced. Most people who have a pierced tongue, in my experience, actually want people to know about it. That's part of the fun.

"I'm still here . . . you bastards." Her eyes were almost completely vacant. "So there's nothing in your drink, okay?"

"You quoted *Papillion*."

"That's right." At last: She offered a smile. And in that smile there was a teenage girl trying to hide behind Satan's makeup tips and a look-how-tough-I-am attitude.

"A knowledge of the Italian Renaissance *and* French penal figures—remind me not to show up against you on trivia challenge night."

The smile got bigger, then vanished, as if she suddenly remembered where she was. "Try some lame oldster's bar, bub. All you get here is bad titties, worse air, and the occasional fine music."

"And, if you're lucky, a free orange juice once in a while."

"Yeah." Ghost of the smile revisited for half a second.

"You know my name. Have to tell me yours."

"Lucrezia."

"Very funny." I sipped my juice. "Why the free beverage, really?"

"If you're still here at closing," she told me in a deep, affected voice, "maybe you can walk me home, and I'll tell you."

"I'm actually here looking for my pal," I offered as clear resistance. "Maybe you know him. Jersey?"

"Risky Jakes? Most of the girls know him." It wasn't a compliment to the guy.

"I see. Happen to know if he's been in here tonight?"

"Somebody said he was over there," she told me, "bothering the band—trying to get Hogan to talk to him."

"Kelly Hogan? She's here?"

"She's about to go on."

"I didn't even know she was in town." Hogan had moved to Chicago. She used to sing at Easy, but up north was a bigger avenue, a newer horizon. Still, when the moon was right, she'd sneak back down South—and the air was always a little finer because of it.

"She's not just in town," the little girl said, "she's plugged in. My offer stands." And she was gone again.

I finished the rest of my juice in a couple of healthy gulps and waded through the atmosphere toward the band.

The singer was nowhere to be seen, but Jakes was sitting the wrong way in a chair, arms over the back, dressed in the same getup as before only with a polyester coat over the loud shirt, pulling on an unfiltered Camel and staring into space.

"Jersey."

He almost went over. He twitched wildly and I saw his hand go inside his coat pocket. Then I saw him remember where he was, and he turned slowly my way.

"Jesus. Tucker." He blew out a long stream of smoke. "Slack off on the sneaking up. It could get ugly with a person more excitable than me."

"Okay. And for the record, you can take your hand out of your pocket now." I took a chair at the table with him. "I come in peace."

"Oh. Yeah." He brought his hand back out empty. "What the hell are you doing here?"

"What the hell were you doing in Easy at four this morning?"

I saw no point in beating around the bush. With the lesser-brained mammals, directness is often intimidating.

"Where?" His eyes shifted to the tabletop.

"I saw you. What's the point in pretending?"

"Look, Flap," he said hastily, lifting his eyes to mine once more, "I know you got to be sore about Dally axing me to help out in a way that you would, ordinarily— but now look here: That's her business. I mean, did you ever stop to think that she might have something she don't want you to know? I mean, like what if it's about a surprise party for you, or some special birthday present or something? Wouldn't you feel ashamed to find out about it and ruin the fun, for instance?"

Beads of sweat had popped out on his forehead.

"Relax, brother," I assured him. "I'm not going to get physical with you. I just want to make sure Dally's all right."

"Sure, sure." He bobbed his head quickly. "But see, that's the problem—and you'd have it too, don't tell me you wouldn't. You don't like to discuss what you're doing for a client in a situation like this type of a deal. Right?"

"Okay," I said slowly, doing my best to demonstrate how he was trying my patience, "so what if you just tell me that Ms. Oglethorpe's not in any danger or weirdness, and I'll let it go at that, for the time being."

He swallowed. He looked around, like somebody might come to his aid. But nobody did. So: "The last thing in this world," he began, "that I need, is to have you mad at me, see? But I can't tell you." He shook his head. "Nothing."

The poor guy looked like he was in front of a firing squad.

He was saved by an angel—in the person of Kelly Hogan.

"Tucker?"

I looked up. "Kel."

"Man"—she hustled toward me when I got to my feet—"what the hell are you doing in a dump like this?"

I squeezed her. "They tell there's music tonight. You know how far I'd go to hear you sing."

She pulled back and gave me the eye. "Across the street, apparently," she needled, "but God forbid you should get on a plane and haul yourself to Chicago to hear me in a really *nice* dive."

"I'd go to Chicago, Kelly." Jakes was standing too.

I let go of Hogan, and turned in his direction. "You're not going anywhere until I get at least one straight answer, pal."

"Is that right?" He'd turned tough in front of the dame.

"Boys, boys," Hogan wise-cracked, "don't fight on my account."

"We're not fighting," I assured her. "We're talking."

"No." He stood his ground. "We're not."

Kelly stepped in between us. She shoved Jakes back into his chair, kissed me on the cheek, elbowed me in the opposite direction, and raised her chin to her drummer, who was at the table in light-seconds.

"Everything all right here?" The drummer was the size of Kong.

Hogan took a step toward the bandstand. "Sure. Why do you ask?" And she was gone inside the smoke.

The drummer stood his ground.

I turned. "You're Toby."

He squared off, then dipped his head a little. "Mr. Tucker?"

"Hey."

"God Almighty." His face was bright as a high beam. "Great to see you. You remember my name?"

"I do better than that," I told him. "I remember your solo on 'In a Sentimental Mood' over at Easy about three years ago. Long, full of quotes, and just like poetry. Hard to play a drum solo like that on a ballad."

"Jesus." He blushed. "That was a night."

"Uh-huh." I checked out Jakes, who was absolutely attentive. I had wanted him to know who was friends and who was in need of the stiff-arm from Ms. Hogan. "Good to see you again."

"Same here. Tell Ms. Oglethorpe I said 'hello,' okay?"

I nodded. He left. Jakes relaxed.

"Look, Flap." His face contorted in silent, empty pain. "I know this is your town. I'm only a moron Yankee visitor—that's a thing you hot-weather types never let a person forget. I know Kelly's your friend, not mine. Ms. Oglethorpe too. A person such as yourself has lots of friends, I'm guessing. Me? I don't got that many. You're lucky. I'm not. That's the way the story goes. But I got my pride. It's not shiny, it's not brand-new, and it's not really large—but it's mine, and you really can't do anything about that. I won't break a confidence. Shoot my kneecap if you have to. It's been done before. But before you get out your pistol to do just that, let me say, by way of being friendly, that the last person who did anything like that to me is now called Popeye on account of somebody took one of his eyes while he was asleep once." He closed his eyes. "Pride can make a man do terrible things. But it keeps him from being a rat. Are we clear?"

"We're clear, Jersey." I tried to make my voice sound as friendly as possible. Not because I was in the least intimidated by his moron Yankee threats, but because he was right: He was in a town filled with strangers—nothing to warm him but the weather. It was my town. I did have friends. And I suddenly thought how awful life would have been without them. So I went even further with Jakes: "Sorry."

He drew in a long breath through his nose and opened his eyes again. "Don't mention it." And he smiled—showed a face that could make a storm trooper cry, filled with forgiveness and gratitude for small favors.

"How about if I buy you something to drink and we listen to Hogan for a minute?"

He leaned back in his chair. "Don't mind if I do."

The kid was behind me like magic again. She set down a glass in front of Jakes and handed me another juice.

"On my tab," she whispered close to my face.

When I turned to thank her, she was gone again, like a ghost.

6

WALKING MY BABY BACK HOME

The kid's name was Lucy, but everyone really did know her as Lucrezia—even if they didn't catch the joke. I thought that's what she appreciated about me—my sense of humor.

"Kelly sounded good tonight." I had my hands in my pockets and she had taken my left elbow. We were walking down Ponce toward Midtown, toward my place and toward her neighborhood—both. All roads lead to home at four o'clock in the morning.

"Kelly always sounds good." She showed no emotion about it whatsoever. "She and I had a thing, you know."

"No." I mimicked her lack of content. "I didn't know."

She slowed a little. "That doesn't freak you out?"

"That you *allege* to have had a fling with Hogan? If I had a nickel for everybody that ever claimed . . ."

". . . that I boinked a girl."

"Oh, that. Well, the fact is, anybody worth knowing's had some sort of an adventure with a girl."

She tightened her grip on my elbow. "If that plus the tongue knob didn't scare you off, then I guess you can come in and have coffee."

We'd arrived at her door. I stopped.

"No coffee for me, thanks." I took my hands out of my pockets so she'd have to let go. "Not at this time of night. I have enough trouble sleeping as it is."

"I didn't really have it in mind," she explained, "that you'd be sleeping much."

"All right, that's it." I'd had it. "What's this about? You ply me with free juice, make sure I know how smart you are—and also that you have a tongue thing—and then invite me upstairs for coffee that isn't coffee. I'm savvy. It doesn't take me more than three hours or so to figure out something's up."

"What *do* you mean?" Deadpan as ever.

"What *do* you really want?" I folded my arms in front of me.

"What makes you think I don't just want you?"

"Because you played your hand too well. I know how smart you are, remember?"

"How smart am I?"

"Smart enough to know better than to get involved with a character type like me, so what gives?"

She took a short breath, watched the high-end car with Lumpkin County tags cruise by, and then looked me in the eye.

"I've got a little problem, and you can help. I just can't afford to pay you, so I thought if you had a personal stake in giving me a hand . . ."

". . . got it." I nodded once. "Excuse me for saying so, but what kind of trouble could you possibly be in that could benefit from my services?"

"You're implying," she told me, "that I'm too young to be in big trouble, but if you'll crack open a newspaper every so often, you'll notice that kids my age are more prone to trouble than any other demographic group on the planet. So stuff the ageism."

"There's an *ism* for that?"

"Are you going to talk to me about it or not?"

" 'Kids your age,' you said. Just what would your age be?"

"I'm sixteen but I look nineteen so I can pass for twenty-one."

I watched her face. Underneath that voodoo base and midnight lip liner there might be a little girl. You really never ought to judge a book by how it's advertised.

"If," I began, "indeed you are sixteen, what on earth would make you think I'd be remotely interested in your post-coffee favors?"

"There is not a guy alive," she shot back coolly, "that doesn't want a sixteen-year-old."

"But see," I tried to explain, "now that I *know* how old you are, the word *statutory* suddenly pops into my head. I hear a judge saying, 'Well, Mr. Tucker, did you or did you not know how old the young woman was?' And I hear myself saying, 'But your honor, she *passes* for twenty-one.' And I hear him say . . ."

". . . enough. I get it. You're the type who always has to tell the truth no matter how whack that is, so I get it. No sex. Is that how this is spelled?"

"In all capital letters," I affirmed.

"So what am I supposed to do?" Suddenly she was a kid again. But I'd gotten a whole lot smarter in the preceding few moments.

"Pouting and acting like a helpless waif will avail you nothing either, kiddo. It is my belief that you could chew up nails and spit them back out as bullets, so skip the lost little girl routine too."

"Well, fuck."

"First off," I rushed in, "I don't care for that word. It demeans an act of inexplicable beauty. Secondly, in a world where every tough guy can speak harshly, there is an advantage in a little thing called *vocabulary*—which is to say that you could find at least seven hundred and fifty-three words in English that would be better to express your current frustration with my demeanor. And finally, why don't you just tell me your problem and maybe I'll help because I've got nothing better to do with my time. What do you say?"

That froze her for a second. But she thawed nicely. "I've got decaf."

"Well, there you go." I opened the door to the house.

The Mouseketeer Vampira lived in a house on Myrtle that had long ago been made into apartments. If you opened the front door to the house, you looked in on a long hall and a staircase. To the right and left of you were apartments, and if you went down the hall, there'd be another. She'd lucked out. She was upstairs. I always liked the upstairs better because (A) you don't get quite so many boosters crawling in your windows and (B) nobody walks on your ceiling.

Her place was a neat-as-a-pin efficiency. That was the first surprise. Next, she popped a very soft CD of Billie Holiday into the stereo beside the daybed. And when she'd said she had decaf, she'd meant she had black, whole decaf beans which she ground to dust in the kitchenette and shoved into a very ornate espresso machine. It began to hiss as she walked back toward me.

"You're not like most kids your age, I'm guessing."

"Each era," she began, throwing herself onto the daybed in an arcane pose, "steals from the previous era. Stones stole Chuck Berry, punks stole James Dean, kids my age are a bizarre amalgam of swing babies and gutter punks."

"Agreed," I said, still standing, "as far as the so-called Swing Revival goes. It may be the old tunes but it's got a punk-a-billy sense about it that's nothing like the days of yore. Ever heard Bowl of Fire?"

"It's new," she agreed. "Sit?"

There was a bent wrought-iron ice-cream chair beside the daybed. I took it.

"Tell me your tale of woe, if you're going to." I leaned back.

"Okay, here goes." She closed her eyes. "There's this guy."

In the history of poor swing-frails like Minnie the Moocher or San Francisco Fan, every tale begins with the sentence: "There's this guy." So I just settled back, prepared to let the story pour over me like the music on the stereo.

"He's the prettiest man I ever saw."

They say that kind of thing a whole lot in those old "he done her wrong" songs—so I was immediately suspicious.

"He won't tell me his name, and he's older, but I don't care. He's the one for me. I've got it bad."

" 'And that ain't good,' I believe is the lyric." I shifted in the chair.

"He came into the Clairmont one night," she went on, only a little nonplused by my demeanor, "just to have coffee. He just sat there and read something or other. He didn't look up once. I had to know about him, but he wouldn't talk to me. I know he's staying in town, but I don't know where. You have to help me track him down, wherever he is. I think it's close."

"What makes you think that?"

"I feel it."

I'm not one to take a feeling of that ilk lightly, especially delivered in such an earnest manner. Not to mention that it's my belief that most southern women have a higher ESP quotient than anyone outside of Tibet. Still, it was the skeptic in me that said:

"You feel it." I looked around her room. It was sparse but tasteful. "Okay."

The espresso machine was hissing like a steam train. I saw a white ghost rise up from it out of the corner of my eye. It was the ghost of other men who'd sat in that chair and stared at that kid's mug and thought about how strange it was to be in her apartment at four in the morning. Guys who'd bought her line.

"Now are you going to tell me why I'm here, or not?" I locked eyes with her.

Her pose grew more Mata Hari. "You're not buying the 'pretty man' scenario?"

"Not by a long shot." You have to be completely honest with a person who has had her share of the opposite.

"Why would I be lying to you?" But her voice was too studied, too deliberately calm.

"I don't know, but you're not the type to be pining."

"I'm not?"

"That's right."

"What type am I?" Her pose on the bed was intended to be increasingly inviting.

"You're the dangerous type," I shot right back, "because even though you think you do, you don't know what you've got."

"What have I got?" One simple lift of the shoulder made the strap of her top fall halfway down her upper arm. I wondered how long she'd sat in front of the mirror perfecting the move.

"You've got a fine sense of the theatrical and a keen eye for suckers," I began, "but tonight it so happens that I'm in a pensive mood, and when I've already started thinking, it's not so easy for the brain to shut off and listen to the rest of the body."

"What's the rest of your body telling you to do?" She leaned forward, eyes looking up at me, top revealing what they used to call cleavage.

"It's telling me to run."

"Man"—she shifted, suddenly sixteen again—"what the hell's the matter with you?"

"Not a thing. Are you telling me that this works on most guys? This B-movie vamp from *Pretty Baby* meets *Taxi Driver*?"

"Never saw either one, but the answer is yes. It usually works. Although ordinarily I've got younger material to work with."

She'd wanted it to be an insult, but when it was forming in her mouth, it seemed to me that she realized what she was saying, and reassessed instantly. I don't know where her mind went, but I'd seen the process before. It's an ability that you have to acquire if you're a teenager and on the streets of an unfamiliar town: instant reevaluation. If you don't develop that sense, the wolves eat you alive and spit out your bones. And there she was: alive and kicking. I actually started liking her more in that moment.

"But that's my problem," she went on, as if the shift hadn't even occurred. "I see that now. I've been hanging out with youngsters. They're thin—in every sense of the word. They've got no substance. I can't learn anything except how to swear and where to cop dope, and I just decided I don't want to do either one of those things."

"Just now? You just now decided that?"

"I think on my feet," she told me from her supine position.

"I can see that. In fact, I was just admiring it. Now how about espresso and some genuine conversation."

"You're staying?"

"I think I'm actually starting to take a shine to you." Once again I thought that honesty was most likely something she was hungry for.

I just didn't expect the effect. She popped out a smile like a kid who just stole third base in Little League. "Really?"

"Yeah." I looked at her rug. "How about that?"

She got up silently and went for the coffee. Inside of three minutes, she was back on the bed sipping and I had finished my first demitasse.

"So why am I here, really?" I set the cup down on the floor. "There's no pretty boy."

"Okay." She settled in. "This guy comes in a couple of nights ago all coked and corners me in the ladies' room. I guess he'd been watching me, and followed me in. He pinned me in a stall, covered my face with his arm and had his zipper open before I could get a good look at him. The light's out, been out for days—you know the deal with the Clairmont. Anyway, luckily, I got out my machete."

She produced, like a thin steel rabbit in a junkie magic act, a stiletto from her sleeve. It would have convinced me to move to South Philadelphia for a little safety—not to mention away from her if I were menacing her in a ladies' room.

"Machete?" I watched her handle it.

"Or whatever you call these things." She looked down at it. "It convinced him to hustle his little two-toned shoes out of my life. That's all I could see—his shoes. But I could see them leaving pretty fast."

With a flick of her wrist she made the evil needle disappear again.

"Looks to me like you can take pretty good care of yourself," I said. "I don't see you needing a guy like me getting in between you and your little adventures. And why, by the way, didn't you just tell me this in the first place."

"Because I thought you'd help the waif-done-wrong type before you help the find-this-guy-so-I-can-kick-his-ass type." Short shrug. End of story.

I had to admit it: "You'd be right."

"And you've got to be willing to help, since I've got

no jack." Then: a lightbulb. "Unless! I can help you. You want to keep tabs on Jakes. I can do that. He comes to the bar every night, he sleeps in the hotel every day. I can be your . . . what do you call those guys?"

"Operative?"

"That's me." Bright as a penny. "That's your payment for helping out: tit for tat. Barter system. Plus." She lifted a finger just like a judge. "Check this out: I was so pissed at the guy, when everything went down, that I came flying out of the bathroom to give him what for. When I did, he was gone. But Jakes was right there, see? So it comes to me just tonight when you walk in looking for Jakes: 'What's this all got to do with our Mr. Tucker?' See? I've got an instinct."

"Is that right."

"I can help!" She sat bolt upright, eyes wide—a kid again.

"Help *what*?"

"You. I can help you." Even more excited.

"Look," I started.

"Hogan's always talking about what you do, but she got especially graphic when I started complaining to her about my masher. And then I asked around about you." She said it like she had connections. What those connections would be, I didn't even want to consider. "You find people."

"In the first place," I went on, "Hogan doesn't know what I do. In the second place I don't need anybody else helping me—I've got enough color as it is. And in the third place, at the moment, I can't even find my own . . ."

". . . what if you need protection?" She went for her blade again.

"Tell me that you haven't had to use Betsy or whatever you call your slinky sticker." Kids often name their blades.

"As a matter of fact, I call it Fang. And it's tasted blood, if that's what you're asking."

"What I'm asking," I began, trying not to slight her braggadocio, "starts with why you'd even give this a second thought and ends with what you think you'd do."

"Okay." She slung herself back on the bed and stared at a corner of the room for a while. "I know how to use the blade, I have good friends, and I know three cops by name. I've been through a grade-C slasher film's worth of crap in my life so far and I've lived to tell the tale." Her lids narrowed. "And when I see a rat, I want it dead—that way I don't have to worry is the rat going to snap at my jugular when I'm asleep. Kill it now, sleep tonight—that's my motto, and it's served me well. It's gotten me this far."

It had gotten her through sixteen years, into a nightmare job at the Clairmont Lounge, a terrible apartment in a more dangerous part of Midtown, and awake at four in the morning confessing her fears to a man she didn't know anything about.

After a moment's reflection, I thought it was actually quite far, and I admired her even more for it. Because for every kid like her awake and alive, there were twenty-five that hadn't made it. I'd known a few of those, too.

"I can be your eye and ears," she went on, "in parts of this town you don't even know exist."

I shook my head. "Let's just stick to the Clairmont, at the moment. Look: Why do you want to do this? You don't have enough bad juju in your life as it is?"

"I want to be just like you when I grow up." You could have sold that attitude, if you'd found a big enough package to wrap it in. She saw my reaction. "I mean it. It'll be cool playing detective, sneaking around."

"I don't need a partner. It's against my code." I heard myself say that like it was somebody else talking, since, to my knowledge, I did not have a code. "But I'll tell you what I will do. I'll try to see where the rat went, and spray a protective ring of poison around you. Preventative medicine."

She fell back on the bed again, exasperated. "You'll shoo him away? You'll be my knight? No thanks. Don't need a dad, if it's all the same to you."

I took that in. And she was right. She didn't need someone to watch over her. I was a little embarrassed that I'd even thought it—even while I was having some very conflicting parental thoughts.

"You're right."

She perked up at that. "So?"

"So, let's think of how you can help me. And if we happen to find a rat, you and I can mess with him so that he feels scared, and then we let him go so that he'll scamper on back to his Dumpster and think twice about shaking up the next kid who looks like easy prey."

Her grin took up most of her face. "That's it. Scare the bastard back to Ratsville. Teach him a lesson he won't soon forget. That's the ticket. Theatre."

"Theatre." I was impressed with her grasp of the subtle possibilities. "Exactly."

"So we've got an arrangement?"

"Of a sort," I agreed, largely just to get out of the situation. "Of a very loose sort."

My expression must have betrayed a little of my thinking. She leaned my way. "You see now that there's more to me than meets the eye. And you're more impressed."

"I was impressed when I saw Fang."

"But the difference now is"—she lowered her voice

and leveled her gray eyes right at mine—"now you're reconsidering my original offer."

And before I could even consider for the first time whether or not she was right, she'd moved far enough toward me to plant a serious kiss on the hard part of my jaw.

7

RATSVILLE

I left the kid's place about three minutes after that kiss. She gave me her home phone number and a typical description of the offender: sweaty hands, scary moves, funny smell. In other words, nothing I could use. I gave her my number and told her to call if she had anything. To tell the truth, I didn't expect to hear from her at all.

The next morning I was over at the Clairmont Hotel asking questions. I usually avoided the whole place in general, and the hotel part in particular. So it was somewhat disconcerting to visit two times in as many days.

"You talking about Jerky Jakes?" The man slumped in the heavily stained overstuffed chair still had his eyes closed, even after at least two minutes of our question-and-answer session.

"I think the moniker is *Jersey*," I told him politely, "but, yes, that's who I'm talking about."

"Jerky I call him," the man insisted with mustered menace, thrusting one hand in the air to swat at a fly, eyes still tight.

"What'd he ever do to you?" I had to know.

"In and out at all hours, late pay, dirty mouth— don't like him."

"I see."

"But he does stay here."

"Which room?"

At last Rip Van Winkle opened his eyes. "You a cop?"

"You know I'm not."

"That's right." His lips parted in something that might one day, long ago, have passed for a smile. "Just wanted to see what kind of a dick you were."

"The kind that prefers to avoid being called a dick."

He looked me up and down, then, in a way that made me feel like he was an undertaker—and I was a potential client. "You're Tucker." He closed his eyes again. "Seen your picture in the *Urinal and Constipation*."

The *Atlanta Journal-Constitution* was known by many such names—especially to those who did not care for its reportage.

"So you're not going to tell me what room Jakes is in."

"You got it."

"Not for a hundred dollars."

"You ain't likely to give me a hundred dollars."

"That's right." I stepped closer to him. "I just wanted to see what kind of a concierge you were."

He opened his eyes again. "Is that so?"

Just as I was about to explain what kind of a concierge I thought he was, Jersey Jakes walked in the front door.

"There's a coincidence for you," I told the old codger. "Speak of the devil."

"Jakes," he called out. "There's a fellow in here asking about you. His name is Tucker. Don't know what he wants." Then he looked at me. "That's the kind I am: take care of my customers . . . whether I like them or not." He sniffed. "I'm a professional." And then he went promptly back to sleep.

Jersey smiled. "Hey, Flap." He seemed tired.

"Hey. I've got a favor to ask. Do you have a minute?"

"A favor?" Jakes looked around. "You talking to me?"

"That's right, wise guy. I think you can be of service."

He cocked his head quickly once to the left.

I motioned him away from the oldster and out into the parking lot in front of the place. I was pretty sure no one could overhear us there. Not that I had anything of tremendous import to say, I just didn't like the idea of nosy denizens of the Charles Bukowski Room or the William S. Burroughs Suite there at the Clairmont knowing even one iota of my business.

On the blacktop, noisy traffic zipping by, I continued my tale. "You know the vampire kid who works downstairs? My waitress last night?"

"Drucilla?"

"Close. Lucrezia, she calls herself."

"It's a free country."

"Maybe," I agreed, "but she's feeling a little threat to her God-given right to be her own person—in the form of some weasel who tried to pin her in the ladies' room just recently."

"Some guy cornered her in the can downstairs? At the club?" He blew out a short disgusted breath. "What kind of a person . . . even I wouldn't do that."

"Hence"—I patted his arm once—"my confidence in you."

"You think I might have seen the guy because I've been hanging around here for a while, and I'm a little more observant than you originally thought I might be. And you think I might also know this rat based on the takes-one-to-know-one school of detective work."

"Not just that. She says he was eyeballing you."

"Really? Zips a kid in the can then stalks me. This guy—he's a real schmoburger. I'll keep my eyes open." He flicked his hand at me. "And I do this as a professional courtesy, see? One dick to another."

"You overheard the concierge call me that."

"I did." He looked down at the asphalt.

"Even before you walked in the door?"

"Well," he began slowly, "when I saw you in the lobby, I stood at the door and listened for a minute or two. Especially when I heard you mention my name. Thanks, by the way, for trying to set the guy right about that. He's a little hard of hearing, I guess."

"Personally I think his whole head has hardened up pretty solid," I said, "but maybe mine would too, if I had his job."

"Yeah," he told me. "You and me, we got it lucky. You've got to love your work."

"So—you'll help me. You'll do me this favor."

"I will."

"Mr. Jakes." I held out my hand.

"Mr. Tucker." He shook it.

"So now will you tell me something?"

"Depends." He folded his arms in front of him.

"I don't want you to tell me what you're doing for Ms. Oglethorpe. I think you made your stand on that clear last night and I'm going to respect it. But I would like to know if she's in any real trouble or danger—I've seen the notes." And I nodded wisely, like I knew all about everything.

It was a good enough bluff. I should have thought of it the previous night in the bar downstairs. A really righteous bluff is something that is true but implies more than the rest of the truth can actually support.

As fate would have it, he was fairly foggy himself, continuing to inspect the pavement in the parking lot.

"She's okay, Flap. She's just got to get out from under some old business. Something she don't care for you to know about, see? And she don't want you to get riled or worried or whatever it is you do when you deal with somebody close. She needs a stranger's help. Me, as I was saying last night, I'm a stranger and don't really have any such person to be close to me, so I don't exactly know what she's talking about when she tells me she's worried about you. But I wouldn't mind having a dame like her be concerned about my welfare. Not a bit. And that's all I have to say on the subject."

"Is it my imagination," I asked him, "or are you and I getting along?"

"I'm not as smart as you are," he started, still looking down, "or as nifty in any way, really. But I'm not a bad guy at the end of the day, and you're just beginning to know that."

"You can always find me at Easy. How will I get in touch with you?"

His eyes darted to the hotel behind us. "Room 212."

"I'll tell you"—I looked out at the traffic—"I'm glad Dally's got you in her corner. I'd had it in my mind—last night and even today—to try and corral a real answer or two about what it is you're doing for her—and why. But now I think I might just let things ride for a little while. It's not even close to the end of my day, and you already don't seem like such a bad guy."

"For a rat." He looked up.

"For a *dick*," I corrected him. "I think that's the word you're groping for."

"Yeah." He smiled and grabbed his belt. "Grope for this."

In the land of the rat, the laughing rat is king—and almost anything passes for comedy.

8

GOD'S BOILED WATER

Next stop was Easy. I told myself another daytime visit would stir things up. It was getting close to an hour when normal people eat a little thing called lunch, so I sauntered into the place. Marcia's Gourmet Chili was advertised on the sandwich board outside—which I thought amusing after the pious day's exchange about just that. Still, hot chili—and corn bread with honey— is the perfect midday summer's repast. When it's hot, eat spicy food.

The place was relatively crowded for the middle of the day, I thought, and there was only one seat available at the bar. Hal was slammed, and only nodded. The noise level was pleasant to me, and the sounds of clinking dishes and idle chatter fell happily on the ear.

Hal brought me a glass of the Puy Blanquet that I'd been saving, and a hand-scrawled piece of paper that was supposed to pass as a "special menu."

Marcia had printed, in big capital letters, GOURMET CHILI, NOT FOR EVERYONE, and underneath she had listed the ingredients, which included anise seed, oriental peppers, dill, garlic, no meat of any sort, and white beans called *cocos* she claimed had arrived that day from Provence. Down at the bottom, in parentheses and a different pen, she'd dashed off: "Perfect with Puy Blanquet."

I looked up. She was smiling at me through the open

window to the kitchen behind the bar. I lifted my chin in her direction. She disappeared.

I snagged Hal. "Tell me that this so-called chili isn't just yesterday's cassoulet with more spices."

"If Marcia heard you say that," he said patiently, "she would cleave your hide and *you'd* be the special tomorrow. You do realize that."

"You're still not telling me . . ."

". . . it's all fresh today, Flap." Hal was rarely in a hurry, and never out of sorts with my banter. I got the impression it wasn't just the crowd that was prompting his discomfort.

"I'll have some. And no hurry." I thought that would ameliorate the scene.

He didn't even give me a glance on his way to the order window.

I drank my wine and listened to the spot talk all around me. Someone was worried about selling his Lexus, somebody else had a kid in college who was majoring in music education; a young woman was quitting her job if her boss didn't stop hitting on her, and an older man was considering assisted living instead of moving in with his oldest daughter, who was a saint but you couldn't live with her.

Which ought to give anyone an idea of how diverse the general crowd at Easy can be, of a summer's day.

And over the din, I could hear a voice coming from Dally's office. I couldn't hear what he was saying, but he was agitated. It was a voice I was still trying to place when Hal brought my chili.

"Somebody's giving Ms. Oglethorpe a hard time?"

Hal stopped for a second, didn't look at anything, then moved on when someone else at the bar mentioned something about her check. She had a nice smile. A twenty-six-year-old woman with a nice smile beats an older regular with a rumpled suit—in any bar in the free world. I put a spoon into my chili.

The flavors were perfectly balanced, and the taste was like nothing else on earth. It was manna.

At about the fifth spoonful, big noise erupted from Dally's office. This time it was shouting and furniture slamming.

I was off my stool before I even thought about it. I moved to the doorway in ten steps and filled the frame.

The guy had his back to me. He was gripping the edge of the desk. There was a chair shoved over out of place. Dally's face was white as Ivory soap, and she had an antique brass letter opener in her upraised hand.

"Hi, kids," I called out.

Very slowly the man turned his bulk toward me. I could see he was the food critic from the previous day, the patron who had taken exception to Marcia's cassoulet. He seemed embarrassed to see me.

"Still complaining about the cuisine?" I did not smile. "Maybe you should try Le Giverny. It's very cozy and they have a fine pork dish."

"Mr. Tucker." His voice was calm. He lowered his head. "This makes two days in a row I've disturbed your peace and quiet." He flashed me the smile that had surely won some kind of award somewhere in the upper-class circles of lower middle Georgia. "I apologize." Still smiling, he folded his arms in a Yul Brynner. "My business with Dal is private, however. Would you excuse us?"

"Love to," I explained to him, "if it's okay by Ms. Oglethorpe."

Dalliance finally spoke, and a little color returned to her face. "I'm okay." It didn't even sound like her voice.

"That's it?" I began again. "No introduction? No explanation?"

"Flap." That's all she said, but it was the way she said it.

I stood another moment, and so did he, frozen. Then I tried his method: I smiled. "You should give the chili another try. I'm eating it, and it's just about the best . . ."

". . . you know, I believe I'll do that," he told me, eyes still lively, jaw a little tense. "Did you happen to mention my apology to your 'wife'?"

Even in her odd state, Dally grinned. "Wife?" She absently laid down the letter opener.

The guy tilted his head Dally's way, talking to her out of the side of his mouth. "I thought that was amusing. He tried to tell me that the cook here was his wife."

She relaxed more, grinning bigger. "What'd you do that for, Flap?"

I didn't like it. Seemed like the two of them were sharing some kind of a private moment at my expense.

"You know how I've always felt about Marcia."

"And her chili," he added.

"*Chili* is far too plebeian a word for what we've got out there today." I glanced over my shoulder, to my place at the bar. "I'm saying it's *Aigo Buido d' Dieu*."

"What's that?" He really seemed to be interested.

"I think it means 'God's boiled water'—but the translation certainly doesn't do it justice."

"You are a charmer." Dally shook her head, then took in a breath. "Would you excuse us, Flap? Please?"

I took one more drink of the whole scene, then took off.

Back on the barstool, sipping my wine: "Hal?"

"Yes?"

"Who *is* that man?"

He turned toward the office. "Bad news?"

"I can't recall ever seeing Ms. Oglethorpe like that."

"Me neither, but Flap?"

"Yes, Hal?"

"It's really none of our business." And he was back to work.

"None of our business? When has that ever stopped me? Where she's concerned?"

But he was taking someone's order, and Dally had closed her door. The noise of the bar was like an ocean wave, roiling over me—and washing me away.

9

MEET THE QUEEN

No doubt about it, I had to find out more about Mr. Wonderful. After I finished my chili, I sat around the bar as things cleared out and waited for the boy to emerge. An hour after the heavy business had subsided, I was still waiting, and the Puy Blanquet was gone.

"Hal?" I called out in a more philosophical tone, "what do you make of a meeting that long with a temper that short?"

He came and leaned against the bar in front of me, toothpick in his mouth. "When somebody's that sorry, I generally don't see putting up with them—unless they're a relative. Or they owe me money."

"Two good guesses. I always thought I knew most of Dally's kin. Didn't you say the guy was asking money questions about Easy?"

"That's right. Maybe he's trying to weasel out of paying Dally some money, and maybe she needs it for something."

"Maybe she owes him money and can't pay it back. Although if this lunch crowd today is any indication, I think maybe Dally could retire to Barbados if she wanted to."

"I don't believe she's hurting," Hal said plainly.

"So rule out money. Let's say he knows something about her that no one else does."

Hal let out a single coughing laugh. "Flap, between

you and me and maybe one or two others, you think Dally's got a secret left?"

"Not likely." I lifted my eyes from the bar to his face. "But you could be hiding something from me."

"I could." That's all he said. But that was Hal, he was just being nice. He didn't like to disagree. Especially with someone who tipped the way I did.

"So you're not keeping some dark secret about our girl?"

"Not that I know of. You already know how she got the money to open this joint in the first place, right? That's good gossip."

"Because she can squeeze a penny until all the copper's gone?"

"That's just how she keeps it," he responded, shaking his head. "How she got it in the first place has something to do with blue blood and the Piedmont Driving Club—old money—which I know you know is not her heritage."

"Not even close. How many stories have I told you about Invisible, Georgia—our hometown?"

"Way too many."

"So you know that kudzu's the main crop, and downtown's a single filling station with a three-hundred-year-old proprietor name of Sonny."

"So what about that blue-blood money, you reckon?"

"Yeah, I've heard all that gossip before," I told him, shaking my head, "but I never put much stock in it. People assume that a woman's got to be given money to start a business, where they always think that a man in the same position probably earned the cash and managed it wisely. Dally earned some money while she was still in college, that was when I was away in the service of my country. She did the right thing with it—investments I guess—and then she had more. When I got back, she made this place. That's the whole story as I see it."

"Okay"—he was willing to go along—"so rule out money. What's left?"

"I don't rule out money, but it's turned around the other way: This chump wants money from Dally. It's somebody she knew in the old days, or somebody she met in business, who thinks he can muscle her around. It's my guess he's the one that's been leaving her those scary notes."

"She told me about the one with the hand." Hal betrayed no assessment of such a package, just that he knew about it.

"She told you about that?" I looked back at the door. "She's worried."

"She told me all about it. So why doesn't she want you *or* me to help?" Hal was staring at the closed office door, too.

"Right." I took in a breath. "It's got to be somebody from the old days. And let's say he knows something about her."

"Something that she doesn't want us to know." Hal's voice was softer.

"Although what that would be, I have no idea." I turned to him. "What could be worse than having me as a best friend, for example?"

"Having you as a boyfriend." Marcia's voice sailed out from the kitchen.

"Quiet in there." I smiled. "What would you know about it, anyway? I've never heard a complaining word from any of my girlfriends."

"Most of them don't have the vocabulary to ask for directions," the ghostly voice shot back, "let alone complain about you. They just can't think of the right words."

"You can't win," Hal informed me.

Marcia appeared. "And when was the last time you had a so-called girlfriend?"

"The Crimean War springs to mind," I told her.

"If that's a long time ago"—she nodded—"then you're right on the money."

Just as I was about to reply, Dally's office door burst open and her visitor moved through the archway.

"You won't like it." He was warm, chipper, smiling—all of which worked to belie the threat of what he was saying. "I can tell you that."

She did not appear behind him, and made no reply from within.

I stood.

"Hey, get everything all settled?"

"Tucker," he said smoothly, "I'm in something of a hurry . . ."

". . . I prefer *Mr.* Tucker from people I don't know."

He stopped dead in his tracks.

"And," I went on, "you seem to have the advantage of me, as they used to say. I don't believe I caught your name."

He pinned me back with a stare so filled with Old South gentility that I almost forgot for a second where I was.

I took a step for him. I had no idea why I was so cranked. I wasn't looking for a fight.

"Do you really want to have this conversation?" His smile grew.

"I do." I kept coming.

"Boys, boys, boys," Hal said calmly from behind the bar, "don't make me come over there."

Out of the corner of my eye I saw he was wielding his big cricket bat. It was a present from one of the old regulars. In times of trouble, mostly late at night, Hal used to hold up a baseball bat—one that had been signed by all the Atlanta Braves. One night he was threatening some guy with it—the regular in question, who was completely drunk and disorderly. Quite a show. Hal was the eternal gentleman—only with a big hard piece of wood in his hand. The drunk started to make more trouble, but then he was utterly distracted by his fascination with the autographed bat. Hal ended up having to sell the guy his "bouncer tool" just to get the guy to go home. The next day the same regular brought in the very cricket bat Hal was holding up. Said it was twice as hard and half as valuable. It had been autographed by Queen Elizabeth. You could see the royal lettering clearly as Hal held the rail up over his head and smiled at me and Mr. Wonderful. "So settle down and let's be friends." That was his usual line.

"There's no need for that, Hal. I was just looking for an introduction, that's all."

"When Dalliance wants to tell you about me," he said softly, "she will." He turned for the door then. "A gentleman doesn't bandy his name about in a bar, now does he—Mr. Tucker?"

He brushed past me just as if I were invisible.

Hal watched him go.

I stood in the middle of the room. "That makes twice today," I said to no one in particular, trying to keep my voice calm, "that I've felt cast off. I'm having a strange feeling I'd like to teach that guy a lesson he wouldn't soon forget."

"Maybe you need a vacation," Hal told me as he put up his weapon.

I turned to him. "A vacation?"

10

VACATION BIBLE SCHOOL

"So while I'm gone," I was saying to Dalliance, standing in her office doorway a few moments later, "I was hoping you'd monitor my calls. I've got some work to do, and instead of trying to compete with my competition, I've taken him into my confidence . . ."

". . . I have no idea what you're talking about," she interrupted me.

"I'm taking a little time off. In my absence I've asked your friend Jakes to help me out."

"Jakes?"

"Don't even start with me, I know he's the one who's helping you out. And so I thought since you'll be seeing him, as you've hired him to do a little work for you, you might just take care . . ."

". . . if you're saying all this, or doing all this just to let me know how much you hate the fact that someone else is helping me for *once* with a problem . . ."

". . . I'm only asking you to relay any messages . . ."

". . . where are you off to, anyway?" Her voice was edged in nervous frustration, the kind you get when you haven't slept and your best friend is irritating you.

"If you'll let me finish a sentence . . ."

". . . and why get Jersey to help? You're just trying to keep tabs . . ."

". . . I don't need *his* help keeping tabs . . ."

". . . Flap, I swear to God . . ."

". . . I'm going home."

That put a stop to elliptical conversation.

"Home?" Her voice was small.

"Yeah. I miss it."

"Remind me to laugh at that when I'm in a better mood. What is it really?"

"Well, I'll tell you." I paused—and in that second, I didn't know what I was going to say next. Ever have one of those moments when you debate the relative merits of the Truth—with a capital *T*—in a conversation, before you go on talking? Ever look back on those moments and wish you'd done better? "I'm working on an angle, see? There's this kid at the Clairmont . . ."

". . . I'm guessing Lucrezia."

"Very good," I told her, impressed. "How would you know that? You know her?"

A single nod. "She's the type who'd find you." Her voice sounded strange.

"I see," I said, leaning against the doorframe, "you've been talking to Mr. Jakes, then. Keeping tabs on me?"

"Jersey reports everything." She leaned forward at her desk. "It's actually kind of annoying."

Her eyes were red at the rims, as if she'd been crying, or maybe she was just tired. Her hair was more disheveled than usual, which was saying something, and her voice was strained.

"I'm just going home for a little vacation, mostly," I told her. "But while I'm there, I hope to get a better perspective on this thing with you, which is vexing me to no end."

"I get it. You'll go home," she began, "you'll do your little cogitation trick. It's like a religious retreat or something. But where will you stay? No monasteries down there."

Neither she nor I had any kin left in Invisible. There

was barely anybody left there at all. Sonny was still around, at the filling station/grocery mart. And some of the old farms were in the hands of the children of the people who had worked them when Dally and I were kids. But for the most part, it was a place populated with memories and ghosts—summer echoes of schoolkids who had long since moved away, running on hot roads that were gone to kudzu and briars.

"I'll stay in Tifton, I guess. Plenty of motels there, and it's not too far." I smiled at her. "I figure there's a Bible in the motel room—so it's kind of like a monastery room—only less comfortable."

"Why are you doing this, Flap?" She finally looked up at me.

"Doing what?"

"Why are you leaving town now?" Softer: "This is what you always used to do. Leave." But she couldn't quite go on with the rest of her thought.

It was funny how we both felt a barrier of unspoken thoughts. We usually told each other everything, and now there seemed to be more and more things we weren't saying, and the gulf was wide.

"I'll be back in a day or two." I thought I managed a devil-may-care smile. "You won't even know I'm gone." I'd meant that sentence to be casual and light. It just sounded hurt, even to me.

I turned and walked out.

The afternoon sun was hot on the parking-lot pavement, and the usual contingent of strays and drunks was not in evidence. I alone was out and about in the hottest part of the day.

I figured Lucy might be up by now, so I made it across Ponce to the pay phones at the side of Green's and called the number she'd given me. I got her machine.

"This is L.L.—I'm here with a gun and a mean-ass

dog, I just don't feel like answering the phone, okay? You still feel like leaving a message?" Then the machine beeped.

"Hey," I said quickly, "I'm leaving town for a few days. I'll catch you at work when I get back. Keep your eyes open."

Then, just as I was hanging up, something shot up to the surface. Sometimes it takes all day sitting quietly and clearing my mind for things to bob up. And sometimes it just takes the heat of the midday sun.

I realized that the gentleman who had been bothering Dally, and complaining about Marcia's food—the one who was probably the actual author of the threatening notes that were in Dally's office—had walked out of my favorite bar in a pair of black-and-tan two-toned shoes.

11

SAILING SHOES

I hate coincidence. It makes me think that I'm putting two and two together incorrectly because I'm confused about the very nature of the number four.

Just because Dally's nemesis wore two-toned shoes, that didn't *have* to mean he was the same guy that had threatened Lucy. In fact, it would be what we often call in the detective game "too much." You can't have one bad guy do *all* the wrong stuff. Evil has to be spread out.

So, as I was making up arguments about how wrong I was to even be thinking such a thing, I was moving just as quickly as I could up the sidewalk toward the Clairmont Hotel. I thought maybe Jakes would still be in his room.

The concierge was snoring when I came into the lobby. I moved silently across the floor and up the stairs.

Room 212 was down the hall on the right, and I stood to the side of the door when I knocked. Old habit. If someone wants to shoot, they generally shoot at the door first.

"Tucker?" His voice was a hoarse whisper.

"How'd you know?" I tried to match his sotto voce.

"I could tell," he explained as the door swung open, "by the footsteps. You got a distinctive-sounding walk. Like dancing."

"I do?" I stepped into his room. "That's funny, because I can't dance to save my life."

"Maybe it's the shoes." He moved away from me

and stood by the bed. He was in striped boxers and a white string tee shirt.

"Shoes?" I looked around his place. It was a wreck: clothes everywhere, empty bottles, take-out cartons, a pizza box with a year's worth of cigarette butts in it, and one lamp lit in an otherwise darkened room. "I'd say that's a strange coincidence, if I hadn't already just been dismissing the entire concept."

"Concept? Got no idea what you're talking about." He looked down at my feet. "Are those Florsheims?"

"That's right, the old-style kind"—I nodded—"with the soles as hard as tap shoes. Got these in a vintage store."

"Yeah." He grinned. "Don't make shoes like that anymore."

"That's right." I tried to think about where I might sit down, then just decided to stand. "Like, say, two-toned shoes. Don't make those much anymore either. The guy we're looking for together? The one who menaced Lucrezia downstairs in the women's room? He was wearing shoes like that, I think."

I could hear the popping and whirring coming from inside his cranium. He could tell I was saying something significant, and he knew that somewhere in the back of his head he knew what it was, but he couldn't quite get it all put together. His brows were knit and his eyes nearly crossed with the effort.

Then, like sunrise on the walls of Troy, a dawning hope passed over his expression, and he locked eyes with me. "Two-tones."

"Anybody you know wear black-and-tan two-toned tormentors?"

He craned his neck my way. "You wouldn't be asking if you didn't already know. That's my belief. So I'll tell you. I do know someone who wears shoes like that."

"And here's where two and two really do come in

handy: I think it's the same person who is bothering your friend and mine, Dalliance Oglethorpe."

He sat on the bed as if he were suddenly taken with a terrible pain in his bean, rubbing his forehead with his fingers.

"Damn, Flap," he finally told me. "You really are good." He cast his eyes up toward me. "Did you do that voodoo thing you do?"

"I love that song," I started, "but the answer is no. I just got lucky, I think. And I'm still wary of such a coincidence."

"That's why you didn't see it right away," he said, collecting his thoughts. "You would have got the connection quicker if it were harder to get, or weirder. This is just too clean, too pat."

"Which is why I'm ready to discard it, but it made me suddenly see other things clearly: such as the fact that the man you're keeping an eye on for Ms. Oglethorpe and the man who just came storming out of her office are probably one and the same. In the first place, Dally doesn't have that many people messing with her, so the odds are highly in my favor anyway. But the fact that you just sat down on the bed and knew or thought you knew who I was talking about tells me that I'm probably right." I shoved my hands into my pants pockets and leaned back against the hotel-room wall. "Man, I'm good."

You could tell by the look on poor Jakes's face that he was just realizing what he'd given away. First came recognition, then surprise, then anger, then resolve—all in a neat thirty-second package. It was entertaining.

"Well," he said, patting his knees with the palms of his hands and standing, "you got me. I thought we were friends, but you did get the better of me there, and I take my hat off to you."

"I'd just as soon you didn't take anything more off,"

I said, trying not to look at those boxer shorts. "Could we just stick to conversation?"

"If there's any possibility that my guy and your guy are the same guy, we'd better know it pretty quick. See anything that looks like pants around here?"

I didn't want to look. "Are you going to tell me your guy's name now, or are we still playing the 'I'm-a-detective-with-a-code' game?"

He stopped, sighed, and looked up at me. "Well, even if I don't, the way you're going, you'll find out sooner or later anyway. Hey!"

His hand shot downward into a pile of shadows, and when he brought it back, his fingers were clutching wrinkled fabric that had once been a pair of blue double-pleated pants.

"Now," he said, shoving one foot into his find, "all I need is a shoe or two, and I'm good to go." He smiled. "Though, they're not going to be as sharp as yours." He locked eyes with me. "Or those two-toned affairs . . . that I hear Ronnard Raay Higgins wears when he's out and about."

"Who Ray What?"

"R-o-n-n-a-r-d. And Raay has two a's in it too." Jakes continued putting on his pants, and spoke, this time almost to himself. "Guy's a real case."

"Two g's in Higgins, as well, I guess."

"Right," he answered absently, looking for shoes.

"So," I continued, looking for shoes too, despite myself, "at least he's got consistency going for him. Terrible name, though."

"Suits him." That was Jersey's assessment. "Did I tell you about the hand?"

"The hand?"

"The guy cut off somebody's hand and put it in a package . . ."

". . . that he gave to Dally, I know all about that, and Dally *told* you that I knew. I've tried to blot it out of my mind. I'm gathering now that she, at first, thought it was Higgins's hand?"

"How do I know what she thought?"

I let it go and moved on. "Where'd he get a hand like that, do you think?"

"How did he keep from messing up those nice cool shoes"—Jakes shook his head—"if he got it himself? That's a good question too."

"Hey." I looked up from the chaos of the floor.

"What?" He looked around, thinking, I guess, that I'd found his shoes.

"I'm sorry I tricked you and I appreciate your telling me Higgins's name. I owe you one."

He halted his search. "You don't owe me, Flap." His voice was warm as the air on the street. For one brief second—it passed quickly—I considered that taking on the occasional partner in my business endeavors was actually a good thing.

Luckily, before I could do anything about it, I beat it out of town. That can sometimes give a person perspective. How was I supposed to know it would give me a rash instead?

12

RASH THINKING

The drive to Invisible via Tifton was tedious, flat, end-less, hot, worthless, stupid—and utterly devoid of any radio relief. Sometimes the static sounds like an ocean and it can be soothing, but you can only listen for so long before you have to turn off the damned radio and commence that most dangerous of travel enterprises: thinking.

It has long been my belief that thinking is the ru-ination of humankind. Once you start thinking about something, it becomes an objectified construct in your mind, and it ceases to be the actual thing it is. Take, for example, thinking about the past.

What are you really doing? You're thinking about *your reconstruction* of events in the past, you're not—as most of us are misled to believe—watching a movie documentary of the events.

Still, when there's nothing on the radio and there's nothing to see out the window and you're driving home at eighty miles per hour, you can't help but think about the past.

Playing in the cinema of my recollection were scenes of the other times in our lives that Dally and I had been out of sync. The first of these was when she was home from college on spring break her first year, and I had just decided to leave the country.

"You did *what*?"

"I enlisted."

She dropped the bundle of dirty clothes she'd had in her arms. We were standing in her mother's kitchen. The old farmhouse was so hot that you could actually get relief by walking outside and standing directly in the sun.

Dally's first year at Wesleyan was going nicely. I'd visited or she'd come home nearly every weekend, so it was more or less like having her still around—only better. Things between us seemed to have been accelerated by her weekly absence. I was twice as glad to see her when she came home; twice as demonstrative about how much I'd missed her. Until I made what turned out to be a fairly momentous decision.

"If you enlist," I tried to explain, "you get to choose what you do. If you get drafted, they just shove you into anything."

"What's there to choose?" She was completely irate. "It's the *army*. That's the opposite of choice."

"I'm going into Intelligence," I told her.

"That's my favorite joke," she said with absolutely no humor whatsoever. " 'Army Intelligence, a contradiction in terms.' "

"But, see . . ." I trailed off. The clarity of my decision was somehow eroded by the ferocity of her opposition to it.

"This is what you always do, you know." She sat at the table.

"I always do?" I wanted to keep up the argument, but she was right. Every time we'd ever gotten to the point of really getting serious about our feelings, I'd take a powder. I'd get a summer job that took me to Ty Ty or a sleepover camp at Pine Mountain. But this was a big one.

The kitchen was like a hundred other farm kitchens

in that part of south Georgia: spotless linoleum floor, big plain wooden table, two refrigerators, and something boiling on the stove twenty-four hours a day.

Dally's mom was leaning with her back against the sink, holding a colander full of purple hull field peas she'd just picked. Her dad had gone over to Sonny's Store to get gas for the tractor.

"Dally, honey," she said softly, "Flap's got to get out of this little town just like you do. He's just got his own way, that's all . . ."

". . . that's not why he's doing this, Momma." Dally's eyes flashed hotter than the flame on the stove. "He doesn't even know what his draft number is, yet. He's doing what he does best: He's backing off, he's getting the big picture." Her shades of irony deepened. "He's the amazing disappearing Zen boy."

That stopped Mrs. Oglethorpe pretty soundly. "Sugar, half the time I got no idea what you're talking about . . . and the other half I don't *want* to know." She turned toward the sink again. The back of her blue dress was like the sky just after sunset.

"Dally," I began, "you've really got this all wrong."

She focused a glare so blinding on me that I took a short step back, right into the screen door.

"Mr. Non-attachment. Every time we get close," she whispered, "you get gone."

Driving the highway home in the heat of the day with all the windows open, air washing around me like whitewater rapids, I was forced to look at a pretty uncomfortable conclusion. Dally was right. The history of our relationship was traced by two steps forward and one step back—a little dance of avoidance, abandonment, and something else that starts with the letter *A*—maybe, in this case, *army*.

13

SUNSET

I pulled into Tifton around sunset. The Lancaster Hotel, a huge old Victorian ship of a house close to the downtown area, had vacancies. It was also known around that part of the state for fine country cuisine—another concept that Dally considered a contradiction in terms. Another way in which we disagreed. I'd eaten there many a time in my youth and had found the fare there aces.

I parked on a side street, in the shade, instead of in the hot lot. I only had a small knapsack with me.

The lobby was cool and dark.

"Evening." The man behind the desk was about a hundred and twenty-seven years old, wearing, I was convinced, a shirt he'd gone to high school in.

"Hey. Got a room?"

"Yes, sir. Just yourself?"

"That's right." I got out my wallet. "I think just one night at this point, but what if I want to stay a little longer?"

"That could happen." He managed a quasi-affable look before his features fell back to their natural gloomy disposition. "A single is forty-seven dollars a night, includes breakfast. Dinner's extra. All the rooms got private baths now. Plus cable."

"Okay, then." I signed the register, gave him cash for one night, and took the key he handed me.

"Top of the stairs, then left."

Room 7 was done in burgundy and green—a masculine room. The Unclaimed Freight–style "antiques" were a little dusty, and the cable television, as it turned out, featured three religious channels, two country music video twenty-four-hour programs, CNN, and the three broadcast channels.

It would be dark soon, and I decided to wait a turn or two before heading over to Invisible, maybe even get a fresh start in the morning. There were a few things I could do while I was in Tifton anyway. I could eat a fine down-home meal. I could take a stroll down Simpson Street and see all the nice gardens. I could call Sally Arnold.

Sally had been born and raised in Tifton, gone to college in Macon with Dally, and come back home to marry and share her knowledge. I'd only met her once, and Dally didn't talk about her much, but she was a fine person, and I had one of my famous intuitions about her. I thought I could get something from her about Dally's past . . . and the strange man who was vexing her.

I pulled the phone over close to the bed, pulled out my spiral-bound memory pad, and dialed Sally Arnold down at Abraham Baldwin Agricultural College. It was the only number I had for her. Left a message on her office machine of a fishing nature.

"Hey, Sally, it's Flap Tucker, Dally's friend. I'm in Tifton at the Lancaster. We met when I was down there in Beautiful, Georgia, a while back for that reunion dinner on the grounds, you know, with the Turner family, and all. Look, I wanted to ask you something about you and your husband Charlie, and Dally, when you all were going to Wesleyan. And I was in the service. I'm trying to—you know, I'm teasing Dally about it, and I can't remember the name of that other guy that was buzzing around her at the time." I didn't think my voice bluff sounded like a barking dog—but that's what it felt like. As far as I knew, there had never been anybody else trying to get next to Dally but Charlie Arnold, and he'd married Dally's college roommate Sally. Ancient history. "She's told me the guy's name, I just can't remember. You could call me at the hotel if you wanted, I'm only in town tonight. Back home visiting—on other business, and thought I'd give you a ring. Maybe even luck out on an invitation for some of your world-famous fried chicken. Or you could call my number in Atlanta, if we miss each other. Thanks, Sally." I gave her the number at the hotel and then my home phone.

Sometimes when you make up a bluff like that, you feel kind of clever, like you've pulled something off. I just felt tired.

I felt like sleep had just sapped me when the phone rang. Groggy, I pulled the receiver toward the general area of my face.

"Hello?"

"Flap? It's Sally. Sally Arnold."

"Yes," I answered. "How are you?" I tried sitting up. The clock said it was six-thirty, but I couldn't tell if that was AM or PM.

"Not that good"—she sounded thoughtful—"considering the circumstances."

She let out a hefty sigh and then didn't talk, so I thought maybe I should start.

"I'm sorry. What's the matter?"

"What in the world are you doing in Tifton?"

"Business, that's all." I rubbed my eyes. "What's up?"

"Why are you asking about Ronnard Raay?"

It only took me another second to wake up completely. "Higgins?" That's all I could manage.

"Yeah," she went on. "How do you know about him? Dally made us all swear we wouldn't talk about him."

"Uh-huh." When you bluff, the less said, the better.

"But since you know. It's kind of your fault, in a way—that's what she always thought, anyway. She was there at college, you were in the service. What with you gone, she kind of went wild, see? So when Ronn started paying her all kinds of attention, she went overboard."

"Go on." It didn't even sound like my voice.

"He was a charmer, I'll give him that." Sally's voice got quieter. "But I guess if you've got money, you always seem a little more . . . what's the word?"

"Rich?"

"Debonair. Ronn was from big money. He bought up a lot of land around here. I think he owns Dally's old place. He doesn't do anything with it, though. He's not here. I don't know where he stays. He's old Macon money, and his mother was a Canton in Atlanta. So maybe he's up there."

Blue blood, old money, Piedmont Driving Club, southern aristocracy, made a mint in old Coca-Cola and ruthless business deals—that's how you spelled Canton.

"Anyway, it was all over a long time ago—that big old fight Dally had with Ronn that night. It was on account of if his parents found out about Dally, they'd have a fit." She lowered her voice. "He called her white trash."

"Dalliance is descended from the man who *founded* Georgia," I announced. "That goes a long way . . ."

". . . it was just a fight, Flap. You know how you say things in a fight you don't really mean—not afterward, anyway. But it was one mean bit of yelling. Charlie and

I had to break it up. I don't believe I ever saw Ronn again after that night. It wasn't until two weeks later that I saw Dally." Softer again. "When I visited her at the hospital."

"Hospital?"

Sally sounded like a ghost. "She was in the Millegeville."

She meant the State Mental Hospital in Millegeville—Georgia's Bedlam.

"Well"—I heard my voice scratch out across the air—"this story just gets better and better."

"You didn't know that either?" Sally paused. "I thought she would have told you everything. Maybe I'd better just shut up."

"Get to the part where Dally goes nuts."

"Oh," Sally was quick to answer, "she didn't go nuts. She tried to kill Ronn—he said—and he had her locked up."

"She tried to kill him?"

"Well," she began, like she was telling me about two little kids fighting, "he came after her first. He swung at her with that thing you use to change tires with. But she had a kitchen knife, they say, and stabbed at him three or four times before he quit coming at her." Her voice dropped ghostly. "I think there might have been liquor or even drugs involved."

"Stabbed him." I could feel the blood in my temples. Were we talking about a person in an alternate universe? "But it was self defense . . ."

". . . his daddy got involved," she explained. "He pulled all kinds of strings, and before any of us knew it, she was carted off to the state hospital. It was a mess."

Sally got so quiet that, for a second, I was afraid she was finished with her story, so I had to prompt her.

"How'd she get out, then?"

"Out?" She snapped back into the picture. "Oh. Ronn went and got her after a week or so. He was pitiful, said he couldn't get by without her. Bad as everything was between them all the time, he couldn't live without her. He wanted her lots more than she did him."

"You can see why," I offered.

"Sure," she agreed. "She started to realizing what was going on. And then your letters started coming."

"Yeah," I remembered, "something about how they got held up for a couple of months?"

"Army," she said, as if it were a curse word.

"I wasn't in the army, exactly," I began.

"Anyway," she went on, "when your letters started to coming, she seemed to calm down a good bit. That's when I knew the score."

"The score?"

"That's when I knew," Sally said softly, "she was sweet on you."

I laughed out loud. "Dalliance was never 'sweet on me,' Sally. That's not the nature of our relationship."

"Well," she said slowly, and I heard the skepticism in her voice, "maybe it ought to be."

"No, see . . ." I started.

". . . *you* see, Flap," she interrupted. "For once, why don't you?"

14

ATTACHMENTS

I wanted to pursue that line of thinking worse than I've ever wanted to do anything in my life, but your Tao has a way of dealing with desires and attachments. In this case, my Tao produced a heavy thud on the hotel room door.

"Sally, can you hang on? There's somebody at the door."

"Okay." She sounded impatient.

I laid the phone down on the bed and made it to the door. In the hall there was a local cop. His uniform was crisp and spotless. His posture was perfect. His head looked shaved under that hat, and the eyes were a cloudless sky.

"Hi, Officer." I tried to sound as innocent as possible. You never know what a small-town deputy might think you've done. "Come on in. I'm on the phone."

I took a step back and he walked in, expressionless and silent.

I picked up the phone. "Hey?"

Sally responded. "I heard you say 'officer'?"

"That's right," I confirmed. "Can I call you back?"

"You still want fried chicken? Come on over."

"I'll give you a ring back," I told her, eyeballing the nice policeman.

Before I'd even hung the phone up, the guy began his speech.

"Are you the owner of the vehicle parked on Simpson Place, license number LNN323?"

"Is that my license number?" I reached to the back pocket of my sleep-wrinkled double-pleats and started to fish out my wallet. Wrong move.

The cop put out his right hand, blew out a breath, took a lunge backward, and had his pistol in his left hand, cocked and pointed directly at my face—all in under a second.

"Whoa," I soothed. "Steady. Just reaching for my wallet to show you some ID and check my insurance card for the license number."

I moved in the world's slowest motion, picking my billfold out of its place with one finger and my thumb. I held it out between us like a dead fish.

"I . . ." he started, trying to compose himself, "I thought you were going for a gun."

"Don't have one." I think I sounded reassuring. "Can I show you the funny picture on my driver's license now?"

He was still frozen in the basic television-style posture of some law-enforcement stereotypes.

"Are you Tucker?"

"Yes," I said slowly. "Do we know each other?"

"No." He seemed very confused. "But we got us a lot of Tuckers around here."

"Right." I didn't move. The young man was obviously tense.

He finally uncocked and replaced his revolver. He reached out, wordless, and took my wallet. He examined several things in it, checked to see how much cash I had, and gave it back to me.

From the wastrel days of my misspent youth I'd had the experience of being busted for vagrancy just because I didn't carry enough cash. It's a way some policemen used to have of messing with you if they didn't like you but didn't have anything else to arrest you for. So I always kept a crisp twenty in the billfold.

I put it back in my pocket, still moving very slowly.

"Your car is illegally parked, Mr. Tucker. That side of Simpson is no parking. Would you mind moving your vehicle into the lot of the hotel?"

Now, a small town is filled with niceties that you don't find in your larger metropolitan areas, but a nervous deputy who was understanding enough to find you and ask you to move your car instead of just shoving a ticket under the wiper blade? That strained credulity.

"Yes," I said with as little irony as I could manage, "I can move my car. And may I say thank you, Officer, for bringing the matter to my attention."

He stood. He fidgeted. He looked down. "You're not buying this, are you?"

"Not really," I admitted. "But it's not you. It's the situation."

"I'm supposed to scare you." His expression still hadn't moved beyond the mask of impassivity.

"I'm a little scared," I suggested. "That gun thing, the pointing the loaded revolver at my head—that was good. Why are you supposed to scare me?"

"I suck at this. Somebody wants you to go back to Atlanta."

"Already?" I looked around my little room. "I just got here. Ordinarily I have to be in a place for at least twenty-four hours before anybody wants to get rid of me."

"Your reputation." That's all.

"I see." The officer's aplomb was beginning to crack, I could tell that. It was my guess that he was doing something he'd been told to do or paid to do—but it was something he clearly didn't *want* to do.

"You wouldn't have any inclination to tell me who

wants to scare me, and who's been impugning my rep, would you?"

He looked for a second like he might do just that—but in the end all he said was, "Move your car."

"Yes, sir."

He turned to leave, then hesitated. "I didn't give you a ticket."

I waited. I knew there was more.

"I think you could return the favor."

"I'll conclude my business here almost immediately. I'm really going to Invisible. Then I'll go right back to Atlanta. And the whole time I'm here in these parts, I'll try to look scared."

"I just meant," he said, softer, "you could not mention my pulling out my gun. It was stupid."

"Not if I'd had a gun myself."

He finally looked me in the eye. "Okay."

And he was out the door.

I stepped into the hall and called out to his back. "Is this last night or this morning?"

He half turned, kept moving. "What?"

"Is it morning or night? What time is it?"

He shook his head, glanced at his watch. "Six forty-seven in the morning." He disappeared down the stairs.

I'd fallen asleep in a strange hotel room and slept nearly twelve hours. Is that one of the danger signs of depression—or just a preparation for going home?

I took advantage of the free breakfast downstairs. Everything was on a haphazardly arranged buffet table: coffee, juice, scrambled eggs with onions and peppers, farm sausage, country bacon, grits and gravy, biscuits the size of hubcaps, and a fruit medley of indeterminate age. I loaded up a plate, sat at a small table by a window looking out on some nice impatiens, and ate quickly.

Then I sauntered outside into the early-morning air and got in my car. I cranked it, sat for a second looking at all the other cars parked along both sides of Simpson—none with tickets—then pulled out onto the main street that ran in front of the Lancaster Hotel, heading a little south, a little west—toward Invisible.

15

INVISIBLE

Twenty minutes later, I was there.

There consisted of a whole lot of kudzu and a little bit of nostalgia. The sky was white-hot, the road was sizzling black, and the pines were thick and motionless. Main Street was totally dead.

Past where the Miss Georgia Dairy Store used to be, I was relieved to see that Sonny's was still open. It was an all-in-one stop: gas, food, gossip, bait, ammo—run by shade mechanic and amateur psychoanalyst, Sonny Griffin. Sonny was the archetype from which all subsequent "good-old boys" had been fashioned. Except for the fact that Sonny was a woman.

She dressed like a man, kept her hair in a crew cut, rumbled in a low, menacing, snake-killing accent, and had lived with the same woman—Bedilia, who ran the post office—for thirty years. It's funny—in fact it's hilarious—that in a little country town like Invisible people will gossip about little things endlessly, but the fact that Sonny was who she was had never once been discussed. By anyone. I don't think the Reverend Mr. Lee, pastor of the New Hope Baptist Church, where Sonny and Bedilia had gone every Sunday for all their lives, even knew the word *lesbian*. Sonny and Bedilia were roommates. And they were decent, hard-working members of a dwindling community that had no business questioning two of the few natives who stayed and kept the town alive.

Although the word *alive* was a questionable one to use for downtown Invisible. Sonny's was, in fact, the only place open at all. And there was nobody there except Sonny.

I pulled in. Sonny was sitting in a lawn chair out in front, watching me. Her tee shirt said "Sh!" in big red letters, and her black shorts were bigger than a tablecloth.

I got out of the car.

"Hey, Sonny."

"Hey," she said warily. She looked me up and down. "Did you used to be Flap Tucker?"

"You remember me?" I couldn't help the grin.

"Shoot." She looked away. "Some of these kids, you don't forget." Another gruff look. "No matter how hard you try. You and that Dalliance Oglethorpe used to snitch my Necco Wafers."

"Did not. That was Valerie . . ."

". . . you still up in Atlanta?"

"I am." I walked around the car and came closer to her. "And it was Valerie Carter who took those Neccos." I looked down at her. "She did share them with us, though."

"How is Miss Dally? Still got her nightclubs?"

"I see you keep abreast of things."

"Okay, enough small talk." She looked up at me. "What you doing here, Flap?"

"Can't just be coming home for a visit?"

"Visit what?"

I looked out across the Invisible landscape. The heat waves rising from the asphalt distorted images in wavy, dizzying patterns. The weeds and vines and termites had taken over. Everything was decayed and overgrown. Somewhere off behind the abandoned barbershop, a dog was barking. But even the dog sounded old and played out.

"Look"—I pulled up a short stool that was beside the door and sat next to her—"you know everything. I've got a few questions."

"You drove all the way from Atlanta to sit here and ask me a few questions?" She closed her eyes and shifted in the chair. The chair complained. "I guess it's something about Dally."

"Something about Dally? You haven't seen me in— what?—more than ten years, and you think I'm here to talk about . . ."

". . . just because you ain't been here in a while," she interrupted, "don't mean we don't know *all* about you."

"All about me?"

"Why don't you get out of that detective business, son? Why don't you get you some real work? Take ahold of that Dalliance Oglethorpe for once in your life, and don't let go. That's what you want to do with your future."

Well, there it was: the small-town know-it-all version of oracular vision. Or maybe even the poor sap at Delphi was just another small town busybody with an opinion. Either way, it wasn't what I wanted to hear at that particular moment.

"You don't have the slightest idea what I'm here for," I began, trying to keep the edge off my voice, out of respect. "I've got trouble, so does Dally, and I'm trying to help."

She opened her eyes, lizardlike, and gave me the overwhelmingly serene gaze. "You found out about Ronnard Raay, didn't you?"

Locusts upped the volume a little, if only to emphasize the strangeness of her vision. A small white stiletto cloud sliced the sun. More heat poured out.

"Yes." When in doubt, say as little as possible. It can give the illusion of knowing more than you do. There is power in silence.

But there's always someone cleverer than you are.

"You don't know jack," she pronounced, and closed her eyes again.

"Sonny," I sighed, "can we start this conversation over?"

"Okay."

"Hi, Sonny—it's me, Flap Tucker, home for a visit." She gave a curt jut of the chin. "Hey, Flap."

"So, how's everything in the old hometown."

"Quiet. Hot." A flicker of the lids. "Still, home is the center of everything in the world."

"Okay, *that's* why I'm home." I sat back. She'd forced me to say something true, almost against my better judgment. "I need a little time at the center of things."

"I know."

"Look, Buddha," I told her, unaware of why I was getting irritated, "it's my turn to say 'you don't know jack.' You've got no idea what's going on, so don't play the wise, silent-seer game with me. I've got no patience for two-bit ghost-town pseudomystical pronouncements."

"Okay, then." She leaned forward and reached into a tub, brought out a freezing Coke in a small bottle, popped the top off with a can opener she wore around her neck, and handed it to me. "How about a Co-Cola?"

I hesitated, but my hand seemed to float involuntarily toward the cold drink. She pulled another out of the ice for herself.

We sat there sipping the beverage that made Atlanta great, watching the blacktop get hotter.

"Dally's been getting some mail that she doesn't really need," I finally said, as if we had been talking all along.

Sonny didn't move a muscle. "You see that patch of grass over there across the road, in front of the wall?"

I looked. Once that patch of grass had been the garden that decorated a dress shop—in an era when dress shops had been a significant part of small-town commerce. All that remained were two scrawny azaleas and a lot of brown weedy fescue.

"I see it."

"Looks like an empty plot," she went on, "but just barely underneath the top layer of soil, there's a whole world: bugs and worms and microscopic whatever. They all march around down there like we don't even exist."

"And?" I suspected she was going somewhere.

"Even a dead town like this—it can have its own little world of things going on underneath."

"Yeah," I brushed her off, impatient, "I get the metaphor—I was hoping for a little something concrete."

"There was a guy down here a few weeks ago, some Yankee boy from New Jersey, they say. Got a speeding ticket in Ty Ty."

Ty Ty was the next town over—around Mysterio and Enigma, Georgia. Invisible did not stand alone in the wan name category.

"Jersey Jakes was down here?"

"If that's his name."

"And he was speeding."

"You remember Denny Martin, the one that was such a good pass receiver that year we almost went to state?"

"No," I told her. "I don't know him. I wasn't that much of a sports . . ."

". . . anyway." She waved a lazy, dismissive hand. "He's a county deputy now. He stopped the Yankee boy—doing better than a hundred. Down Tifton Highway. You know how dangerous that is?"

Tifton Highway was deserted almost all of the time, and farm boys flew their pickups down it in excess of a hundred whenever they traveled it. But I wasn't thinking about that. I was thinking about the deputy.

"What's Denny look like?"

"Big blue eyes, shaved head—ain't gone to fat, yet. Very nice posture."

"They used to show us a film in elementary school about posture," I said.

I guess her description could have fit a hundred deputies in Georgia. It didn't have to be the same one who came to my room and left so suddenly. Still, I couldn't resist pushing it.

"I think he might have paid me a visit in Tifton this morning."

"He don't usually go over that way too much." She took a healthy slug of Coke. "But you don't never know what that boy might do. He's got twins, and he don't sleep well." She inclined her head my way. "I think he's got financial concerns."

"Anyway, you tell me about this speed-trap thing because?"

"The Yankee boy was down here asking a whole lots of questions just like you. About Miss Dally. About Ronnard Raay. It's probably just a coincidence."

I sat back. "How's Bedilia?"

"Fine." No expression. "She's got that sciatic nerve, and it troubles her a whole lot. She goes to church more than she used to over it."

"Brother Lee still preaching at the Baptist?"

"He is. He's got less hellfire in him than he used to. His wife passed on, you know."

"I didn't." I hadn't even known he was married.

"Are we back to small talk?" She leaned forward.

"Because if we are, I'm getting a little hot. I feel like going inside in the air-conditioning."

"I think I'm going over to the school."

"It's all closed up, you know."

"I know. But I just kind of . . ."

". . . Sentimental journey." She leaned back and closed her eyes. "Come back by here on your way out of town."

"Sonny?"

"Yes, hon?"

"Were you expecting me?"

"In what way?" Her eyelids fluttered a little.

"In a way that would make you tell me about Jersey Jakes, or the way you brought up Denny Martin. It was all just a little too much like a setup."

"Oh." She blinked her eyes. "It's a setup all right." She leveled a solid stare my way. "You've got no idea how much money some people have."

Trying to keep up in the non-sequitur department, I said calmly, "So speaking of which: Tell me a little something about this Ronnard Raay."

She settled back, closed her eyes tighter—as if she were seeing the vision she was recounting to me in her mind's eye.

R. R. Higgins was a Macon boy. Macon was the home of Wesleyan College for Women—now simply Wesleyan College. Macon was also the home of Otis Redding and the Allman Brothers. And Macon was the home of Machine-Gun Ronnie Thompson, a certain archetype of southern mayors: white face, red neck, black gun. If you were white and rich in Macon in a certain era of southern grandeur, you were like the petite royals of Europe in another grand older time.

His mother was from a fine old family. A hybrid azalea had been named for her. Her cotillion at the Piedmont Driving Club in Atlanta had been the talk of the town for a week when she turned eighteen. She worked, noblesse oblige, with wayward girls—the then-current euphemism for pregnant unwed teens—and helped found the ladies' adjunct golfing society of the South's finest country club.

When she married a Macon Coca-Cola executive, a new empire was born. And Ronnard Raay was born right into it.

Rich as a Rockefeller, good-looking as a Kennedy, smooth as a julep—and just as covert. You drink a mint julep, all you taste is the magnolia-sugar-isn't-life-grand-here-on-Tara mint. You never even know about the bourbon, until it's too late and you can't walk because you don't know what your feet are.

Ronn met Dally at a mixer. A gentleman always meets a lady at such a function, or in church. That's it. And Dally wasn't much of a churchgoer, so her only shot at finer society was a sorority party on a polka dots and moonbeams Saturday night.

The usual "May I have this dance" later, he was wining, dining, charming, farming—whatever it is you do if you're that rich and that smooth. Dally dug it all the way down to the ground. Who wouldn't?

Things were entirely apple-blossom time for a while there, but they turned about as bad as it gets in the end. And then I came home, and all was forgotten.

"That's the short version," Sonny concluded. "For the novel—talk to that Sally what's-her-name. You know."

"I know, her college roommate. We spoke briefly, but I'm planning to stop by her place on my way back to Atlanta." I sat back. "So you're saying this Ronnard Raay—he was something, then."

She only nodded, staring at the vacant lot across the street where bugs and worms and microbes waxed biologic in their dance of decay.

16

GLOSSY ABELIA

Sometimes you take a trip home to find something there, and end up finding something in yourself instead. Pine Heights Elementary School was almost as ruined as the rest of the town. The only thing that made the old brick building seem alive was the abelia out front. Abelia is a swell bit of shrubbery that has glossy leaves and little white flowers that smell like your childhood on a hot summer day.

The smell was something I'd taken in maybe a thousand times, staring out the window of the fifth grade classroom, thinking about getting away from everything in that humid little podunk. But standing there that morning, all I could think about was how much I missed that time, those days. The Buddha truly said: you don't miss your water till your well runs dry. That's Blind Boy Buddha—also from Macon.

As I stood there, maybe it was the abelia or maybe it was the heat—maybe it was even the influence of Sonny's visions—but my own mind's eye was activated—flooded with images of quasi-childhood.

Dally was running down the long, hot alley in back of the row of stores downtown. We were playing hide-and-seek. She tripped and cut her shin on a green piece of glass, Coke bottle I guess.

She sat in the dirt, rocking back and forth, squeezing her leg and whispering under her breath.

She didn't see me come up behind her.

"What are you saying?"

She jumped. "Flap! Damn it."

"Sorry. I thought you knew I was here. What were you saying?"

She looked down at the blood. "I was praying to God to make it stop bleeding."

"Praying? I didn't know you did that."

"You don't know everything about me."

I glanced down at the cut. "Didn't work."

She looked up at me. "Uh-huh. It was going way worse before I started praying."

"That's not it. You just slowed down bleeding because your blood is clotting, is all." I was blessed with a memory of our biology homework.

She steadied herself on my side and got to her feet. "What would you rather believe in, Flap? God or clots?"

I was still looking at her leg. The bleeding had all but stopped.

"Both," I told her. "God is in the clots."

At least that's the way I remember it. We were a fairly precocious pair, but I may have let memory color the dialogue a little.

I nosed around the building, letting the feelings from a long time past wash around me, thinking I might get a boost of something from it.

The sun was nearly overhead before I realized that I had already gotten what I'd come for: Dally saying, "You don't know everything about me."

17

MIXER

It was around twelve-thirty when I arrived at Sally Arnold's office at Abraham Baldwin Agricultural College. It said "Prof. Arnold/Poultry Science" on her door.

I'd called her from Sonny's, after Sonny and I had exchanged a few throwaway scraps under the heading of "catching up." Sonny'd already told me everything she was going to. She didn't even say good-bye when I left.

I stood in Sally's doorway. She was on the phone, brightened when she saw me, pointed to the only chair in the room.

"All right, Syd," she was saying, "I'll be there. Got to fly, now. Bye."

She set the phone down and leaned forward. "Flap, it's so good to see you."

"You too, Sally. Lunch?"

She grinned. "I brought us some fried chicken—since you were bragging on it—and some livers, and some vegetables. We could eat right here."

The office was as small as a closet, cluttered with years of books and dust and papers and boxes and snapshots and cards and memos and grade books and junk. There wasn't a window. The light was fluorescent. It didn't seem like the greatest place in the universe to have our repast, but I assumed Sally had her reasons.

The chicken was on plates wrapped in tinfoil. She'd

kept it in a small fridge she had in her office so it was as chilly as it was heavenly. On the plate were also baked beans and yellow potato salad. She had silverware, cloth napkins, and a glass pitcher of iced tea. She'd thought about the meal.

I ate. She tried twice to start a conversation, and stopped herself in mid-thought. Finally, she found the right words.

"Flap," she announced, "what goes on between you and Dally is none of my business."

"Okay." I finished the drumstick.

"What went on between Ronn and Dally," she went on, "is none of your business."

"Unless Ronn is the person responsible for leaving notes of a threatening nature, not to mention packages of a gruesome sort, at her place." I set the bone on the edge of the plate. "Then we've got concerns."

"You think it's him that's doing something like that to Dally." It wasn't a question.

"I do. He's trying to scare her. And I don't know why. He's trying to muscle her, and . . ." I trailed off.

". . . and she don't want your help. Or else you wouldn't be down here running all over creation trying to find out something you think you should already know." Sally sat back. "But don't you think"—she lowered her voice—"that she might be just a little bit embarrassed about everything that went on between her and Ronn."

"Embarrassed?" I put the plate on her desk. "What went on between them?"

As it turned out, I ended up being sorry I'd asked, because Sally told me.

I was away, Dally was in college, Sally was the roommate. Wesleyan College was sedate, but you can't go to college without experimenting in things you never thought you'd do when you lived at home. Dally's version of that experimentation involved a rich boy, common recreational drugs of the day, and the heaviest flirtations this side of Mae West.

Sally and Dally were in their room on the night that changed her life, folding laundry and avoiding book work.

"Damn that Flap," she said to Sally. "He won't call. He won't write. He won't tell anybody where he is." She stopped in mid-fold. "What if he never comes back?"

"He'll be back." Sally finished her pillowcases.

"But what if he never comes back, I'm saying. Or what if he's killed or something. What am I going to do then?"

"It sounds to me like you've got it bad for him." Sally sat on her bed.

"I think I like him a whole lot better than he likes me." She sat too.

Sally sighed. "Well, it's like that sometimes. Me and Charlie's lucky. We both have the same pull, I guess you'd say." She patted Dally's shoulder. "You sure you don't want to go to this mixer tonight? Might be fun."

"I don't want to horn in on you and Charlie."

"Shoot," Sally said, "once you get there, you'll have men buzzing around you like crazy, and me and Charlie can sneak off." She blushed.

"I don't know."

An hour and a half later, Dally met Ronnard Raay Higgins. He was dressed to the nines, jazzing all the girls, shaking hands with all the boys, swilling martinis instead of beer, and making himself the focus of nearly every conversation.

When Dally came into the room, he shut up. She could have that effect—still can—and everyone noticed.

Sometimes there's a visible electricity between two people. Everyone stayed out from between Dally and Ronn for fear of being electrocuted by it.

By the end of the evening, Ronn was saying things like, "when we go to Paris" and "our place in the mountains" and Dally was as bowled over as she could get.

Their dates went from weekly to nightly inside of a month, and since she still hadn't gotten any of the letters I'd written, Dally had signed off on me.

"Even when Dally found out about Ronn's drugs and all, she just kept right on." Sally swallowed a little of her tea. "I think she liked it. Some girls, you know, are drawn to a little badness." Another grin. "Why you think she takes to you so much?"

"I'm not bad," I corrected, "I'm just wrong."

"Anyway," she continued, "Dally liked an occasional little bit of cocaine and she liked the romance of the rich-boy crime scene in a small town." She took a serious sweep of my face. "Everybody likes to live dangerously once in a while. Isn't that what you were doing in the service?"

I had no answer for that.

"The fact is, except for when they were really wasted, Ronn and Dally were a real fun couple. And I believe if you'd have met him under different circumstances, he might have been the type man you'd run with up there in Atlanta."

I had to stop and think about the borderline-criminal element I often took for consorts. I didn't want to agree with her, but she was probably right.

"The only thing he couldn't stand was running out

of money. When his folks cut him off, which they did every so often if he got real wild, he'd just do some bad deal again, and get a bundle to tide him over until he could talk his daddy into letting the money gate open."

"His parents cut him off?"

"Every so often. He usually took it in stride. I'm sure he's grown out of it by now, but sometimes it used to get to him. He could be kind of panicky if he thought he was going to run out." She leaned back. "You know, me too. Everybody's that way, I guess."

"But you don't deal coke when you get economically challenged, I'm guessing."

"Shoot." She laughed. "I got animal tranquilizers, what would I want with cocaine?"

The phone rang to punctuate her joke. She picked it up. After she listened for a second, she looked right at me. "Send him up, please."

She hung up. "I was talking to my friend Syd Martin before, when you came in? I wanted her to do me a favor. She did. She sent her son over to talk to you."

That's all Sally would say. But when I saw who came to the door of her office, I understood what the favor had been.

"Officer Martin? I believe you know Mr. Tucker?"

The kid was standing in the frame of the door, but he looked like he'd rather be almost anywhere in the universe.

"So," I said, standing up, "you *are* Denny Martin after all. I was just talking about you over in Invisible just this morning."

He nodded curtly, once.

"You want to come in, hon?"

He stood firm in the doorway.

"So, Officer Martin, I understand you gave a speeding

ticket to one Mr. Jakes a while back." I saw no point in beating around the bush.

"I don't have to tell you about that." He saw no point in cooperating.

"You don't," I said, coming to stand in front of him like a drill instructor in front of a recruit. "So I'll tell you about that. You were given money by a Mr. Higgins to mess with anybody who was down this way asking about him." I was bluffing, and I was doing it boldly—but it wasn't a stretch. "And then you were given more money to mess with me. You could go to jail today, see—because that's what they call illegal."

"Mr. Jakes was speeding . . ." he started lamely.

". . . shut up," I interrupted. "Everybody speeds on that road. And, by the way, everybody parks on Simpson. Look, you tell me what I want to know, or we go talk to your sheriff. I'm ready either way."

He stared. I think he was having visions of how life would be in jail.

"It wasn't Higgins who gave me the money." He let out a breath. "But that's who it came from."

"Who actually handed it to you?"

"Some of his employees. I don't know their whole names. One is called Chuckie."

"Why did Higgins do this?"

He looked me in the eye for the first time. "I honestly wouldn't know that, Mr. Tucker. Maybe he doesn't like you."

But I could see all the chinks in the kid's armor. He was about to cry. His eyes were red and his chin shook a little. Let's say you live in a double-wide and you've got twins who want to eat a whole lot more than you thought they would. A couple of extra dollars just for handing out traffic tickets doesn't seem all that bad. But when you're forced to look into yourself and see that you've betrayed something about your basic nature—that can seem like the crime of the century. And it was my guess that Denny Martin's basic nature was kicking its own guts out. It only took me a second more to come to the conclusion that messing with a kid like that was much worse than hassling me or Jersey Jakes.

So all of a sudden I really wanted to talk to Ronnard Raay Higgins about so many things—in the worst way.

18

DÉJÀ VU

Déjà vu isn't such a bad thing. The eerie feeling is kind of nice in a metaphysically reassuring sort of way. It can say, "You're on the right path. You've done this before. It's good." It's comforting.

On the other hand, when you've driven all afternoon to get home, fallen asleep on your sofa, and then you get a hysterical phone call at three in the morning, and then you get up and get back in your car and drive as fast as you can through the hot air along Ponce—air that won't have had a chance to cool down by the time the sun comes up the next morning—and you go to a deserted nightclub to help a friend open up a grizzly package just like you did a few nights previous, the feeling of déjà vu can seem more like a needle than a quilt. Or more like a run-on sentence, maybe.

The new lifeless hand crawled out of the wrapping when I cut the same old butcher paper. This time it was attached to an equally lifeless body, still sporting a golden wedding band at the other.

Dally caught her breath, then sat at a stool.

I looked up at her. "Is this why you called me?"

"Did I know there was a body in there? No." Blink. "Was I worried about what *was* in there? Yes."

See? Déjà vu.

"Have any notion of telling me where this one came from?" I searched the package.

"Flap." She sounded like a zombie.

"I see." I stopped looking and rubbed my eyes. "Same deal as before? You were alone, you heard the door?"

She nodded absently. That's all.

I may have mentioned that I have three rules. I've already made it clear that, no matter what, if she calls, I come. One of the other rules has to do with respecting her silences. Which proved a tough rule that night, given everything.

"Okay." I took in a deep breath. "So is it about time to call our old policeman friend Detective Huyne, now? A dead body is a little more of an event than an errant hand." I looked down at the mess. "Or should I unwrap the rest and see who this is?"

I already had my vote in mind. Open first, call later. Detective Burnish Huyne was a can of worms. Now, I don't mean to disparage the guy by calling him that—or to imply anything about going fishing with him either, for that matter. I only brought up the term to say that calling him at that time of the morning—what with him sweet on Dally and me put off from the sorry way that he sometimes liked to treat me—would bring with it some difficulty. I was certain Dally wasn't in the mood to handle it right then.

"Oh." She was breathing funny. "I think we know who it is."

"We do?"

She wasn't looking at me, so I didn't know what else to do but kneel back down and slip my little penknife past the heavy rope and thick butcher paper. Soon enough the body was laid out, sprawling nearly six feet tall. He was dressed in a swell blue suit, no hat, no glasses; his face was in rigor mortis, but I still recognized him— maybe it was the two-toned shoes. The dead body was none other than our food critic and all-around bad guy with double letters in all his names. Speaking of which, there was a letter sticking out of his breast pocket.

She made an ungodly, barely human noise. I thought it was just because of the way the hard face looked, a mask somehow distilled from a life of constant sorrow.

"Care to see what this letter in his pocket says?" I sat on the floor.

She nodded again.

I pulled the letter out of the pocket, ripped open the envelope, and read it out loud. "Consider this payment in full."

I stared up at her.

She closed her eyes.

"Dally?"

"What?" Her eyes opened again. She really hadn't quite heard what I'd said. I could tell from her face she'd been that far away.

"Are you going to tell me who this gent really is now?"

"Yeah." She stood, took in an even deeper breath than before, and nodded one last time. "I know I never formally introduced him to you." She looked away. "That would be my husband."

19

HUSBAND?

Now, under ordinary circumstances, one of the greatest things in the world is discovering something new about a person you love. Some new bit of information just when you thought you knew it all—that's what keeps surprise alive and fire in the heart of every good relationship.

Unless this fresh discovery includes a cold corpse. I think that's a safe rule: New information that involves a corpse is seldom "one of the greatest things in the world."

"Husband?" That's the first thing I could get myself to say. And only then because all I had to do was repeat a word she'd said—not have to come up with some new thought all my own.

"Yeah." She was apparently having the same verbal dysfunction that was plaguing me. "Husband." I still hadn't digested all the business about their *dating*.

Just then, because timing is everything in the entertainment business, and because Dalliance and I were in her top-notch club where entertainment reigns, Mug Lewis busted in the front door with his automatic in his left hand.

Some parts of that image were not unusual. Mug was left-handed for example, so it was natural that his gun would be in that particular appendage. On the other hand, he was the last person I might have expected to see at that time of the morning in Easy, mostly because the last time I had seen him was at his funeral.

So I said, to the room in general, "Well, this is certainly a surprise." Which I thought was a fair statement.

"Yes," he agreed, idly nodding, "I suppose it must be. I myself am a little surprised as well. I thought it was past closing time, and didn't expect anyone to be here." His eyes traveled two feet south. "Who's the stiff, by the way?"

"Dally's husband," I told him, but it didn't sound like my voice.

"Really?" He lowered his gun a little. "I never knew you were married, Ms. Oglethorpe."

"It was a well-kept secret," I conceded.

Dally remained strangely mute.

"Well then, I suppose you are wondering what I might be doing here," Mug went on casually, "at this time of night—and being dead and all."

"Now that you mention it"—I stood slowly—"I was kind of wondering about that."

"It goes like this." He took a small step in, toward the bar. "I was shot in the head by men who thought they were doing me a favor. But as luck would have it, the bullet didn't hit anything important. I've been recuperating in a distant land."

I looked at Dally. She just stared.

I turned back to Mug. His face caught the light just right, and anyone who looked at him then would have understood his given name. He had the prettiest face of any straight man I'd ever seen, even with his new stubble. Not handsome: pretty, like angels are, or Raphael heroes. In his black suit, with his gun pointed at a jaunty angle, even I would have to admit he cast something of a romantic image.

Mug Lewis had, in fact, been the apple of many an eye in both high and low society for quite a number of years in Atlanta. About a year before, he had thrown some sort of cotillion at the Piedmont Driving Club for his eighteen-year-old "niece" when she'd wanted one. How he got in there was anybody's guess. The rumors were, of course, that she was his paramour. But he tired of her after a few months, and that particular debutante ended up with a film career and a home in California, married to a prominent audio technician, with a small baby boy, first name: Lewis. All also, according to the wagging tongues, courtesy of our boy Mug.

That's the sort of mishmash Mug was known for. I never understood how he even had time for his nefarious activities, given his amorous adventures. But he was quite the mover in the more mannered fringes of Atlanta's gentleman crime, where it was often difficult to tell the difference between that and just plain good business. Big money was always involved. For example, years back he had promoted a huge land deal—or scam—around the block of Peachtree between Tenth and Eleventh Streets. First it was supposed to be an urban mall. Nearly the whole block was razed. Then the alleged Nordic developers went belly-up, and the only thing left standing was some poor little live theater. Mug felt so guilty that he sponsored a production of *Beowulf* there—a musical version of *Beowulf,* if you can believe it. I saw it. Mug invited me to opening night. Quite a hit, I thought.

Anyway, Mr. Lewis was a complex man, a beautiful man, and—until just a few moments previous to his busting in on Dally and me—a dead man.

"Mug," I finally said, "there's so much about your little story that I call to question. First: Somebody thought they were doing you a favor by shooting you in the head?"

"I owed some money to some very bad drug men, and I couldn't pay it back," he explained. "They thought if they shot me in the head, it'd be one way out of my dilemma."

"All right"—I shrugged—"but then: The bullet did you no harm?"

"They shot me in the back of the neck"—he put his own gun up behind his head to demonstrate—"but when they pulled the trigger, the bullet ran, if you can believe this, between my skull and my scalp—excuse me for the description, Ms. Oglethorpe."

She waved her hand.

"And it popped out right about here." He put the gun at his left temple, where there was something of a charming scar. "I have a very hard head."

"This is some kind of an amazing story." I had to shake my head. "But now tell me about how we all thought you were dead, and where you've been these . . ." I turned to Dally ". . . six months?"

She shrugged.

"Well, you thought I was dead because you went to my funeral because someone shot me in the head."

"That's not what I meant."

"What you meant is this: I thought it best to leave it that way—people thinking I was dead, which was my *own* idea of doing myself a favor . . ."

". . . I think I can see that," I agreed.

"So I went South, as they say."

"Right."

"A little place called Cumberland Island. I was a custodian there. It was . . . refreshing work."

"Refreshing?"

"I was in the out-of-doors a lot," he explained, "and it calmed me down a good deal. They have wild horses on the beach there."

"Yes, well," I began slowly, "you do seem calm, but I guess I have to wonder, then, why you have your automatic out."

"Oh, this." He looked down at it. "As I was saying, I was casing the place to make sure it was closed and no one was around. I'd seen the bartender leave. Then, all of a sudden, there was a guy."

"A guy?"

He raised his eyebrows. "Lumbering across the parking lot, with a rug or something over his shoulder. He barged into the very door I was about to enter. I only stood there a second or two, trying to figure what to do, before I saw him run out again. He zipped across the street and took off, in a van or something."

"You saw the guy who delivered this body?"

He inclined his head.

"Well?"

"Are you asking if I could pick him out again in a crowd? I think, actually"—he blinked—"he looked a little like you. But as you are here and not in an escaping van . . ."

". . . so you have the gun out now . . ." I prompted.

". . . oh, yes," he picked up quickly, "the gun. It was a kind of talisman, if I may use that word—protection against whatever else weird might be in here. At this time of the night. After such a spooky event."

"Talisman?"

"Okay, just a precaution, then." He shrugged. "To call a thing by its proper name."

"By all means, let's be proper." I looked at Dally again. "Sugar . . ."

". . . thanks," she interrupted, then turned my way, "for not asking me any stupid questions right now, okay?"

"Okay." I turned back to Mug. "So how about if I ask you what you've been doing since you saw the guy split."

"How do you mean?"

"Why didn't you come in here then? That had to be, like a half an hour ago. Dally found the body, called me, I drove . . . you see my problem."

"Linear time," he nodded.

"Exactly."

"I'm a cautious man these days, Flap. I've got patience, too. I peeked in here through the front door and saw Dally all agitated, I thought she was calling the cops. Naturally, I wouldn't want . . ."

". . . naturally," I agreed, "but why didn't you just split, I'm saying."

"Patience is a funny thing," he began, philosophically. "It can give a man curiosity—which is what I got." He tossed his head. "It's like a disease."

"Not that I'm buying this . . ."

". . . but when I saw it was only you, and not the cops, I got comfortable, and came on in."

"Just not comfortable enough to come in without your pistol." I took a short breath. "I'm going to call the police myself, now. And I hate to ask, but it would certainly help out, here, if you could . . ."

". . . sorry, Flap." He held up his hand. "I'm back in town on secret business of my own. And even if I wasn't, I couldn't be known to your police friends."

"They're really more Dally's friends than mine, actually, but I see your point." I stared. "Still, I'm really hoping that maybe you could help us out, then, on the sly."

"I could do that—while remaining dead to everyone else, you understand."

"Of course." I shrugged. "So, by the way, who was in your casket at your funeral—which was quite a nice affair."

"Yes, I thought it was pleasant." He smiled. "I paid for most of it myself, you know. And in the casket? It was all the records of my transactions with the certain parties I owed money to. Do you see the poetry in that?"

"Dead and buried, I get. And I see now why it was a closed-casket affair . . ."

". . . is there any other?"

"In the South? Sure. Everyone wants to look at a dead body." But I wished right away I hadn't said that, because there was a dead body nearly touching my right foot that, really, no one wanted to see.

20

TWO GOOD REASONS

There were really only two good reasons to call Detective Burnish Huyne. First, he was the presiding homicide detective for the area and there was a corpse on the floor. Second, we'd sort of worked together before, he and Dally and I. So he might not think it was as strange as it might seem for people like us to have such a thing special-delivered to the club at that hour of the AM—and he was known as something of a night person so I figured he'd be in his office. There were, on the other hand, dozens of reasons not to call him. To mention just two: He didn't think much of me, and he thought a little *too* much of Dally—at least for my money.

But, ultimately, my money was no good: A stiff on the floor beats a jealous friend any day in the week. So I found myself dialing up his number before I thought too much more about it.

"Hello." It wasn't a question with this guy, it was an accusation. *That's the way a real police detective answers the phone,* I thought.

"Well, Detective Huyne, I thought you might be in. It's Flap Tucker calling."

"Oh." He seemed more puzzled than anything else. "It is?"

"It is, and it's something about a dead body, the reason I'm calling."

"What sort of a dead body?" He was calm.

"Well, for instance, let's start with the fact that it's right here on the floor, in Dally's club."

"You're at Ms. Oglethorpe's?" He was more interested than he had been.

"Yes, and I hope you're sitting down for this: The body is none other than Ms. Oglethorpe's Mister. Ex-mister, I guess, at this point, since it's been dead for a while. It's stiff."

"What are you talking about?"

"I'm talking about Ms. Oglethorpe's husband."

"Husband?"

"That was my first response," I told him, smiling. "Try as we might, we do think kind of alike, you and I, don't we?"

"Her husband is the dead body?" he shot back.

"Yes."

Mug had put away his automatic and was sitting at the bar. Dally had gotten him a Glenfiddich, his choice of scotch. He seemed content.

Dally was standing still behind the bar. She seemed the opposite of content, whatever that would be in a situation like . . . like what? I really could come up with no simile whatsoever for the situation. I was, in every sense, stumped.

"So?" Huyne's voice was buzzing in my ear.

"Ah. Yes. So, perhaps you'd like to come over and visit in your official capacity?"

"Flap?" Which startled me. I couldn't remember that he'd ever called me by my given name.

"Yes?"

"What's really going on? You sound . . . you don't sound like yourself. Are there other people there?"

I looked at Mug. "No. But you know how surprised you probably are to find that this body was the former spouse of our Ms. Oglethorpe?" It wasn't getting any easier, no matter how many times I tried to say that phrase, how many ways I tried to say it.

"Yes."

"Double that, and multiply by a factor of, let's say, *pi*—and maybe you'd get just how perplexed I am at the moment."

"Isn't *pi* an infinite number?"

"I think so."

Silence at the other end. Then:

"You didn't know she'd been married." He couldn't hide the incredulity. He wasn't trying to. He was only trying to hide something else, something like delight, I thought—Dally had a secret that big and she'd kept it from me. That, it seemed, actually made him happy.

And that statement, especially framed in the sound of that voice, stuck an ice pick or a meat cleaver or some equally sharp and tough cliché right into the middle of my solar plexus. For a second, I couldn't feel anything else but that. My mind was trying to form the response: "That's right, I didn't know," but my voice was stuck in a rock of dry ice.

Dally was watching my face. She read it like a newspaper column, and reached out her hand, took the phone away from me.

"It's Dalliance," she said, but it didn't sound like her voice. "Could you just come on over, now, or send someone. I don't like to leave the place in a mess like this. You understand. It could be bad for business if people had to come in tomorrow and step around . . ."

She trailed off, I guessed because Huyne had started talking.

After a few seconds, she lifted her head. "Okay. See you then."

I found my voice again, looked over at Mug. "I assume you'll be wanting something like one more for the road, and then you'll be on your way—as you'd like to remain dead, at least to the cops—but I'd really like to keep in touch. I'll be moving pretty quickly to find out who brought this thing in here, and I'm going to need some timely confirmation from you about the culprit's identity *before* I show the guy his own liver in an effort to learn more about what's going on."

"You don't like to do a thing like that, that liver thing," Mug agreed, "without being sure you've got the right guy. I understand." He knocked back his scotch, Dally poured another to the top. He smiled. "I'm staying just across the street, as it happens, at the Clairmont. Ask for Curtis."

"All right"—I squinted, trying to ignore the fact that I might have to go to the Clairmont *again*—"but then here's my question for you: Don't you realize how recognizable you are? Nobody's got a face like you. You can't be hanging out around these parts without somebody knowing . . ."

". . . I have a disguise." He reached in his pocket and pulled out a pair of glasses. "Clark Kent." He put them on. "Plus." He got something else out of his suit coat pocket.

He grinned, and snapped something into his mouth. When he moved his hand away, I could see that he had popped in a gold tooth on top of one of his front incisors.

"*And,*" he went on, "I'm growing a beard, as you can see. Soon even my mother, if she were still alive, wouldn't recognize me."

I had to admit that the gold tooth significantly lowered his IQ, and the glasses, remarkably unflattering, took a lot away from his much-touted demeanor.

"Okay, then—Curtis." I smiled. "I'll be looking at the moon . . ."

He nodded. ". . . but I'll be seeing *you*."

That was a sample of the game that Mug and I had played since the old days when my band used to grease up a few of the dance floors around town. We played old jazz, swing—before it was an MTV craze—with a kind of a punk sensibility. What else could you do if you were young, playing jazz, and the Sex Pistols had just come to Atlanta? But I digress. Mug was a fan from those times, and we'd often try to stump one another with occasion-appropriate lines from the great songs.

Mug stood, kicked back the last of his scotch, and adjusted his coat so that his pistol wasn't too obvious.

"Ms. Oglethorpe." He smiled at her.

She didn't move.

He was out the door like a ghost, vanished into the shadows.

Now, ordinarily, that would have been the kind of exit to end a moment—clear and clever and clean. But there was nothing ordinary about that night—and nothing clean. Before I could even sit down on the barstool closest to me, three quick shots, like firecrackers in a barrel, ripped the air just outside the place, and something heavy bumped against the door.

I thought, *Now there really* are *two good reasons to call homicide.*

21

MOONLIGHT

Soft moonlight in the doorway spilled across the dead man's face, stopped at the collar of his short-sleeved, loud Hawaiian shirt. I hated seeing it. Mug stood over him, his automatic still in his hand, the hand shaking a little.

"Man." He had the voice that most people get when they kill somebody, no matter how tough they are: hollow and cold. "He just came right up on me. From behind. He got his arm around my neck, and I was pretty sure he had it in mind to squeeze until I couldn't breathe anymore. I started to black out. I don't even remember firing, exactly."

There was a black ooze coming from the guy's middle that proved Mug had, in fact, fired. I was glad the moonlight didn't go far enough down to make that any clearer than it was.

"This isn't by any chance," I asked Mug slowly, "the person who delivered our package inside?" I was afraid that the answer was really not what I wanted to hear.

He stared, but I could tell he couldn't quite get his eyes to focus. "I don't know."

"You know him?" I said softly, staring down at the face myself.

"Looks familiar." Mug lowered his gun hand at last.

I looked around at the streets. "The police'll be *right* here, you know."

"I know." He managed to get his gun back inside his

coat. "I've always been wise as to what kind of guy you are, and I know that since I've asked you to keep my presence here mum, you'll do it. So this is the kind of guy I am: I'm going to give you a good reason to do it." He reached into his coat. "So I'm a customer, get me? Take the money."

I wouldn't. He stuffed it into my outside breast pocket anyway.

"That's not going to do any good in a court of law."

"I know," he agreed, "but I know you'll keep quiet about it as much as you possibly can, and I appreciate it—economically."

He jammed the money farther into my pocket. I didn't object. Never resist a man with a tough nickname when he's got money in one hand and a gun in the other. That's another one of those rules you always hear about.

"Okay, then." He looked out toward the street. "I'm gone."

And before I could explain just how much I wanted him to stay, he was. I didn't really even see him move. He was just there one second, and in the next second I thought I could hear faint footsteps behind the building, moving away—but it could have been a bird. Dally feeds the birds out back.

Then, her voice: "Flap?"

"I don't know if you want to come out here or not," I said. "It's another body . . ."

". . . not Mug?"

"No. Mug's gone."

"Then . . . he shot somebody?"

"Somebody attacked him, and Mug shot the guy, yes."

She was standing right there at the door, I could tell—but there wasn't a chance she would come out.

"Is he dead?"

I tried not to think about anything, I just leaned over

and put two fingers at the side of the guy's neck. Nothing. Nothing at all.

"I guess so."

"Who is it?" Her voice was barely audible. "Do you know?"

I stared at the white face. "I know," I told her, "but could you just wait a second for the rest of this little talk. I can hear the cops . . ."

". . . this is certainly shaping up to be quite a night."

I tried to sound lighter—I didn't succeed. "I'm wondering what Detective Huyne will say about this."

"This new wrinkle." She was game too, or trying to be.

"Exactly," I agreed. "I don't think he'll see the humor."

"Don't all policemen like gallows humor?"

We both knew we were just talking because we didn't want silence, didn't want to talk about another dead body. Neither one of us really knew what we were saying at that point. Shock makes any conversation stupid.

That's why it was almost a relief to see the flashing blue lights appear in the parking lot and the men with drawn service pieces charging my way.

"Stand real still, there, Tucker." Huyne's voice was almost friendly.

I held my hands out in plain sight and made as much like a statue as I could.

Police swarmed. One knelt beside the body. Huyne was close behind, staring down at the body next to me. "I thought you said he was on the floor inside."

"Well, see," I began, hoping not to sound as hapless as I felt, "this is new."

"New?"

"I mean there is a body inside—from when I called

you a moment ago, all right—but this one just got here . . . at the door."

Huyne looked up at me. "There's another body inside?"

"Yes. There is."

"Besides this one?"

"Look . . ." I began.

But he was suddenly in no mood to hear anything else I said.

"Check him for weapons," he told the man standing closest to me.

The guy moved fast, patted me down carefully, then shook his head.

"Tucker," he began again, steel-voiced and razor-sharp, "if I look around in these bushes and leaves around here, and I find any sort of a gun . . ."

". . . it won't be mine because I don't have one; it won't have my prints on it because I don't even touch the things anymore; and I won't know whose it is, because I'm too stupid tonight to know my own middle name. Okay?"

"You don't know who this is lying here?" He looked down at the body at the door.

"Oh, yeah." I closed my eyes. "I know that." Funny how images of the guy were zooming through my head whether I wanted them there or not. Funny how I'd just gotten reacquainted with the guy—only to look at him dead.

"So?" Huyne had no patience with my sojourn down memory lane.

I opened my eyes. "This used to be a guy called Jersey Jakes." That was also a surprisingly difficult sentence to get out. Who could ever have imagined that I would get attached to the guy?

"I've heard of him." He let out a heavy breath. Then: "Ms. Oglethorpe inside?"

"Right here." Her voice was strange, muffled by the closed door. I didn't know whether she'd heard who the stiff at the door was or not.

"Are . . ." His voice was high and he moved his hand quickly to the door handle, then stopped and shot a quick look to me, like he'd given something about himself away. Then, calmer: "Are you all right?"

"All right?" Her voice was beginning to get an edge of hysteria that any person might have achieved under the circumstances, and it grew worse as she continued to talk. "Well, no, Detective. I can't say that I'm all right. I can't say that at all. I have no idea how I am, in fact. Are you coming in this door? I only ask because I'm using it to hold me up at the moment, and I guess I'll need to step back if you *are* coming in, to keep from getting knocked down, see? Which would just make me even less all right than I am now. That is, if I were on the floor, here, beside . . ." and she trailed off.

I didn't wait for Huyne's response, which, given that there were still guns pointed at me, I probably should have. But I heard the terrible shatter of her voice, and I just moved.

". . . that's right, sugar"—I touched the handle, spilling moonlight into the club—"we're coming in now, so take three steps backward."

I heard her move right away, and I was inside, holding her in my arms, before anyone else took another breath.

22

HEARTS

Much as I might have often wanted to, I'd hardly ever held Dally as tightly as I was holding her then. Our hearts were beating against each other like one big drum.

Even Huyne could see the righteousness of the moment, and remained mute.

After a second that lasted a lifetime, I stood back. "Let's go sit down."

She nodded, I put my arm around her, and we made it to the bar. She sat. I grabbed the scotch and poured her a shot. Not ordinarily her drink, but it seemed called for.

I turned. Huyne had stopped at the package on the floor.

"This is Ms. Oglethorpe's . . ." He spoke softly, like he was in church, in the direction of the corpse.

". . . yes," I finished for him. "And you might want to check the little letter in his pocket. It's got my fingerprints on it since I just handled it a little while ago to read it to Ms. Oglethorpe."

Other policemen were coming in. Some were making calls, arranging for wagons. Some were checking out the door, the floor. Some were still outside. Huyne bent over, picked the note out of the dead man's pocket with a gloved hand, and read it silently. His men began to swarm all over the place then. How many men were there. Six? A hundred?

After what seemed to be an interminable degree of activity around us, Huyne found his old voice again.

"I don't suppose you'd even care to try to explain this?" He had a little smile on his face.

"How could anybody explain something this bizarre?" I looked around.

"Well"—he absently scratched the back of his neck—"I'm going to have to try—you know."

"I guess." I wasn't sure what he was saying.

"I have to consider you a prime suspect in the deal, at this point." That's what he was saying, but he didn't mean anything by it. He was just stating a fact.

"I know." I shrugged. He had his job to do.

"And you know I'm not going to bother Ms. Oglethorpe much tonight."

I wasn't quite sure why he said that, but she responded.

"Can we just get it over with?" She was sounding really tired, at that point, so her voice was more harsh than ever.

It even startled Huyne, I could tell.

"Just tell me what happened," he said, moving toward her, getting out a small spiral pad.

She related the facts as coldly and quickly as she could, and Huyne kept quiet, except for the scratching of the pen on the paper. She told him about the delivery. She omitted Mug. She described the gunshots at the door. Then she stopped talking.

The ambulances arrived. Men moved. The air stirred. It all had the feel of a dream. Sounds were disjointed, images were blurred, voices didn't seem to be speaking English. It was all in slow motion. I felt every nerve ending in my body—and it wasn't good.

By the time the room was emptying out, I felt like I

had the worst case of the flu on record: fever, achy, dizzy, thirsty, and cold.

"Tucker?" Huyne could see I was in a state. He got a firm look in my eye and tried to speak as clearly as possible. "I'm not taking you in."

"Thanks."

"But don't go anywhere."

"Except home to bed," I agreed.

He stayed frozen on my eyes one more moment. "We'll talk."

"I'm sure we will." I turned to Dally.

She had her head down on the bar. Maybe, I thought, she was even sleeping.

Huyne gave her one last glance, lingered a second too long, then split. He was the last one out.

I felt myself moving toward the bar, and I ended up beside Dally.

She lifted her head then, and an alien's face met mine.

"Flap?"

"Yes?" I was afraid, from the sound in her voice, of what she might say next.

"You didn't do this—did you?"

"Do what?" But I knew what she was going to say, even though it defied everything I knew to be true in this life.

"You didn't kill my husband, did you?"

23

BROKEN

There's not much you can say to a question like that. Denial would have sounded a lot like I was being defensive, given the mood I was in. And my traditional blend of cool shots and laugh lines seemed out of the question.

So I did the only thing I could do. I stared back at her like I didn't know who she was. And in that silence, I felt a circle break between us.

"I'll find out who did this." It didn't remotely sound like my voice.

"I'm tired." Her voice didn't even sound exactly human.

So I drove her home, and we didn't talk anymore.

The second I got to my place, instead of dropping in bed like I should have, I found my old band contact book—under books and magazines and unpaid bills—and dialed up an old phone number. I hoped it would still be current.

"What?" That's the way he answered the phone, but it wasn't mean or tough, it was just a question.

"Daniel?" I tried not to sound too surprised to get him. "It's Flap Tucker."

"Flap? What on earth are you doing calling me at . . . five o'clock in the morning?"

"I've got a problem and I need help." A sentence

that seldom came out of my mouth. I was always the one who was supposed to solve problems and give help. I was thinking what a, pardon my language, coincidence it was that I had only recently considered taking on partners.

"Oh. Well. That's different." His voice shifted gears. "Tell me what your problem is."

"Dalliance."

"I think I know the nature of this problem." He smiled into the phone. "I should have such a problem."

"No"—I let go of a hard breath—"I don't think it's what you think it is. Dalliance is currently under the misimpression that I killed her husband."

I was glad he didn't answer right away, because I needed a little moment to adjust to having said such a thing.

Then: "Well, Flap—that's a mouthful, isn't it? Let's start with 'I didn't know she was married,' and end up with 'he's dead'?"

"Not just dead"—I closed my eyes and slumped down into the blue sofa—"dead and delivered to Dally's club. Dead on the floor. Wrapped in brown paper, like a present. And there was a note."

"A note? What do you mean?" He was completely awake, even though I knew my call had gotten him up. God bless him.

"The body had a note in the pocket. Said something about a final payment."

"I see. Somebody's trying to be what they call ominous."

"Or something."

"Well, Flap." I heard him sitting up. "This is a problem, and you do need help. And so if you're asking me to lay on the aid, I'd have to say, 'Can do.'"

"Daniel . . ." I started.

". . . Flap." He stopped me. "When I needed gigs, and wasn't worth much, who hired me? And when I got a coke habit that wouldn't lay off, who thumped me in the back of the head until I quit? And then . . . when I wanted to bust up Lorraine's marriage . . ."

". . . I see where you're going with this, Danny . . ."

". . . no, I don't think you do, Flap. Let me finish. My thought has a different ending than you think it does." He shifted a little. "The answer to all the above questions is: Flap Tucker. Now my debt quotient is high in this regard, but you don't ordinarily give a person any shot at returning the favor. You're like the Lone Ranger, see? No thank-you-masked-man . . ."

". . . to quote Lenny Bruce," I finished for him. "But I don't do these little things so that . . ."

". . . so that a guy will owe you, I know that. But what I'm talking about is not you. I'm talking about me and my sense of what's right. You don't quite get that this will be doing me a favor—if I help you. Like I've got something broken and this will fix it. It'll release a little of my karma, as you and the mystics of Asia are always saying. Don't you *want* me to have a little karma release, Flap?"

And God bless Daniel Frank again. He made me smile.

"Yes, all right, Daniel—I want very much for you to get off the wheel of death and rebirth. And if, by helping me out with my little situation here, I can be of some service to you in that regard, I suppose it would be selfish of me *not* to make you help me out."

"My point exactly. I'm glad we got that settled. You want sleep or you want me to come right over?"

"Well"—I sighed and smiled deeper—"I've said it to myself but now I say it out loud: God bless Danny

Frank. I think what I need now is a little shut-eye. See you around noon?"

"Noon's good. At where? Mary Mac's?"

"How about Krispy Kreme? I predict I'll be needing fried sugar when I wake up."

"There at noon. Get some sleep."

"Daniel . . ."

". . . no thank-you-masked-man either way, okay."

"So . . . good night then, Danny."

"Well," he said quietly, "okay. Good night, then, Flap."

24

HOT DOUGHNUTS NOW

Whenever the red neon sign was lit, you knew the doughnuts had just come out of the cooker. But if you had been a blind man, you would still have known, because the smell lifted the air like low-rent lilies, and the spirit would rise. That smell was yeast for my soul—the taste was my communion.

I sat there with the terrible coffee and the miraculous food—so hot it had already burned my tongue and the roof of my mouth and I didn't care, in fact it was blissful—waiting for Daniel Frank.

I'd walked over, since Krispy Kreme was only two blocks from my place, and the weather was as hot as the doughnuts. But on some certain days, the air has a kind of clarity that even pure water can't achieve, even if that air is in the middle of a city on an old, old street. It's renewing, that air. And I needed a little renewal.

Danny didn't keep me waiting long. He strolled in, took a stool beside me, and ordered something for himself before he'd even acknowledged my presence.

"So," he began as if he were continuing a conversation, "you got here early. Good. Now, as I see it, the real issue is why would Dalliance think you did this—even though it would seem like the issue is who did do it. That's what I've been thinking. Am I right?"

"I would never have thought of it in exactly that way,

but yes—I guess you are accurate in some respect." I took a last bite.

"Did you sleep? You look tired." He sipped his coffee.

"I slept on the sofa. It's never a true night's sleep that way. Sofa sleeping."

"I'd say you need better food, too." He took a quick glance at my sugar-glazed breakfast. "Otherwise you would have already answered my question about the real issue."

"Why would Dally think that."

"Right," he said. "While that's something that is disturbing you and keeping you from your rest, I'd have to say that it is also a clue."

"A clue? To what?"

"To what's in her head. Also to what's surrounding this—the ominous note; to what's the deal with her—excuse my language—husband."

"Well"—I straightened a little on the stool—"you certainly have a strange vision this morning. Even strangely clear, maybe."

"Isn't that why you called me last night?"

"What do you mean?"

"You can't be clear about this at all, because it's broken your connection—like with your muse . . . something like that. You need someone else to see *for* you—for just a little while. You need someone else to ask questions about Ms. Oglethorpe that you can't or won't ask yourself. Maybe you're even afraid she might not give you the right answers. Not lie, exactly . . . just avoid." He lifted one shoulder.

I stared at Daniel's profile for a long time. I wondered, then, why I'd lost track of the guy for a while. It brought up all kinds of mud from the band days—and it made me take a square look at my life with Dally. As long as I had her, what did I need with any other friend?

But it had made me lose touch with my circle. It had made me a loner.

Dally and I used to have a circle of friends so close we wouldn't go out of the house without calling each other to see who else was stepping out, and where we were all going. Where does that go?

He finally turned to look at me. "Stop staring. People will talk."

"Yeah"—I smiled at that—"but Daniel, I love you."

"Lay off." He smiled back. "You're spooking the straights."

But no one in the place was paying the least attention to us. In a joint where drag queens and psycho killers with devil tattoos are the average customer, you really have to go the distance to make any kind of impression at all.

"Dan? This has all happened a little suddenly for me."

"Yes"—he nodded—"you wouldn't have called me otherwise. If things had moved at their normal pace, you would have had time to digest, to consider—you'd be perplexed, but you'd be fine. You've got a whammy on you."

"Yes," I agreed, "I do."

"So," he continued, "let's examine the worst parts first. Dally had a husband that nobody knew about. Not even you. Which, could I say, I would not have taken even money on—your not knowing something about that particular person. Now, not only did she have one—but now he's dead in her club. Okay, before we can even get used to that, Dally jumps to the bizarrely erroneous conclusion that you had something to do with it. And all this takes place at the speed of light."

"Not to mention the second body."

He almost dropped his coffee cup.

"What?" He twisted on his stool to face me squarely.

"Yeah," I told him, looking down at the crumbs on my plate. "Before we could even get the cops there, somebody else got popped—at the front door."

"Who? Do we know?"

"Poor old Jersey Jakes. Remember him?"

"He got dead? Another dead body got dropped off?"

"No"—I shook my head slowly—"this one was alive for a while, then somebody shot him."

"At the front door?"

"Yes."

"While you were staring down at the dead husband?" His voice was getting loud enough then to actually concern the ice-cool wait staff, so I looked him in the eye.

"Dan," I said quietly, "don't ask me too much about this right now, okay? There are a few things I can't tell you because I promised I wouldn't."

He held my stare for another minute or two, then nodded. "Fair enough. But when I find out these things on my own, you can discuss them with me?"

That was Daniel Frank. I already knew where he was going with his thinking. He knew I was keeping a confidence, and that I wouldn't break it. But he also knew that he could probably find out what it was. Because he knew he could find information about a single penny in a desert sandstorm if he wanted to. That was his gift: information.

"We'll talk." It was evasive. I knew we would talk about it eventually.

"What's your next move, then?" He went back to his coffee.

"I'm going to speak with Huyne," I told him, "strange

as that may be. I want to find out some hard information about the letter, the body, the wrapping—that sort of thing."

"Will he give?"

"No"—I shook my head, smiling—"but he may share."

"Ah." Danny understood. "You know, Flap? For a man who likes to think of himself as something of a mystic, that's talking an awful lot like a detective."

25

DETECTIVE WORK

I shoved my plate and cup away, the ancient ceremonial indication that I would have no more, and tried my best not to be insulted by what Daniel Frank had just said to me.

"I'm merely going about my daily work," I told him as I stood.

"Good." That was all.

I wasn't surprised that Dan and I had passed so few words between us. It had been the way we had communicated in the old days. Once you have a kind of understanding like that—at least with some guys—it never goes away. Years can zip by like birds snapping past your window, and you can take up right where you left off like no time at all had intervened. And I'd say thank God for that, when it happens.

"I'm off to the police." I dropped a five on the counter.

He stared at my oversize tip. Then: "I'm off to see a man about a doggerel. Call me at two."

That was something I'd forgotten about Danny. Sometimes he thought he was being clever, when he was just being strange. Still, wit is subjective, I guess. I didn't even bother asking him to explain. I just took off out the door, back into the hot air.

From the doughnut place, it was a good five city blocks to the police station—if I walked it, maybe it would be enough time to get my thoughts together.

Which would have happened except for the fact that as I walked, all I could think about was what had gone wrong. Not sleeping can make a person see the world in a different light—or less light, really: more shadow. I considered the possibility that Mug had been the one to deliver the dead body of Dally's Mister. Or that the second stiff, in the person of Jersey, had been his henchman. And that Mug had iced him too, to keep him cool. It would have made sense. Jakes was hardly the type to pop somebody, wrap him up, and deliver him all alone to Dally.

Or maybe it was just the heat.

What didn't figure most of all was Dally's wild leap. What do you call the opposite of a leap of faith? Leap of doubt? And how, I was left wondering, after everything—everything—could she possibly think what she did?

That's when, about block three, Danny's words started making more sense to me. What I had to get clues to, besides the facts about dropping corpses and parking-lot jazz, was something about Dally's internal landscape. It was a place I would have bet everything on, only a few days earlier. But at that moment, it all looked like a new part of the forest—something I barely knew at all.

I needed, in short, to know how her mind had worked in those wee hours the night before. And for that, I needed to know why she'd never told me about her Mister. And for that, I needed to know about him. And for that, I needed a phone.

Once I thought that, my steps quickened. I saw clearly what my path was—or my two paths: one in the city, one in Dally's mind.

So by the time I got to the station house, I was feeling ready for Detective Burnish Huyne.

I walked into the station house like I knew what I was about. Huyne saw me coming.

"Well, Mr. Tucker." He wasn't smiling. "Have a seat. This is good, your coming in like this. Saves me a few steps, you know." He offered me the seat in front of his desk.

"Let's see if I can guess." I sat. "You found my prints on both stiffs, the letter in the one guy's pocket, and all over the wrapping paper."

"For starters," he said.

"Okay, now you tell me the rest." I wanted to see what he had.

"Fine." He obviously didn't mind sharing. "We also found evidence of a third pair of shoes by the body at the front door—that is besides yours and the deceased's. Oh, and some shell casings that might be involved."

"What does this mean to you?"

"If I look at it from your point of view, it could even mean that you're off the hook. I mean to say that there was obviously someone else there besides you." He scratched his face. "On the other hand, if I look at it objectively, which I ought to do considering the obligations of my chosen profession, I'd have to say that it could also mean that you maybe had what we call an accomplice. Because this other person was there last night, I'm pretty sure, and you didn't share that information with me. Not a mention. So I have to wonder why you'd withhold such valuable and potentially self-serving information from me, unless it actually does you more harm than good for me to know."

I smiled. "I see your problem: You're a man who likes to look at something from all the angles."

"That's right."

"Especially if it messes me up." I didn't mean that to come out as aggressively as it did.

"Flap"—his voice was much quieter—"if you knew me just a little bit better, you wouldn't underestimate me like that."

And for a second, I stared at the guy like we'd never met.

I was still trying to adjust to what could have been a new attitude when he started talking again in his old voice.

"At any rate," he went on, not looking me in the eye, "I am going to assume you've already started your own investigation, for what that's worth. If you know what's what, you'll keep me apprised."

"Yes"—I smiled—"and I can start right this minute. Man number three in the parking lot with me and the dead body? That's my client." I took a small second to respect Mug's foresight. "That's why I didn't mention him last night, you can understand."

Huyne leaned back. "Oh. Your client. Like I care." He nodded. "Unless he knows who killed these guys."

"I didn't say that." I had no expression on my face whatsoever. It's a good trick. "And by the way, do we have a cause of death for the gift-wrapped corpse?"

"Stabbed in the heart."

"His clothes weren't that messy."

"Stabbed in the heart, bled to death, bled some more, cleaned up, changed, wrapped, and then delivered." His eyes were barely slits.

"Well." What more could I say?

"So I guess you'd *better* tell me about your client's . . ."

". . . I don't know what he did or what he didn't do," I interrupted, "from any firsthand knowledge." True. "I'll have to start my investigation and see where it goes, just like you do."

"Just like me?" He didn't bother to cover the irony. "Aren't you going home to cogitate or whatever you call it is—what you do?"

He was making fun of my ability, my talent—my way of putting two and two together in a quiet moment of contemplation. He thought it was something mysterious, like most people did. But the more I did it, the more I realized it was just another cold trick of the mind, and I felt cold enough as it was there in the police chair.

So I leaned forward. "My trick?" I got a good look locked right into his eyes. "Not today."

26

TODAY

A whole lot of people will tell you that today is the only day there is. Live in the moment, they'll say. The moment is all. I've tried. I really have. But I always worry a little too much about what's going to happen next. And then there's the problem of what if today stinks. Are you stuck in that? If misery is all there is, why would you want to be in that moment—when there are so many other pleasant moments at your disposal, in your mind's eye, when memory whispers its pale joy.

So as I sat there across from Detective Burnish Huyne, I found my mind wandering to a day long since gone. Dally and I were staring down at a lake where turtles were swimming. The sun was pouring over us like spun honey, and the turtles were lazy and skimming the lake. She was wearing a skirt with a funny blue pattern all over it, and when we stood I happened to turn just the right way at the right moment and our lips had brushed. Like we'd been shot with a house current, we both snapped our heads back and stared.

That was a day way better than today, I was thinking.

"So what are you going to do?" Huyne's voice was a nasty awakening.

"Well, I was going to try to be clever and trick you into telling me what you know about the note—and whatever other evidence you have, that sort of thing."

"How were you going to do that?"

"By appearing to be disarmingly forthright." I smiled at him. "Is it working?"

"Tucker." He shook his head. "Can you tell me why I didn't arrest you last night?"

"Yeah." I leaned forward. "Nine times out of ten, the killer doesn't call in to the cops. Now, I'm pretty smart, as we've just discussed, so I could be suckering you. But then you're pretty smart too, so I think you'd see past that. Plus, you wouldn't arrest me like that in front of Dally. She wouldn't take it well. It would imply that she was lying because she'd tell you the stiff in the package was there before I arrived, and the one at the door was bopped while I was inside right next to her. So you couldn't pop me, in short, without impugning her veracity . . ."

". . . which I would never do," he agreed. "So. Here's what we've got: The note's got your prints on it, fresh, and that's it. That body remains officially unidentified, but we've already called Ms. Oglethorpe in for questioning, so that's coming up. As to the body at the door, the second guy, that was none other than Jersey Jakes, as you told me last night."

"Poor old Jersey." I shook my head.

"You knew him, I'm guessing." Huyne was staring.

"Yeah. He was a tropical."

"Oh for God's sake." Huyne was clearly not in the mood for whimsy—or explanation of same.

"What do you make of all that, then?" I wanted to see what he'd tell me.

"I have opinions." That was all he said.

"You think maybe this Jakes was the delivery boy for the body, and that he was popped by an accomplice or a higher-up." I realized after I'd said it that my sentence was more a bold indication of my own wishful thinking and little to do with what Huyne might have in mind.

"No"—he blinked—"I was going with the fact that Jakes had been watching the place and had seen the delivery, surprised the delivery boy, and got the wrong end of the deal."

"Why would he have been watching the place?"

"Because"—Huyne was looking at me sideways—"he was in the employ of Ms. Oglethorpe to do just that."

27

I SLEEP WHILE THE CITY BURNS

"What gives you that idea?" I tried to sound steady.

"She told me? When I called her this morning to come in?" He was asking me questions like that because he seemed to think that I was the densest person in the Southeast at that moment.

"Okay." I was calm. "So you know about that." Bluff: "Did she tell you the other thing?" Sometimes an outrageously vague lie like that can actually work.

"Yes, we know all about the other letters." He sounded like he was tired of playing with me.

"So." I know for a fact that my voice didn't sound right, then, because Huyne looked up at me with actual concern.

"Flap?" He was searching my face. "You okay?"

"Tired."

He looked back down. "It's the hours you keep." He got a piece of paper. "This is my warrant for you. All I have to do is sign and send, and you'll be here with me permanent. I tell you this to explain how close you are to the edge, and to make sure you know not to mess with me on this thing, right?"

"The last thing I need from you," I managed, smiling, "is information about how close to the edge I am at the moment."

"Good." He mistook my meaning. "So you go ahead and do your little investigation or whatever it is that you do, and you tell me everything I want to know, and by and by we'll get the evil bad person that's scaring our girl."

Our girl.

He leaned forward. "Deal or not?"

"Yeah." I rubbed my eyes. "Fine. Look, let me just think a second, here." I looked hard at my hands and tried to focus my thinking. "Try checking out the inside elbow bend on Jersey's body for some kind of skin or fiber evidence."

"What?" He tilted his head.

"Like he'd had his arms around someone's neck, for example. Would that show up, something like that?"

"Could." Huyne looked away. "Your so-called client . . ."

". . . stop. Okay?"

He was about to say something else when he decided on: "For now."

I nodded.

"Anything else you might want your personal service to look for?"

"Is there any way of telling where the wrapping paper, the stiff's packaging, is from?"

"Looking into just that."

"Being who the dead guy is, and all—Dally thinks it might be down south. Invisible, or maybe Macon, Georgia." Once again, I didn't see any point in letting Huyne know that the guy had actually been in Atlanta for a while. Or that I had been to Invisible.

"Could have been wrapped there. But the paper wouldn't have been made there."

"No"—I smiled—"I guess it wouldn't."

"Are you just stalling, now?" He squinted. "Because this is all pretty much par for me . . ."

". . . sorry." I nodded quickly. "You're right. I'm . . ."

". . . you need sleep."

"Yeah. Maybe I'll go take a nap."

"Just the thing. You sleep while the city burns."

"That'd be a good thing for my business cards." I stood. " 'I sleep while the city burns.' "

"Keep in touch." He didn't stand.

Back out on Ponce, the air seemed closer, and the traffic was like bugs swarming. Stopped in at Green's liquor store. When in doubt, *cherchez le vin*. I had to see if my '86 Cantenac-Brown gold label was in. It wasn't. There was all manner of explaining to me just how convoluted the French are about some things, and plenty of my reminding everyone within earshot just how good my business was with Green's—but in the end my wine still wasn't there.

"Well this is shaping up to be quite the day," I told the guy as I was walking out.

"And many more to you," he shot right back.

Yeah. That's what you need when you feel like your guts are kicked in: one more little punch. Like I even felt it.

Since I was near my favorite telephone, I thought I ought to give a ring to the kid, see what was what. I dialed. The heat was suffocating. Her phone rang longer than it had before.

"Uh-huh." Sounded like she was asleep.

"Hey, it's Flap . . ."

". . . oh, God. Oh." She woke up quick. "Jesus, did you get my message?"

"Message?"

"I just, like, left a thing on your machine maybe a half an hour ago."

"I've been at the . . ."

". . . you have *got* to get up to the Clairmont and check out some dude named Curtis. He's so fishy cats follow him around."

I had to smile. "Nice turn of the phrase. And how did you come across this Curtis?"

"He was in the club last night, and he was acting weird, and he was ducking Jersey like he owed him money." She was really excited—like a kid playing detective.

"Okay, you got it," I played along, "I'll go check out the mysterious Curtis."

"Cool. By the way, how was your sentimental journey—your trip home? Get anything?"

"Yeah," I said, "I got a free Coke from lesbian Buddha."

"Okay don't tell me."

"I'm telling you."

Déjà vu—like we'd had that part of the conversation before, until I realized that it was something that had transpired between me and Dally. The heat was frying my hair.

"Got to run," I told her quickly, "but we'll talk."

"Okay." She lowered her voice. "Flap?"

"Yes."

"This is so cool."

"Yeah." Despite the temperature, her adolescent enthusiasm painted a big old smile on my face.

So I was halfway into the front parking lot of the Clairmont to confront "Curtis" before I realized that I wasn't going to make it all the way inside. I just wasn't up for another slap of new information or a difficult confrontation. Not without some kind of fortification.

I turned around, got across the street—with no small risk to life and limb, Ponce being busy—and found myself, moments later, fumbling with the door at Easy.

A little of my cheap Côtes du Rhône at midafternoon, that's what I needed. Then I'd be able to explain to any man alive just *how* convoluted the French could be.

28

CAUTION

Now, any person whose ancestors hail from just above Provence will tell you that a modest table wine for a midday pick-me-up is more in the way of sustenance, on certain occasions, than air or light. Still, caution is tossed to the wind when any person slugs back a half a bottle or so on top of three doughnuts, four hours' sleep, and enough angst to choke a Tennessee Stud.

So I was in fine fettle, as they sometimes say, when Hal gathered up a pile of receipts and papers for his usual afternoon round of inventory and ordering.

"Flap?"

"Hal." I spun around on the stool. "Just the person I need." I got up, walked behind the bar, and found a glass for him. "You're going to keep me from drinking this whole bottle by myself."

"No I'm not." He was registering something like amazement, as far as I could tell. "I'm going to do a little work and I'm going to worry about you."

"But you're not going to have a glass."

"It's three in the afternoon, Flap."

"Just the time French farmers are cutting open a wheel of brie and splaying a baguette to spread it on." I raised my glass. "*Vive.*"

"Uh-huh." He came closer. "You're a mess."

"You know what Robert Frost said?"

" 'Miles to go before I sleep'?"

"Yeah"—I smiled—"he said that too, but what I was thinking was a line something like 'Home is the place where when you go there, they have to take you in.'"

"He said that?" Hal turned his head, eyed me.

"That's not the exact quote," I agreed, "but it's the sentiment. And, anyway, if that's true, that sentiment— then here I am. Home. Much more than Invisible, Georgia."

"Because despite the fact that I don't think you should be here right now doing this," he told me, "you know I'm not going to ask you to leave, I'm not going to say anything, and I'm just going to go on about my business."

I smiled. "You're really too sensitive a man to be in the bar business."

"I'm gruff on the outside," he deadpanned, "to cover it up."

"Does that work?"

His face softened a little. "About half the time."

"Thanks, Hal."

"Please." He winced a smile and headed toward the office. "Don't even mention it."

So I had another moment's peace before the door slammed open and Mug Lewis, in his ridiculous Curtis disguise, stormed in.

"What the hell's the matter with you?" he wanted to know.

"Me?" I looked around, as if the answer might be in the air somewhere. "I give. What?"

"I *saw* you coming up the lot to the Clairmont."

"And?"

"Why'd you turn around and come over here all of a sudden?" He came closer quickly. "What's up?"

"What's up?" I twisted on the stool, still not standing to face him. "I really couldn't tell you that. But let's just get this out of the way: The cops have your shoe prints and shell casings, they know someone else was here last night, they know that that someone is my client, and—by the way—Hal's in the office and will be back out here in a second. So maybe you don't want to be here right now."

"Who's Hal?"

"The bartender. He has a really big cricket bat, and he likes to bop troublemakers in the head with it."

"Jesus." He blinked, then slowly took the stool beside me. "Sorry. I jumped to conclusions." He grabbed off his phony glasses, talking mostly to himself. "I do that when I'm nervy: Get my dander up, I lose my game. Wow. I must be flipping. If I wasn't half-nutty I would never have barged in here like this."

"You've got to stay cool," I agreed. "But, as your employee I'm going to have to ask you a few questions now, if you insist on staying. Questions that might make you hot all over again. And by the way, what did you *think* was up?"

"Think?"

"When you saw me start into the Clairmont and then veer away."

"I thought you were leading somebody to me," he told me straight. "I thought you might have ratted me out. So I slipped out a secret way I've got, and made it over here to foil your plan."

"I see." I smiled. "Nice confidence you have in me— and I thought you said last night that you knew what kind of a guy I was. But the real facts are these: I got jack for sleep last night and all I've had to eat in twenty-four hours is three doughnuts. I was headed up to talk to you to tell you our deal was off, because it's too much in the way and because you're so bad at this incognito game that a kid who doesn't even know you spotted you acting strange last night. But then I stopped here because I felt like a glass or three of wine. That's all."

"Oh." He stared at my glass. "Is it good?"

"It's okay. Want some?" I got up and went behind the bar again.

"In the middle of the day?" He followed me absently. "It makes me sleepy. And I'm not in a position to nap at the present time."

"Well then let me get right to my questions . . ."

". . . your hot questions," he added, leaning forward on the bar.

"Would you consider my job done if I told you everything about the guy you zotzed here last night?"

"Depends on your definition of *everything,* I guess." He shrugged.

"He was a guy named Jersey Jakes. You might have heard of him." I tried to gauge his reaction out of the corner of my eye—see if he had known Jakes. He didn't seem to have any reaction at all. "Dally had hired him to watch the place because she'd gotten some threatening letters of some sort and I think she might have suspected someone was coming—although I don't believe she knew it would be her husband dead—I could be wrong. How's that for instant information?"

He leaned in on the bar. "That's quite a bit of research you've done . . . on short sleep and no food." Then his voice hardened a little. "It's almost like you knew some of it already."

"We have mostly the police to thank." Modesty, I thought, became me at that moment.

"The police? You talked to the police?" He straightened up.

"I want to move as fast as I can on this. I have a kind of an *in* at the station, and I used it." I slugged back the rest of my glass, kind of to prove the point. "You just tell me if you're satisfied and our business arrangement is done."

He stared at my profile a good minute or two. "No," he told me finally. "No I am not satisfied, because I am not stupid. I see that you want out so you can tell the cops about me with a clear conscience. But I can't have that. And your job's not finished. You don't know squat, in fact, about this Jersey guy. You didn't even know last night about what he was doing here, is my guess—which means that Ms. Oglethorpe didn't tell you. Which means something is weird."

"*Rotten* is the word." What profit would there have been in my setting him completely straight at that moment?

"Let me finish." He held up his hand. "I will give you an extra grand for one more day. One. In that day I would like for you to find out why the guy was here, why you didn't know, and get some bearing on whoever delivered Ms. Oglethorpe's dead husband . . ."

". . . I'm going to do that anyway—I'd do it for nothing," I told him quietly.

"Which you don't have to do now," he brushed on.

"Why in the world would you want me to . . ."

". . . because if Jersey was watching and I didn't know, then what's to say that this other pug, this delivery boy, didn't see me? I can't have that. It's worth it to me to pay you the grand. Too many people have already have seen me. Including this whoever-it-was who saw me last night that you just mentioned. . . ."

As luck would have it, just at that exact moment Hal came barreling out of the office, if only to prove Mug's point about how many people had seen him.

"Okay, Flap," he was saying, staring at some order forms or other, "just take a look at—"

He stopped when he looked up and saw me and

Mug standing by his cash register. "Flap," he shook his head, "we can't have people behind the bar like that."

"I'm not people," Mug started, giving out with a deep hick accent, putting his glasses back on, smiling to show the fake gold tooth. "I'm Curtis."

He held out his hand.

"Curtis," Hal said, nodding once—not taking the offered hand.

"Curtis was just leaving, anyway," I said. "As was I." I stuffed the cork back into the bottle, took it back around to my stash spot under the register, grabbed my glass, and put it in the bus window. It was a smooth dance, one I'd done many times. Hal and "Curtis" were watching silently.

"I feel better." I stood behind the bar, feeling the wine build up my blood. "Send in the lions."

They thought I was drunk. But I wasn't. I was thinking of Daniel.

29

LION'S DEN

The hour nearing four in the afternoon, past which time I was to call Daniel Frank, I made a quick walk of it back up Ponce to my place.

I swung open the door and looked around. I'm usually an orderly sort of a guy, but the joint, I had to confess at that moment, was a dump. I just thanked God for air-conditioning.

The phone was ringing, which seemed to add to the disorder of the room.

I waded through the discarded clothes and wads of newspaper to the bedside and the telephone.

"Okay," I breathed into the phone.

"Flap?" It was Daniel. "You okay?"

"Fine. A little winded from my walk, but I'm fine. You're calling me."

"I am," he confirmed. "I have news."

"Should I sit down?"

"Sounds like it to me," he told me. "Did you know that Dally had received other letters like the one in the stiff's pocket last night?"

"Yes." I nodded.

"Okay," he went on, "so they're all this 'You owe me so much' and 'You know what I can do to you' and stuff."

"Okay." I sat. "Go on." I knew he had more.

"You're in a fast mood. Not usual for you."

"I am today. Fast."

He rattled some papers. "She turned them all over to the cops, these notes. Of course she never said a word about you—but I guess you know that this Huyne guy is all over you, for some reason."

"Remind me to tell you the reason someday," I rushed, "but right now I have to know about the letters."

"I have Xerox copies here." That's what he was rattling.

"How the hell did you get those?"

"Oh"—his voice was matter-of-fact—"I have friends."

"All right. Are you coming here or am I . . ."

". . . don't you think the cops might be watching your place, maybe?"

I sighed. If I hadn't been so sleepy, I probably would have figured on that myself.

"And I have no secret passageway out of the building," I told Danny.

"So you've got to lose them, if they come behind you."

"Well"—I smiled—"I can do that."

"I have some other information, but, you know, are you also paranoid?"

I started to ask him what he was talking about—it only took me one more second to realize that he was thinking the phone might be tapped.

"Naw, Dan." I tried to sound casual. "I'm just tired. I think maybe I'll grab a nap for before I leave to meet you—and lose the police. Should we meet at our usual place?"

I was hoping that would be the giveaway for Dan—I was polishing one off for anybody else who might be listening, as Danny and I *had* no usual place.

"Yes," he told me, trying not to sound stilted, "our usual place. Perfect. Around 3:20, 3:30? You know they're tearing things down over there. There's *more land* than ever . . . at our usual place, so watch out, okay?"

His voice didn't betray amusement, but I was certain he was smiling. There were huge open vacant lots around the three hundred block (320, 330) of *Moreland* Avenue—just up Ponce, past the Majestic Diner.

"I don't need to watch out, Dan," I told him plainly. "I've got friends who watch out for me."

"That's a good feeling. Have a nice nap."

"Can do." I hung up.

I didn't even take a breath before I slipped out my front door. There were only four apartments in my building, mine was one of the two upstairs. If the front and back doors were being watched, there was no way to sneak out that way, or out the windows down on the street side of the place. But if a person could be quiet and careful, that person might just slip out of the downstairs apartment that was right beside the next building over—in the shadows—and he might make his way through the bushes that would hide him from anyone watching at the outside doors.

So downstairs, I tapped quietly on Kane and Paula's door. Kane answered.

"Flap." She was in her usual cheery mood. "What's up. Were we making too much noise again?"

I put my fingers to my lips. "Can I come in?"

"Sure." She lowered her voice. "Paula's asleep." Big smile. "I think I wore her out."

"Good for you. Can I slip out your window?"

"What?" Then: "Oh—work."

"Thank you." I nodded my appreciation of her quick grasp of the situation.

"Let me go in first," she whispered. "No telling how Paula would react to a strange man in her bedroom. And you're stranger than most."

"Uh-huh." I followed her.

The room was black. I could barely see her lean over the still form in the bed.

"Paula, honey? Flap's going to sneak out our window, okay, baby?"

"Hm?" Paula roused herself a little. "Flap?"

"Hey, sweetheart," I told her softly.

"Flap?" She smiled, I think her eyes were still closed. "You sneaking out?"

"Yup."

"Okay"—she settled back into the door to dreamland—"don't let the bastards get you."

"Thanks."

Kane helped me with the window, being the perfect hostess, and I slid out the window and down onto the ground. She peered down at me.

Then she mouthed, "Good luck."

I smiled and slipped into the bushes.

Once I was around the back of the building next door, I could see, through the tall shrubs, an unfamiliar tan Buick in the back parking lot. There were two guys sitting in it. One was reading a magazine, the other was sipping Krispy Kreme coffee.

So.

I made it around to the front, still nestled in shrubbery. The cops were parked right next to my car.

So I kept to the shadows and shrubs up my little street and made it across Ponce to the bus stop without being seen, as far as I could tell. I guess it was a little bold, sitting there when policemen a block away were looking for me, but I had a way of being invisible. I settled in with the rest of the group at the stop, turned my face away from the street. Then we were all just working stiffs waiting for a bus.

30

Jazz

I got lucky: Five minutes later I was on my way down Ponce to Moreland. The ride didn't take long, but it gave me a second to gather my thoughts.

Something mammoth was going on in Dally's head. Something had been happening to her that she hadn't told me about. And she hadn't told me because she was afraid. Afraid of me. Which meant she wasn't in her right mind. Something was altering her perception of reality. Although what that reality would be—in a world where Dally was married and never told me—I wouldn't know.

When I was a callow twenty-or-so, Daniel Frank and I talked about how easy it would be to slip acid— LSD—into the Atlanta water supply and thus liberate a million minds. I was wondering if someone had gone that far with Dally. I was thinking that she might actually be in biological danger. Or dire stress, or physical threat. What else could provoke her to so misapprehend me and my ways? So I put off being hurt or angry or whatever other stupid man-thing I could have taken on. Later for those. Not that I completely let go of my suspicions, but Dalliance needed me, needed the things I could do for her. After everything was all over and done with, I could find out what had happened. Work first, then philosophize.

I was off the bus and down Moreland toward Little Five Points less than fifteen minutes later.

The vacant lots on the left were high up off the sidewalks, and if you went far enough up onto them, you would be invisible from the street.

I was up on the hill, far away from the madding crowd, when Danny just appeared, smiling, from behind one of the few oaks left standing on the lot.

"Are we clever or are we clever?" That was his question for me.

"We're pretty hot," I agreed, "but let's not congratulate ourselves too much. We need action. Not quite time to be smug yet."

"I'm not smug." He shook his head, came right up beside me. "But I ought to be. Guess what I know?"

"What?"

"Jersey Jakes has been working for Ms. Oglethorpe for *six months*. He's had one assignment and one only: to keep an eye on her husband."

I actually had to sit down in the grass. Danny thought a moment, then sat down beside me. It was like we'd decided to have a picnic.

"How the hell did you find that out?" I stared at the ground.

"There's more," Danny began explaining. "It's about a guy named Mug Lewis, who once was dead, but is now in town to take care of some sharks once and for all. You remember him?"

I looked down at the dying grass on the hillside.

Dan only watched my face for a second for reaction before he went on. "He had a clever scheme, this Mug did: play dead, let them go away. But he was a haunted man, see? He's thinking all the time, 'What if they find out?' and he can't live with that. So he comes back from the dead to put them down good. Which is easier for a ghost to do."

"Okay, so you know about Mug Lewis," I said slowly. "I was just thinking that your special gift was information retrieval. Fine. Mug's stupid anyway—sticks out like a sore thumb. But you're saying he's the only ringer? That he's only a coincidence?"

"That's *exactly* what I'm saying." He pounded my arm. "See how you read my mind. You've got to discard him from your thinking. He's a red fish of some sort and he'll mess up your little trick . . ."

". . . when and if I ever decide to do it."

"We should work together more often. We've got a sync. Anyway"—he shrugged—"Dally had Jersey there that night because she was worried."

"Not worried." I shook my head. "For that I would have been the one she'd asked. You mean she was nervous about the husband. That's the only reason Jersey was there."

"Okay, right."

"So then when the package got there"—I squinted—"why did she call me? And where was Jakes all this time?"

"Take a look," he said quietly, reaching into his breast pocket. "You're in the letters. I think she was worried about you."

He held out Xerox copies of letters.

I stared at them, then took them. The were all short, with no address and no salutation.

The first one in the stack said:

You are aware of how much you owe me. I only want what's mine. Please disabuse Mr. Tucker of his holdings—or I will.

RONN

The next was even more fun.

I saw Mr. Tucker drive you home tonight. I know
where he lives now. Time to do what I say. You
know I mean it.

And it was unsigned. The last one was the most fun.

I'm coming. I'm done with asking. Get the papers
right or that's it. For you and for Mr. Tucker. You
know what I mean.

RONN

"Spells his name with two n's." I handed the copies
back to Dan.

"Are you ready?" He smiled. "His whole name is
Ronnard Raay Higgins. Ray's with two a's—Higgins is
two . . ."

". . . I know. That's got to be some kind of a weird
name game his parents . . ."

". . . you're the one from Stump Jump flatlands
down in the gnat belt. You tell me: Do they deliberately
name their children like that down there, or do they just
not know any better?"

"Stump Jump?"

"The problem is," he went right on, "that Mug
killed Jakes before we could find out what Jakes was
doing there."

"That's our problem?" I turned his way.

"Well"—he shifted a little, too—"we really need to
know why Jakes was there, if his gig was to keep tabs
on the husband and the husband in question was as
dead as he was. I mean, I hate to speak ill of the dead,"

Danny said softly, "but could Jakes have been working both sides against the middle?"

"He didn't seem the type . . ." I started.

". . . could Jakes have iced the husband to make his gig easy, then shoved it through the door in such a manner as to make Dally call for you—since she was expecting a live visit not a dead fish? And could he have been keeping an eye out so that he could later rat you out, or something?"

"Then he was just unlucky that Mug showed up?" I continued. "And Mug couldn't say last night if Jakes was the delivery boy or not."

Danny looked over at me and smiled. "This is fun. I mean, I know it's screwed your life all to hell, but if you look at it a certain way, it's like riffing, here. Remember how we came up with that cool arrangement of 'Sentimental Mood' at the old Downtown Cafe that night?"

I had to smile, because I remembered exactly what he was talking about. "Yeah. Great arrangement."

"That's what this is like—this talking and wild supposition."

"But there are a lot of mistakes in our thinking, here, Danny—lots of holes and wrong guesses. It's not an arrangement today. It's a . . ." But I trailed off because I didn't know what it was.

"Don't you even remember what you always used to say to the crowd," he interrupted, smiling. "You'd say that if you did it once it's a mistake—but if you did it twice? It was jazz."

31

TWICE

Dan carted me back to his house in East Atlanta and let me pass out on the sofa, with Chet Baker singing to me: "What'll I do with just a photograph to tell my troubles to?" Chet: fallen angel, lost boy, ghost—just the thing I needed in my head while I was falling asleep.

It was dark when I opened my eyes. Dan was gone. I couldn't think what the hell had happened to my living room for a second, then I sat up and remembered where I was. I managed my way into the kitchen, thinking about coffee.

The moon was painting lilies across the sidewalks outside. The breeze was filled with magnolia. On another night, in another place, I had stood watching moonlight like that, with Dally, talking about what she should plant in her spice garden. "Let's try tarragon," I'd told her. "Why?" "Because I've never gotten it to work before, but maybe that's because it never got to be with you before." So she'd planted some, and it was a foot tall in two months.

But my thoughts were interrupted when the front door of the apartment exploded open and men—I thought two—stabbed into the relative silence of the house.

I took a step to the refrigerator, and opened the door. The light clued my visitors as to my whereabouts immediately, which was partly what I'd had in mind. I wanted them to come to me.

"There," one of them said.

I was right about the number: Two men moved quickly into the kitchen. I had the refrigerator door in front of me, and the light was in their eyes, so I could see them much better than they could see me.

"He's behind the refrigerator door," one whispered.

"I know." The other sounded irritated.

"I think that's far enough," I said, loud enough to startle them.

They both froze.

I could see they each had a gun, but the light wasn't quite strong enough to tell much else. Still, no matter what sort of fire power they were holding, icebox doors are hardly bulletproof.

"Care to discuss this?" I wanted to know.

"Look," one began, "this is going to go hard no matter what, I'm not lying to you."

"So just come on over here and take your medicine, okay?" The second was speaking like an impatient parent.

I grabbed tighter onto the handle of the door. "No. I think I'll just stand here for a second."

The first one moved quickly, and came a little too close for his own good. I closed the door on him. You can be as tough as you want to be, but when a refrigerator door tells you where to go, that's where you'll be going.

The second one didn't seem to understand what was happening, which was a break for me. While I crushed the first one as hard as I could with the door, I tipped my right toe up like some Fred-Astaire-Meets-Kung-Fu movie and popped the gun out of his hand. He watched it fly across the room like he was watching the sudden flight of a bird.

I opened the door, then, and thug one fell to the

floor. I didn't know where his gun was, so I took a few steps back. Then I kicked him in the chest hard enough to knock the wind out of him. He rolled out of the way. I closed the fridge door, and the room was suddenly dark.

I took advantage of that blackness to duck farther back, find the broom I'd noticed by the stove, and poke thug two in the solar plexus. When he doubled over, I just pushed hard on the back of his neck, and he ended up on the floor too.

The whole thing was over in under a minute.

I saw thug one's gun, and kicked it away toward the living room. Then I turned on the kitchen light. The glare was brutal after the darkness.

The first guy looked up then, squinting, and moaned, holding his chest.

"Damn, Chuckie, look," he said. "This ain't even Danny."

"I thought his voice sounded funny." Chuckie managed a glance my way, and then repeated a carnal insult I'd heard once or twice before.

"You were looking for Daniel?" I stared down at them.

Chuckie grimaced.

"He's not in right now." I watched them carefully. "Could I take a message?"

Not-Chuckie shook his head. "No. We were supposed to rough him up, though. Would you mind doing that for us when he comes home? I figure you could handle it." He groaned again, to prove his point.

I wasn't completely myself, rest- and strength-wise, or I would have smiled a little at that, and maybe helped the guy to his feet. But as it was, I was on the cautious side of paranoid. That's what sleeplessness can do for you.

"How about if I just tell him off?" I held my ground.

Chuckie was starting to get up. "Not good enough."

I watched him move. "You wouldn't want to tell me what this is about, would you?"

"He's been asking questions," Chuckie said, holding on to the countertop to steady his rise. "When you ask questions around big money, big money gets nervous. Right?"

"I guess," I told him. "I haven't been around that much cash in a while."

Chuckie got his bearings and finally got a good look at me in the light. "Well." He shook his head again. "You're definitely not Danny."

"Nope."

"So." He smiled. "Tell him it was Chuckie that came by." He stared down and his cohort. "And Rimshot."

"Chuckie and Rimshot." I shook my head. "Very colorful. I'll tell him. He knows you two?"

"Oh, sure," Rimshot managed. He was finally getting his voice back. "We asked for this gig. We like Danny."

Chuck explained. "We thought he would take it better from somebody he knew."

"I see." I balanced myself. "You're not upset with me?"

They looked at each other.

"What for?" Rimshot answered. "You're not Dan. Case of mistaken identity. Big deal. Fact is, you saved us a little work, here."

"Plus," Chuckie went on, "I hate beating up the wrong guy."

"We've done it before," Rimshot confided. "It was a mess."

"Well"—I still didn't relax—"I suppose you don't feel much like telling me any more about all this."

They checked with each other again.

Then Rimshot shook his head. "Not really."

The air around us all was tight and coiled.

"Okay, then." I tried to shrug it all off. "If there's nothing more, I guess this is good night. I have miles to go before I sleep."

"Robert Frost," Chuckie noted.

I showed them to the door, without mentioning my appreciation for Chuck's erudition, and bid them a good night like they'd just been over for dinner.

32

RIVER OF NIGHT

Sometimes the night is like a river. Sometimes it runs, and you jump in, and you're pulled along, whether you want to be or not.

That night was black and cloudy. I was determined to find out, before the sun was up, what had happened to Dally and me—despite the importance of all the other things I wanted to know. She was on the other side of the river, and that hadn't happened often. So all I wanted to know at that moment was what had happened: I was ready to swim over.

Just a quick check out the door before I left told me that Rimshot and Chuckie were not apparent. Still, I was cautious—for example: A rim shot is where you take a drumstick and pound it really hard on the head and the rim of the snare at the same time. Makes a crack like a gun. I figured it had something to do with the guy's nickname. And when you're in a Tom Waits/Charles Bukowski part of town, you never underestimate a Chuckie—so, caution was on my mind.

I couldn't say that I enjoyed waiting on the dark bus corner just up the block from Dan's place. Too many shadows, too many strangers in slow-moving cars.

By the time the bus got there, I was ready to sit in a semicrowded bus and watch the streets roll toward Midtown. It gave me time to think.

Dally was scared, that's what I came up with. She'd

really been taken out of her usual panache by the res-
urrection of a husband she thought she'd buried—or
at least kept hidden. That's the only thing that made
sense. She hadn't told me about it all because there was
something about it she wanted to forget herself. And,
knowing I'm not one to pry, she would never imagine
the subject would come up. But she also knew that I
was on her side no matter what.

So let's suppose, I was thinking as the bus lurched to
a stop, that she figures I have secretly done something
about the threatening notes from her surprise husband.
She figures I'm protective, I'm mad—I get jealous. I
don't tell her about it, I just go off half-cocked and do
something about it. Especially after my most recent
confrontation with the guy when Hal nearly had to in-
troduce us to the Queen Mother of all bats. I have been
known to jump to such conclusions.

A jump to conclusions and a leap of faith are often
the same thing to me.

Still, even if all that were in her head, she would still
discuss something like this with me—under ordinary
circumstances. Something else besides her own doubts
had thrown off her Tao.

Someone had planted a seed of doubt about me.
That's where my thoughts were by the time the bus
brought me to the stop just past the corner of Moreland
and Ponce.

I hopped down into the street and headed up toward
Easy. Even with the cars and the streetlights, the night
seemed dark. Maybe it was the mood of the night, not
the amount of light at all.

By the time I got to the club, I was in need of water
before wine—not to put too fine a biblical point on my
thinking. The place wasn't crowded, and the band hadn't
even finished setting up.

Hal was talking to Phillip Raines, one of the best sax players in the city—he'd found contentment being a brick artisan by day, blowing blues by night. Each occupation kept the other one honest

I took a seat next to him. "Phillip."

He nodded, then looked at Hal. "Since he's here"—he inclined his head my way—"I'll sample whatever wine he's got hidden under there." He smiled at me. "If I may be so bold."

"You're as bold as you want to be." I smiled back. "It's a pretty okay Bordeaux tonight." I glanced at Hal. "Château Tonnelle."

"All right, then." Raines approved.

I shrugged at Hal. "For two, plus a glass of water for me. And is Dally in?"

"Office." He reached under the register and pulled out my bottle, poured two glasses, and set them down. "Phillip, here, was just telling me that he's got a gig in Savannah."

"No kidding?" I turned his way.

"Yeah." Raines got the glass in his hand. "Some new club on River Street."

That was all. He sipped and remained silent.

I took the whole glass of water, then the entire glass of wine down—it made both the other men stare. I didn't care. I was in a hurry, and nervous about talking to Dally in this Doubting Thomas frame of mind. So: gulp.

"Be right back." I tapped the bar, stood, and headed for the office.

I stood in the doorway, and watched her, for a second, bent over the desktop writing checks.

"Hey."

She jumped.

"Sorry." I didn't move. "Didn't mean to . . ."

". . . Flap." She stared.

"Yes. Correct. Flap." I tried to remain steady.

"What are you doing here?"

I looked away. Then I stepped into the office and I closed the door behind me.

"I'm here to get things straight." I shot right over to the desk.

She put her pen down. "Well, I don't know how you think you're going to do that." She looked up at me, pale as the moon.

"I think I'm going to start," I told her, "by asking you just what the hell is going on between you and me that you think you can't tell me you've got a husband and that husband's got a bad disposition. Then we progress to what's going on with your getting little Jersey Jakes to watch out for you when that's usually my kind of thing. And last but not least"—my voice was getting louder, but I couldn't help it—"I've got to ask you what the *hell* is the matter with you thinking that I would *kill* your husband . . . without at least telling you first."

I could see right away that I'd made the wrong move. It works about seventy percent of the time, this barging in and confronting thing. The rest of the time, you end up with the kind of reaction I got from Dally.

She slid her chair away from the desk, stood up, looked away from me so deliberately that it nearly burned a hole in the wall behind me as she brushed past.

She opened the door to the office. "Hal!"

He jumped. She hardly ever yelled that loud.

I knew where she was going with this little scene.

Hal was at the door in two seconds.

"Would you please," she said calmly, "get Flap some more of that wine and make sure he leaves me alone while I'm trying to do these payouts?"

He grinned. "Flap's in the doghouse."

I stared.

He stopped smiling.

Dally moved back to the desk without looking at either one of us.

I left the office.

Hal closed the door.

Phillip Raines had taken off, but he'd left me a note: "Thanks for the wine, good luck with your misery."

My head shot up. "Hal? Did you tell that guy what was going on with me and Dally?"

"No." He grabbed a bar towel and started fussing with the countertop so that he could avoid eye contact. "But it's not like it isn't written all over your face."

"It is?"

"You don't play the kind of sax that guy does and not be able to tell when somebody else's melody is off, you know."

I finished the rest of the bottle slowly, with Hal carefully making charming albeit one-sided repartee. I had no idea how much time had passed, but I was on my last glass when Daniel Frank sat down beside me.

"I thought I might find you here."

Hal brought Dan a soda water and lime. When Danny quit one habit, he liked to quit all habits. Since his drug days he had not had anything stronger than coffee to drink—or anyone stranger than Lorraine to love, but that was another story.

"I tried the direct approach with Ms. Oglethorpe," I told him. "It was fairly disastrous."

"You're off your game." That was his assessment.

"Oh," I agreed, "I'm absolutely off my game."

"You're moping."

"I am?"

"You're sitting here drinking that French varnish"— he shook his head—"when you ought to be off chasing down fragments."

"Fragments?"

"You know what I mean."

And I did, in fact, know what he meant. But I was too confused to put anything together. So I finished my last glass of the Bordeaux and turned to face the music.

"Dan," I said plainly, "I think I lost my thing."

"That is a dilemma." He sipped his water without looking at me. "You mean your trick."

"It comes and goes, anyway," I said. "And now with this thing about Dalliance—I don't think I have it anymore."

He looked at Hal. "How often does he go through this?"

"Let's see." Hal leaned forward onto the bar. "A while back there were a couple of dead girls hanging in Piedmont Park, and he had a little trouble like this." Hal looked at me. "But now that I think of it, he goes through something like it almost every time."

"So it's a part of his process." Danny shrugged.

"Are you talking about me like I'm not here," I started, "because you want me to go away?"

"Not *away*." Dan turned to face me. "When everything about you is turning to ashes—go to *work*. That's what you want. Not moping and drinking and trying to muscle Dally. If"—he held up his index finger as if to make an important pronouncement—"you wish to prove to Ms. Oglethorpe that you've been to the ocean—then why don't you get her a shell."

"Nice metaphor." I smiled at Daniel. "You've got the soul of a poet, you know."

"Yeah, well"—he turned back to face Hal—"I'd like to give it back to whichever poet I got it from. It makes me itch. Now you can tell me what happened to my house."

"What happened . . ."

". . . I get home not half an hour ago, and I find evidence of a tussle in my kitchen."

"Oh, that. Sorry. I should have cleaned up." Although I couldn't think what had gotten messed up enough to clue Dan to what had happened. Still, he was the observant type. "A couple of boys called Chuckie and Rimshot came by. They wanted to clip you for asking the wrong questions around town. They thought you wouldn't mind it coming from them, being as they were old friends."

"I'd call them more acquaintances." He finished his soda. "So this means I asked the right questions somewhere."

"I guess."

"If only I knew what they were—or where I'd asked them." He stood. "Call me if you get anywhere. I'm going home."

33

ITCH

Danny was right: If I wanted to prove to Dally—and, much less consequentially, Detective Huyne—that I'd had nothing to do with killing Ronnard Ray, then I had to find out who did do it. The situation seemed just that simple to me, finally.

I was standing out in the parking lot in front of Easy, staring at the doorway to the place. There was still evidence of a scuffle—kicked-up dirt, a torn bit of moss between cracks in the sidewalk. So the idea that Jakes had been lying in wait for Mug to come out seemed a likely scenario.

I took the few steps toward the place at the far curb where Mug had told me the alleged delivery van had been parked. You never can tell, I thought, maybe somebody had dropped something. I wandered around in the street staring but not looking. That's the way to do it. If you're looking, you'll overlook. If you're just there to stare, things jump out at you.

But nothing did.

So I wended my weary way homeward. A nice walk in the sticky air ended in an unexpected bit of luck: There were no cops in evidence in front of my pad.

I turned, therefore, where any man in my situation might go in celebration of such good fortune: I hopped in my car and went to the county morgue.

A short drive later, I was inside the building. The

security guard barely noticed me when I came in. He'd seen me there before, usually with policemen. Maybe he even thought I was a cop. I waved, he nodded, and I made it down the dry, fluorescent hall to the "new arrivals" section.

Reese was the attendant that night, which was a break for me. He was a good kid—under five feet tall, and looked like a teenage girl, even with his short-shock hair. He'd boosted a couple of cars in my neighborhood a few years back, and some of the neighbors had asked me to look into it. I did: I caught Reese with his hand still on the brick that he'd used to smash the window of a steel gray Volvo station wagon.

Instead of taking him right to the police, I made him go meet all the people whose cars he'd skimmed. It had turned out to be a pretty good idea. Reese was bopping the cars for drug money. And because my little Midtown neighborhood was filled with some pretty decent people from all walks of life, he'd gotten into a methadone program, been offered a job, and eaten a great meal from the caterers in my building—the aforementioned Kane and Paula duo—where he'd met Drexel, a goth-scene hairdresser who was to become his significant other. And that was just in the first week. I remembered thinking at the time that I ought to go into the rehabilitation business.

Now Reese was working at a job with dead bodies all night, which he loved. That always said something to me about the basic deficiency of his personality, but he was happy so who was I to dwell? He was taking cooking classes, and he and Drexel were happy as clams. I'm told clams can get pretty giddy when they want to. But I digress.

"Flap!" Reese was always delighted to see me.

"Hey, kid," I nodded. "What's it all about?"

"It's all about time, Flap." He smiled. "When you're young, time's the slowest thing on the planet. By the time you're a grandpa, it looks like it's racing for the finish line."

"You're saying it's been a long night," I guessed.

"Until now, yup." He got up out of his chair. "Where are we going?"

"I'm going to look at what's left of Jersey Jakes. Shot three times."

"Okay." He shrugged and turned around to check some papers on his desk. "Here he is, suite number seven."

We went into the room beyond. It was dark and smelled like formaldehyde, a smell I could live for seven or eight lifetimes without.

He strolled over to the big drawer marked with a number seven and rolled it out.

There was poor old Jersey Jakes, and he was just about as dead as you can get. Under ordinary circumstances, I think I would have been relatively uncomfortable about jabbing at a dead body, but I was too tired and too weird to stop and feel anything at that particular moment.

"Can I get some gloves, Reese? I have to check a few things."

"Sure." He moved immediately to a little cabinet by the door. "You want more light?"

"Can I?"

He swiveled and flipped a switch. The place was flooded with white ice light, and I couldn't see for a second.

"You see why we keep these off at night." He was laughing.

When my eyes adjusted, I put on the gloves Reese had brought me and stared down at the man whose given name had been Risky. My first thought was to check his arms, just what I'd suggested to Huyne. I wanted to see if the inside of his elbows had anything on them—which they might have had, I thought, from his attack on Mug.

I lifted the right arm.

"You want a magnifying glass, Flap." Reese was peering under my shoulder, staring at the arm I'd just lifted.

"Well, yes I do." I smiled down at him.

He zipped to the cabinet again and was back at my side before a second had gone by.

I held the glass to the inside elbow of Jersey's right arm and stared for a good while. Then I checked his fingernails, his legs. I just kept looking, but nothing revealed itself to me.

"What are you looking for?" Reese whispered.

"I guess"—I let the arm rest on Jakes's chest—"maybe I'm looking for something that's not there. I was hoping to find some shirt crud or a bruise or a scratch . . ."

". . . like he'd been tussling with somebody before he got shot," Reese finished.

"Right."

"I've seen a lot of that." He stared at Jakes. "But I didn't see anything like that there."

"Me neither."

"What does that tell you?" He could see that something was troubling me.

"Nothing . . . by itself."

"So." He got it. "You're not done tonight. You have more things to do."

"Yes."

"Well." He smiled. "It's a nice night for it."

"Yeah," I told him right back, "I know your ghoulish predilections."

"For instance," he seemed delighted to report, "Drexel and I have decided to drink each other's blood. It's like a wedding."

"That's just the kind of thing I was talking about." I stepped away from the corpse. "You can put Jersey back to bed, by the way."

He closed the drawer. "Did you want to look at the list?"

"List?"

"Of other people who had a gander at him." He started toward his desk. "I have to get full identification and everything. It's official."

"More than the police came to see him?"

"Uh"—he turned—"yeah. Come on."

I followed him back to his desk, and he picked up a clipboard.

"Am I going to be on that list?" I stared at him.

He looked away. "Well, Flap . . . I owe you a lot. But, like, the security guy saw you come in, and . . . you know, I like this job, and all . . ."

". . . okay, okay," I told him, "put me down."

He did, then handed me the board.

Risky "Jersey" Jakes had been quite the attraction in the previous twenty-four hours—and it made me itch all over. Besides the police, he'd had visits from Daniel Frank, Mug Lewis, Chuckie Barnes, Rimshot Harris, Hal Beasely—and Dalliance Oglethorpe.

34

VISITORS

Hal and Dally had come to the morgue together, and in the company of the police. The goons, Reese told me, had taken notes, if you can believe a thing like that. Danny had only stayed a second.

I took myself out of the morgue the way a good dentist would extract a tooth: very gingerly. Barely said good-bye to Reese.

I was on a pay phone outside within three minutes.

"What?" Dan's usual greeting.

"I got somewhere—not sure where, but you told me to call. If I had something."

"Where'd you get this something so soon, if I may ask," he said calmly.

"I visited my young ward, Reese. Know the kid I'm talking about?" In case *his* phone was bugged, I thought I was playing it cagey.

"I know the boy." I thought I could hear him smile. "Just so happens I saw him recently myself."

"I know. I saw on a list that he had. Who else was on the list? Would you care to guess?"

"The cops, of course."

"Yes." I shifted to the other ear. "But also: You know your two recent visitors, the ones I greeted for you?"

"Them?"

"How about that," I answered. "Also a bartender and his boss."

"That bartender I was just talking to earlier? And *his* boss? Well, isn't that a little something extra." It wasn't a question.

"Yeah," I agreed. "I thought it was."

"What do you make of it?"

"Well, they were there with the police," I answered him, "but I'd certainly like to discuss it further."

"Okay." He took in a breath. "And just for laughs— I think you will find this amusing—let's meet at your house, shall we?"

"My house?"

"Don't you think it would be the last place anyone would imagine that we'd meet?"

"Sure." I smiled into the phone. "I guess I do."

I hung up without another word and made it to my place.

Danny was sitting on the curb outside the place when I walked down the street to my apartment building. He was talking.

There were two guys in a car across the street. They didn't seem to be responding to him, much, but he was having a great time talking to them.

"So," he was saying, "then when I was eleven, see, I had a vision of St. Thomas. Did you ever read the Gospel of Thomas? It's great. It's in the apocrypha sometimes, and in the Gnostic texts, of course. Now, my rabbi, he gets upset when I go to him and say, 'I want to know more about St. Thomas.' But, you can understand his pique, you know: He was named Levi, so he was kind of an old-school type. You can always tell by that name."

"Danny," I interrupted, "leave the nice policemen alone and come on inside now."

"Okay." He hoisted himself up and stood on the curb. "Good night, boys."

The two men stared straight forward. I figured they were rookies—no sense of humor about their jobs. They wouldn't last in stakeouts, I was thinking, without a sense of the absurd.

Dan and I beat it inside.

"You know, Flap," he told me as he sat hard on the sofa, "we haven't really talked about this Ronnard Raay character. You know he was kind of a sick package—if you'll excuse that phrase—under the right circumstances."

"Espresso?" I gave him the patented wry smile.

"Naturally."

I headed to my own little galley kitchen, straight for the espresso maker, and ground the beans while Dan shouted from the living room, over the noise.

"He was known to be into bad stuff upon occasion, I mean." Dan's voice rose.

"I know." The noise of the grinder stopped, and the house seemed like a tomb for a second. I started the espresso machine and joined Dan in the living room. He'd turned on the lamp beside the sofa, and there was moonlight pouring in across the windowsill.

"I've got to find out more about Dally's marriage—and I don't know how I can do that, since nobody alive except her knew anything about it." That's all I could say.

And all Danny could do was nod.

After a couple of minutes of ocean noises from the kitchen, our brew was ready.

I fixed it and brought it in.

Danny stared forward the way he always had when he was about to say something he knew the other person wouldn't like. I'd seen that look before once on a guy Daniel was supposed to shoot, and I'd have to say it worried me to see him looking just that way in my living room.

"Flap," he began slowly, "you know you have to see all sides of this story, right? I mean, you have to take everything into consideration."

"Okay." I had no idea where he was going.

"Did you ever consider"—he went on staring, his voice barely above a whisper—"that what with all the threats and secrets—did you ever consider the possibility that the reason this is all so weird is—that Dally killed her husband?"

35

THREATS AND SECRETS

The problem with being a southern-fried Taoist is that you have to try to look at all phenomena as just that: an occurrence, devoid of any meaning except the one you impart to it—that particular instance in that exact moment. But then, you ask yourself, where's discernment, where's moral choice, where's social responsibility in all that? If you say God's in everything and everything is holy, then how do you explain the Holocaust?

I'm saying that philosophical questions of that magnitude were blossoming in my head because of Danny's question. And because of all that, I found that I actually did have to consider the possibility that Dally had killed her husband. That would certainly explain everything, even her accusing me of same. Dally was the smartest person I had ever known, and she would have figured out that if she wanted to throw me off the scent of a thing like that, there would have been no better way to do it than to accuse me—because it would have knocked me down and stomped on me hard. As it, in fact, had.

Danny was right with me. "See, you might have detected odd things about her when the body showed up, so if she threw you way off your game—by insinuating to you that she thought you were the killer—you'd lay off her."

"None of this," I began, "remotely fits into my knowledge of a person I've known most of my life."

"Everybody's got secrets, Flap."

"Not me." I shook my head. "Not from her."

He sighed. "You told her all about your band days?"

"I told her I had the occasional bump from a fan and the odd brief encounter, sure. Our relationship, mine and Dally's, it goes way beyond that kind of stuff. You know that."

"You told her about Lorraine?"

Oh. Well. Lorraine. That was another story.

She'd been a fan. She loved Daniel's playing. None of the other girls could get around him when she was there. She was all over him. When he found out that she was married to a rich lawyer who was running for state senate, he really got inventive with his coke habit. He even talked to me about popping the husband, setting up a big score so he and Lorraine could beat it out of the country and live like robber barons in Costa Rica. He even talked to me about my going in on all of it with him. That's when I had to whack him in the head with my philosophy stick.

"Dan, you will now get off the dope and on the wagon," was my line, "not to mention getting far away from Lorraine, who is the worst news since Pearl Harbor."

There was a tussle involved, but he finally saw it my way.

In retaliation, Lorraine spent a few wild moments spreading it around town that she and I had been involved. It wasn't remotely true, but it wasn't the kind of rumor a guy like me can have wafting about the city. So:

"No," I told Dan. "I have not told Dally everything about that. Thanks for reminding me."

"Just saying . . ." He trailed off.

Further thinking on the subject was interrupted by the harsh pounding on the door.

One of the things about all this that I really didn't care for was the nearness of all these policemen. I didn't mind hanging out with people like Daniel, or Mug Lewis—even Chuckie and Rimshot, when it came down to it. But having rookie policemen around me all the time made me feel ill at ease; downright unsafe.

"Mr. Tucker?" The one standing squarely in the doorway was the one who had been in the driver's seat of the car downstairs. Could have been the city cousin of Denny Martin from down-home way.

"Yes?" I smiled.

"Detective Huyne would like to see you. Would that be all right with you? You're not under arrest, or anything. You're not even wanted for questioning. He'd just—like to see you."

"And I'd like to see him," I answered. Then I turned away from the cop to face Danny, still speaking to the rookie. "Can my friend come too? He likes policemen."

Daniel grinned. It seemed to make the poor kid nervous.

"No." The cop shook his head. "I don't think so. Just you this time, okay?"

"Sorry, Dan."

Dan was affable. "I'll just stay here, then, if that's okay by you. I'd like to finish my espresso, catch up on a little reading, that sort of thing."

"What's mine is yours," I said, shifting my eyes to my little memory pad that I'd left sitting on the coffee table.

He barely flashed his eyes and then he smiled bigger, mostly to throw the cop off, I thought.

So I turned and headed out the door. "Bye, then."

Danny didn't answer.

As I followed the cop down the stairs, he suddenly stopped and turned back to look up at me.

"That was pretty good, giving us the slip like that earlier." He didn't mean it as a compliment.

"The slip? Is that what I gave you?"

"It won't happen again." He squinted hard, trying, I thought, to look a little like Clint Eastwood.

"Fine by me." Never rile a rookie, especially in the middle of a celebrity impersonation. That's a law of nature.

We were down onto the sidewalk before he spoke again. "Detective Huyne has the idea that you know more than you're telling him. That's why he wants to . . . talk."

The sound of his voice was another clumsy attempt at intimidation. But since we were out in the open air where I had a better shot at moving out of the way in case he tried to pop me, I thought I'd whistle back.

"Well," I told the guy, "as it happens, I always know more than Detective Huyne, and it gripes him."

"Is that so?" He didn't even look back at me as we were crossing the street.

"Yeah," I said quickly. "It's like a little game we play. I solve his problems for him, and he takes credit."

"Get in the car." That's all. He was done playing.

The ride to the station house was silent, thank God.

Huyne's desk was a mess. He looked up long enough to make a sour face, and then went right back to the pile of papers in front of him.

"Sit." He didn't even look back at me.

"What is it?" I wasn't irritated with him even though he was so perfunctory. I could tell something was up.

"I'm worried about Ms. Oglethorpe's husband."

"No need." I tried out my best Baptist minister: "He's past worry now."

"Shut up." He looked up then. "I mean I've gotten some odd news about him."

"Okay." I sat.

"At the time of his death, he wasn't tied up and he hadn't been drugged—not that way, anyway—not knocked out. I mean, he was loaded with coke, but it seems to me that would have made it even harder for him to sit still while somebody else shoved a knife into him."

"You mean the killer was standing right there with the knife pushed up in poor Ronnard's chest, and Ronn didn't seem to object. That brings up questions in your mind."

"How did the killer get that close? Why didn't Higgins struggle? You understand. It doesn't make sense. From what we know, it looks like this Higgins was, on occasion, a bad citizen—drugs, wild temper, rich-boy poor behavior . . ."

". . . rotten penmanship . . ." I flexed my eyebrows, looking at Ronnard's notes on Huyne's desk.

". . . and my mind wandered," he finished for me, "to some very uncomfortable conclusions. I was saying that Higgins was no good. He was tough, he might even have knocked off a few people in his travels. We know he absolutely roughed people up over the drugs—especially when people didn't pay him. Coming, as he did, from a wealthy family, he had a rich guy's greed—no compunction about getting the dough any way he could. His favorite instrument was a tire iron, they tell me. He was apparently some sort of virtuoso with it."

"Not the sort of person who'd sit still while someone stabbed him." I looked down. "And incidentally, you don't have to go out of your way to convince me to dislike the guy, but the fact is, all I've heard about him is that he was charming. So the tire iron thing . . ."

". . . just tell me what I want to know." Huyne's voice got too calm for me.

"Tell you what?"

"Somehow convince me," he said, not making eye contact, "that I'm an idiot for thinking that Ronnard Raay Higgins might sit still like that for his wife."

36

PENMANSHIP

I felt a little sick to my stomach for a second, and I thought maybe the poker face had let me down, because Huyne was staring a hole in my forehead. But after another moment or so, I glanced down at the papers on his desk.

"Not likely in this case." I was hoping I sounded something like *breezy,* whatever that would be. "When our Ms. Oglethorpe gets letters like those you've got there on your desk, she's not the type to hide her feelings. Ronnard would have seen her coming a mile off. She wouldn't even have gotten into the building with him. She's loud, she's not subtle when she's mad, I'm saying. All the world knows her disposition."

I saw absolutely no point in letting him in on the fact that I'd been thinking how Dally might just stab a man in the heart if she had the right motivation and the stars were lined up just so. And I thought it best not to even bring up Lucy and her friend Fang, so I was even afraid to ask what kind of blade had done old Ronnard in.

"Well that's another problem," Huyne went right on—even though I was pretty sure he hadn't completely bought my act. "These letters—they could be from several different people."

"What are you saying?"

"Well, look." He turned one my way. "The handwriting is maybe from two different guys—different penmanship, different spelling skills. They look completely separate."

"They do?"

He looked up at me. "You get an eye for that sort of thing if you're any kind of detective."

"Ah." I cocked my head at him. "I see. Very informative. But could I just tell you that, for example, I write a lot differently sober than I do when I've had more than half a bottle. When I'm mad I press down hard, when I'm not I've got a different touch. When I'm in a hurry I don't always check grammar or spelling the way I do when I've got the time. This stuff? It's all up to rampant interpretation."

"Is that so?" He leaned back in his chair. "Well, it happens that we've got a team of rampant interpreters to tell us that these notes came from, at the very least, two different people."

"I see." I folded my hands in my lap. "That is impressive. But I remain a skeptic."

I was trying to lead him as far as I could from thinking that Dally had anything to do with bopping Ronnard—but every time it slipped back into my mind, I was tense at the neck and had a little twitch in my left eye.

Huyne finally looked at me hard and pronounced, "You look tired."

"You know how it is"—I smiled at him—"when you're slipping away from your police tails and consorting with criminal types. That's not the kind of thing that happens during ordinary business hours."

"Flap . . ." he began.

". . . okay." I stopped him. "I actually do have my suspicions about something, but I need more time and a little less police escort, if that's okay with you. At this point, really, you don't think I had anything to do with Ronnard's getting dead."

"Anything to do? I didn't say that. I don't think you killed the guy, that's true. But I think you've got something to do with this mess, all right." He sniffed. "Still. I guess—given the nature of our relationship—I can cut you loose a little."

"Our relationship?"

"Yeah. If you don't call me within twenty-four hours and tell me something I want to know," he told me plainly, "I'll have those two kids—the ones who were supposed to be on you when you gave them the slip—I'll have them throw you in the trunk of their car and drive around in circles until you feel like talking to me."

"Oh," I said. "*That* relationship."

37

THAT RELATIONSHIP

Back out on the street, I headed up toward Easy once again. Maybe it was because Huyne had thought the same terrible things I had, but for some odd reason, I was feeling a little more steady than I had in a while. I thought maybe I wasn't going nuts after all.

In fact, I felt so steady that I thought I'd try again to talk to Ms. Oglethorpe one more time.

Isn't it just the funniest thing ever the way the human mind works?

By the time I was crowding the doorframe at Easy, I was downright giddy. I nodded at Hal as I walked past him toward the office, and he smiled big. He reached under the bar. I nodded. He poured. That's the kind of relationship everybody wants: one where words are only a nice accessory—thoughts are the true coin. Hal and I? We had a single mind about the important things: wine, music, and his boss.

I walked in on Dally. She was staring blankly into space. A rare idle moment. I found myself watching the blink of her eye and thinking that in a single blink you can lose something you need to have in order to live. And in another blink, you can get it back. That's just how funny the human mind is.

"Hey." I stood my ground.

She looked up. "Flap?"

"That's right. And don't bother calling for Hal. He's on his way in already."

"Oh." She looked down. "Sorry about that. You don't know . . ." But her voice weakened and she didn't finish her sentence.

Hal broke our silence. "Here you go, bud. Next to the last glass of this bottle, so savor."

"Will do." I smiled at him.

He took one look at Dally, then a glance back at me, winked, and split.

So.

"Mind if I sit down?" I moved toward the chair on the business side of her desk.

The lamplight was sepia like from an old photograph, and for a second I felt time slip and decades mesh.

She looked up at me and just stared.

I sipped and stared right back for a while.

Then: "Dally? We really need to talk."

"I know." She broke her gaze.

"It's come to me that you don't really think I killed Ronnard Raay—and can I just say that it's a whole lot easier to talk about a dead guy if he's got a funny name?"

She didn't see the humor. "It's possible that you didn't kill him."

"Good. But I already knew that, like I said. It's come to me that you only said that to throw me off. So I had to ask myself why you would want to throw me off."

"Well." She looked up. Her eyes were narrow and her voice was hard. "Barely takes a Blue Ribbon chef to cook that up. I've been lying to you about myself for a really long time, and it's something really big, and I thought if you pried into the matter enough, then you'd find things out. Things about me. Things you wouldn't care for."

"I understand." I tilted my head once. "You had a crisis of faith. Me too, welcome to the club. And could I just say that I didn't much care to be handling your dead husband? That right there would have been enough of an evening for me—that would have been enough of a *thing*, I'm saying, to find out. But no, I had to pry, as you mentioned—and sure enough: I found out things. Things about you. Things I didn't care for. And what do you know? I don't give a damn about them. I only give a damn about you. I only give a damn about I love you."

Well, there was a sentence absolutely as filled with grammatical misgivings as it was with surprising results: Dally started crying.

"The last time I saw you cry," I told her, only baffled, "was at a water fountain in Rich's about a hundred years ago when we were kids."

She shot her hand up and flicked a tear. "I'm not crying. I'm just tired and my eyes are a little watery."

"I see. Probably the pollen."

"That's it."

"So what I found out," I went on, "is barely a shock. You are not, in fact, St. Dalliance of the Azaleas or whatever. You're a real live girl. Had a bit of a coke habit a while back. Who didn't? Got messed up with the wrong guy. Talk to little Lucrezia about that sometime, probably. You're in good company there, too, I'm saying. And you lied to me?" I took a sip of wine. "Who hasn't? Flash: I don't care about any of that. I don't care if you're lying to me now. I have a very . . . what's the word? Existential? No: phenomenological viewpoint about the so-called truth—in this particular case, anyway. I think this truth is just a phenomenon and it's largely up to my own personal interpretation as to how I'm going to see it, right? So I choose to see it . . ."

". . . do you ever take a vacation from thinking too much?" She smiled a little.

"Thinking too much *is* my vacation."

"I see." She blew out a little short breath. "Well now would you care to hear a little more of the story?"

"Story?"

"It's a story about marriage—about that relationship."

"Oh." I finished the rest of the wine. It seemed like a good preparation for what I expected she was about to tell me. "That relationship."

38

EXPECTATIONS

"There's a time in your youth," she began, "when you start to think to yourself, 'I can do anything I want to in this life.' So you take a look around and you assess. My assessment at a particular time in the past was that I was ready for some fun with a capital *F*. This was, or course, after you left, so I'd have to admit that my fun was partially to get back at you. I was just pissed off enough about your leave-taking to take a ride on the tilt-a-whirl."

I put a silence into the room like the one before the earth was formed and there was, as I understand it, a void upon the deep.

"And there was Ronn." That was all. Seemed simple. "Ronn was rich and handsome and charming—old South in one hand and Kennedy-forward-thinking in the other. As much *unlike* you as he could be. Knew everyone. And, *God*, you should have seen him dance."

"I'll just try to picture it."

"Ronn must have told me twenty times a day," she went on, "that he couldn't live without me. He would ask me all the time: 'Do you really love me?' And he would always say, 'Let's get married.' But my favorite was: 'What happens when Flap comes back?' I want you to get this right." Her voice was steel. "I liked it. I liked Ronn—the high end of things. I even liked looking into the yawning chasm when it all got a little too wild, if you can believe that."

"Yeah," I shot back, "everybody likes a scary ride."

"So long as we understand where I was." She made a sudden flurry of activity. "So, so, so. Long and short: His parents found out that we were going to get married. They were on a rampage. Threatened to cut off our boy—no trust fund, no free ride."

"Which is why you married in secret."

"And the secret stuck. I think the truth of the matter was that even Ronn and I didn't want to know we were married. The secrecy just made it more wild."

"But the marriage was not," I said as matter-of-factly as I could, "an entirely happy affair."

"How much looking into all that have you done," she managed, "just to save me time in case I can skip over gory details—which I really wouldn't mind skipping."

"I believe that the main body of my knowledge on the subject includes the aforementioned rec drugs, some money troubles, a tire iron, a kitchen knife, and a visit to the state hospital at Millegeville."

"Oh." It was an entirely dispirited syllable.

"What I don't know is the aftermath."

"The what?"

"Divorce. Continuing harassment. Threatening notes. That sort of thing. Things that have, at this point, invaded my life."

"I see." But she didn't.

"You were divorced."

"No."

I sat in that chair, then, with a sudden sensation that I was sitting in an electric chair just before lights-out. It took me a minute to collect.

"So you were still married up until the night he died?" I tried to sound calm.

"That's right." She finally made eye contact and

leaned toward me over the desk. "Look, Flap, the fact is, when that hand was delivered here—with the wedding ring on it? I thought for a while it was his hand."

"What?"

"You don't know what kind of people he was mixed up with. He got further and further into this weird world of big-money drugs—especially whenever his parents cut him off. I didn't care. When I got out of the hospital, and you came home, I buried a whole lot of this. I told Ronn in no uncertain terms that if he didn't stay away, if he ever messed with me again, I'd go straight to his parents and tell them about the marriage—certificate in hand. That scared him more than anything else. That's one of the main reasons I stayed married—bizarre as it seems—it was insurance to keep him at bay."

She sat back in her chair, and her face was barely a shadow.

"He'd call me sometimes," she went on after a moment, "here at the club, whispering, begging me to come back to him, talking about how miserable he was and how much he had to have me back. I'd hang up. He'd call right back, then, and he'd turn mad and yell— mostly about you, about how you were part-owner of the club, and I was always with you, and if you knew all about me, you'd run screaming in the other direction. And how he could pay to have you killed. Wouldn't even take a hundred dollars, he'd say. Then I'd threaten him with going to his parents here in Atlanta, and he'd shut up. But I swear to God, Flap"—her eyes were almost entirely flame—"part of the problem—part of it—was that you looked at me all the time—always—like I was some kind of . . . like I was the perfect . . ." And then she ran out of steam.

". . . St. Dalliance of the Azaleas."

She didn't cry. Somehow she seemed all out of crying. She was shivering a little, and she folded her arms in front of her like she was cold. "What did you think it was that was always slowing down our . . . that part of our relationship?"

"So when did old Ronn start to threaten you with these letters?" I thought it best at that point to just brush over the emotional content of the situation and try to get on with the facts. They tell me that's what most guys do.

Heavy sigh. "These letters started about six months ago." Her voice had nothing in it. "Something big had happened—someone had gotten away with a ton of his money. He was in real trouble. He needed some major collateral. He was going to take the club away from me."

"What?"

She eyed me. "Georgia's community property laws: He's the husband, he's got the best lawyers money can buy, and he's got judges who play bridge with his parents. He was certain he could have taken it real good . . ."

". . . except for the fact that I was part-owner." I nodded. "Now it all comes clear. I always wondered why you did that." I thinned my lips. "Now I know."

"No, Flap." And for some reason, *that* was the moment she chose to start crying in earnest. "You don't know anything. I gave you part of the club because I wanted to, because you've got no real income and no kind of retirement and you need a little something. I gave you part of the club because it was a tangible way I could try to tell you what you give me . . ."

". . . but it didn't hurt that it also kept Ronn at bay." Okay. That was a little harsh on my part.

"Right." She pulled back on the tears, sat up, and took in a breath. "Okay."

See, when you want to make a person stop crying, you have to use any means necessary. Harshness worked in that case, as I had hoped that it would. And I wanted to get on with what I considered to be the real issues at hand.

"So about these letters. I guess I get why you didn't just come to me about them, although when this is all over we're going to have such a long talk about this—but what I don't get is hiring Jersey Jakes."

"Hal knew him from the old music-union days"—she shrugged—"and he was someone I knew Ronn wouldn't know. I mean, Flap, you don't know the kind of people Ronn had around him sometimes—they would have known, somebody would have known if you had gone looking for Ronn. And they would have killed you. Ronn would have seen to it. Happily. It's just that plain."

"And you thought they *wouldn't* kill Jakes . . ."

". . . because he wasn't a threat. All I wanted him to do was keep an eye on Ronn—and an eye on me so that never the twain would meet. If Ronn came into town, I'd be forewarned."

"Did Jakes make reports? You know, like a P.I. would?" I was working overtime, by that point, trying to stay above the swirling tides of bizarre feelings and thoughts that were having a significant pull on me.

"He did."

"Anything interesting?"

"Well." She steadied herself with a good solid breath, put her hands on the desk, and looked a little to the side, so that the amber light in the room caught the side of her face and turned it into gold. "One of the reasons I was in the club by myself that night is that Jakes told me Ronn would be paying a visit."

Which, as it turned out, he did.

39

VORTEX

"So, we knew Ronn was coming?" I sat as still as I could.

"Yes." She didn't look at me. I may actually have seen her skin crawl.

"So it's quite clear to me—this was at least one of the things that's contributed to the strain on our relationship of late."

She let out a breath. "It's tough," she agreed, "to have a phantom husband and a . . . person like you—in the same town at once." She was trying to get back up from being knocked down to the ground.

Person like me? I'd have to get more information on that score at my earliest convenience.

But for the time being, all I said was, "You know eventually you're going to have to tell me *exactly* why Ronn was here, and what he wanted."

"I did. I already told you." Dally tilted her head and I watched her think. "He wanted money. He was scared. And he wanted me. So, I was scared too." She looked up at me, finally, to punctuate her assessment of the situation. "That's really it."

"You were scared?" I understood the money angle, but was she afraid Ronn would have hurt her?

"I was scared of what I was like with Ronn," she began, "and I thought how easily it might have come back to me. It's funny how you can feel a slip in your personality, sometimes, just by the sound of the wrong person's voice."

Once again I found myself thinking about Daniel Frank. There wasn't a more upright guy on the planet nine times out of ten. But on that tenth orbit? He was capable of serious drug incapacitation, mindless marriage busting, and threatening a friend within an inch of his life. What made that kind of stuff happen to two such fine people as Daniel and Dalliance? I found myself thinking that in both cases the culprit was a virus version of that crazy little thing called love.

Love isn't always shining. Just as often, it's obsession, it's dark water that swirls downward into some hollow vortex that keeps wanting to be fed evil fruit.

"Well." I roused myself from the black reverie and tried something like a smile. "Sometimes, also, you can feel the opposite: a tug toward heaven, just by the sound of the right person's voice. So let's just leave off second thoughts and remorse for the time being, and get down to the heart of the matter—if that isn't an ill-chosen phrase in this regard."

"Okay." She was unsteady, but game. "Right."

"Where was Ronn staying while he was in town. Let's try that."

"I don't know."

"I see. Then how often did you see him?" I was trying to keep the questions short and simple. "Any ideas about that?"

"Would 'too often' not answer it for you?"

"He wanted money from you," I pressed on, "how? He wanted you to give him money from the club . . ."

". . . that's right. As the husband," she continued, "he could get what he wanted out of the profits, he thought. But he also thought that it would be invisible money—because it would look like it was only my money. So he thought he could have all he wanted without it ever showing up anywhere else."

"Like the IRS or something. How much was he looking for?"

"Seven hundred fifty thousand."

I tried not to blink. "Correct me if I'm wrong, but wouldn't that be roughly closer to ten or twenty years' worth of personal profits?"

"I do a little better than that—but not much." She looked at me again. "See, that's why the subject of your share came up."

"My 'share' just goes back into the operation of the place. Right?"

"Mostly." She licked her lips. "But there's a little account I haven't told you about. Your retirement fund. It's not much."

I stopped her. "So Ronn wanted my 'share,' which would screw up your operating expenses, and my retirement, which would leave me alone and penniless in my dotage. I get it. But if I really am a silent partner in the place, he would have had to convince me to turn over my part to him—or have me . . . oh." Ronnard Raay Higgins might have considered shuffling me off.

"He didn't care what he did. In fact, if it messed me up, he liked it better." She closed her eyes. "He thought it could get me back."

"Get you back for what?"

"No." She squeezed her eyes tighter. "He thought it would get me back into the marriage with him. He thought we could go on like we used to. He's always wanted that."

"All right." I folded my arms. I tried to sound jaunty. "You've really led quite a double life. Must have been kind of a strain."

"Yes." She was sinking into her zombie voice. "That's the understatement of the century."

"Well, then," I told her softly, "it's got to be kind of

a relief to get it all out in the open." I got even quieter. "And to know that it all doesn't make one bit of difference to me—not in the way I feel about you."

She opened her eyes, then. "Flap."

And there it was: that voice angel that could tug a person up to heaven. The same voice of which I had to be so careful—in case I was wrong about it.

40

WRONG

Since I was so completely off my game, and the falcon could not hear the falconer or whatever else there is in that poem about not knowing where the center is, I thought it best to repair homeward about then and see if I could polish off a quick trick.

My little trick is nothing more than sitting back and watching a parade of daily events stroll by the mind's eye. If you can pull back far enough, settle down deep enough, and not mess it up with a whole lot of thinking, you can see things in the parade that you missed the first time. Then you have what some people like to call an epiphany.

I can sometimes go on and on about what the trick is. That's because I don't really know what the hell it is. I remember being quite enthusiastic when I saw Van Morrison's record called *Enlightenment* in the stores. I bought it and rushed home to see what Van had to tell me, at last, on the vital subject. And what was it? "Enlightenment," he said, "don't know *what* it is."

Right. So if the man himself is fuzzy on the topic, who am I to spout off?

Still, I thought it was worth a shot, at least to sink into the center of the storm, the eye of the hurricane, the middle of the miasma, and so forth.

I took my shoes off. I loosened my skinny gray tie, the one with the poised heron on it. I sat on the floor in the sunporch, three sides of light, with home at my back. I stared. That's all there was to it.

I stared and waited for the light to create a curtain. Eventually gold was everywhere. Light came from all sides. All I could hear was my breathing. All I could see was golden haze. I didn't taste or smell anything at all. And I'd completely forgotten about the floor I was touching.

But here's the funny thing about your human being: It's like an uncontrollable child sometimes. It sees candy, and rushes for it, even across a traffic-crowded highway. Sometimes you see the kid run, and catch it. Sometimes the kid gets away. And sometimes the kid gets hit by a bus.

Which is exactly what happened to me. I suddenly found myself in the middle of some images that I always had to avoid—Dalliance with another guy—especially if that guy was Ronnard Raay Higgins.

I found myself, in fact, in a state only slightly less atomic than Chernobyl, and just as poisoned.

My eyes popped open and I stood up like the house was on fire.

"Woof." Sometimes you have to growl out loud at the demons to make them go away. Even if you're all by yourself in your apartment.

Luckily, the cordless phone in the very next room rang before I could even focus out of the trouble.

Without thinking, I got to the phone and picked it up.

"Hello?"

"Flap? It's Lucrezia." I could hear the noise of the Clairmont Lounge in the background. "What the hell is going on?"

"Well," I told her, flopping down on the sofa, "I have news for you."

"Is that right?" She sounded mad—but who wouldn't be, I figured, at her job?

"Yes, that's right," I shot back. "I'm pretty sure the guy who messed with you is dead and gone. Happy?"

"What?" She didn't sound happy. "You killed the guy without getting back with me first?"

"What is it with me this week?" I looked out the window. "Everyone seems to think I'm capable of icing somebody. I'm really a whole lot nicer than that, you know."

"You didn't kill the guy."

"I most certainly did not. And I'll thank you to consider how you speak to me at the moment. I'm ordinarily a gentleman, but I'm in a terrible mood at the moment. So unless you have news for me, I'm hanging up."

"You," she said, then softened her tone, "already turned down my good news."

"Yeah, yeah, yeah," I answered quickly, but I was smiling by that point. You can't stay mad at a kid. Any kid. "But did you hear *my* actual news? Your guy won't be bothering you anymore. And the fact that your reaction was what it was goes a long way to convince me that you had nothing to do with it."

"What the hell would I have to do with it?"

"He was stabbed." I slouched down on the sofa. "If I were you, I wouldn't be flashing Fang around too much for a while."

"Jesus." Her voice took a dark turn. "Somebody could think I killed the guy?"

"They could." I didn't see any reason to tell her I'd thought it myself.

"So—that case is closed?"

"It wouldn't hurt for you to look at the body and make absolutely certain it's the guy."

"I never saw the guy, Flap . . ."

". . . you look at the clothes, maybe—or the feet, the shoes—you see what you can see. And you need to go right now, if you can. I happen to know the guy you've got to see at the county morgue who will let you in. His name is Reese. I think you'll like him."

"Where is it?" She sounded a little scared, like she wanted me to take her there, but I had bigger fish to fry.

"Hey." I finally focused. "What did you call me for?"

"Oh, yeah." She had the mad voice again. "I saw you chugging up Ponce toward the Clairmont and then I saw you chicken out at the last minute when I told you to talk to that Curtis guy."

"Somebody already got mad at me about that," I told her. "In fact, Curtis himself. I'll tell you the same thing I told him: I wanted a little wine, that's all. And I deserved it after the day I'd already had up to that point. As it happens, Curtis came into the club, which you would have seen if you'd *kept* spying, and we had our little meeting there."

"Oh." She breathed into the phone. "Well that's okay then."

"Go look at a dead body."

I gave her directions to the place, a sentence to say to Reese to let him know she was coming there at my behest, and I hung up.

My hand was still holding the phone when it rang again.

"Hello."

"It's Dan." His voice was barely audible. "Do I have

news. Can you meet me at the Clairmont now? We were wrong."

"Now?"

There was a bumping noise, a scrape, and then the phone went dead.

41

DEAD

Ordinarily after a failed attempt at my trick I don't like to rush out into the fray. It makes for a tough transition. But when you've got a pal on the line and the line goes dead, you generally have to rouse yourself, trick or not. Trick or Treat. Trick or *Gnosis*.

See, that's the kind of head you have when you hope to see beyond the pale and instead you stick your head *in* a pail. You go through linguistic peregrinations like that. You're a resident of Flip City, in other words. And I was that city's mayor.

Still, I took charge of my body, made it stand up, made it find my shoes, and I was on the street before I knew what time it was. Seemed late. The moon was high, the night was old, and I felt like I was a little of both myself.

I would usually have walked the long city blocks to the Clairmont from my street, but time seemed of the essence, so I tossed caution to the wind and hopped in the old auto. I was still groggy from being ripped out of my calm state by ugly visions of the young married couple and the jangling of the telephone.

My street dead-ends onto Ponce. The light there was red, but I knew it would take forever to change, and I wasn't in a mood to sit, so I looked both ways, saw nobody, and turned left onto the empty thoroughfare.

I was barely three blocks down, but nearly halfway to Dan, when I saw the blue lights in my rearview.

I pulled over. The cop car came up right on my bumper. I got out—which was my first mistake. Never get out. I scared the guys: the same guys who had been staking out my pad earlier, the same kids Dan had scared, the ones who had taken me to see Detective Huyne.

"Hey, guys," I told the driver, waving my hand as I approached. "Miss me?"

The poor schmo was startled. "Jesus! What the hell are you doing? Get back in your car."

"What's the problem?"

"Running a damn red light," the one in the passenger seat told me angrily, ducking his head down so he could see me out the driver-side window. His face was red, almost as if to demonstrate the color of the light I'd violated.

"I see." I looked around. "Now let's just think about this thing for a second, shall we. If it happens to be, say, Judge Kincaid in traffic court tomorrow, which I believe it is, you realize he'll never buy this ticket. I mean, it's got to be four in the morning. Ponce is deserted. The 'prevailing conditions' caveat would seem to apply. I came to a full stop. I looked both ways. I proceeded slowly onto Ponce with no traffic in either direction. And I was driving exactly at the speed limit. Would either of you happen to know what that is on this stretch of Ponce?"

They sat.

"Thirty-five. So I'd say my bank of lawyers would come to some sort of heinous 'harassment' lawsuit against you two, maybe even the department, and you poor dinks would be under investigation before noon. Or at the very least in Huyne's office with him yelling at you, don't you think?"

I stood.

"So," I concluded, after I'd given them just barely

enough time to consider what I'd said, "if you'll excuse me, I've got a friend in need over at the Clairmont. In fact, if you'd like to follow me over there, that might be nice. It's your friend Danny, to whom you were just speaking earlier. The guy on the curb. You remember him."

As they could, apparently, think of little to say, I waved good-bye and got back into my car.

I was a block closer to my goal when I saw the blue lights flashing again.

This time, before I could get out, they used the speaker system atop their chariot.

"Remain inside the vehicle! An officer will be with you shortly!"

I sat. Hours passed—in a single thirty seconds.

Finally Tweedle Whichever stood at my door.

"License and registration."

"What's the problem, Officer?" I tried to sound as much like Gomer Pyle as I could.

"Fleeing the scene while under an officer's scrutiny."

"Oh for God's sake." I jabbed my little auto into first. "That's not even worth my making fun of. Come on. We've got to get to the Clairmont. See you in the parking lot."

And I took off.

Okay, it wasn't the best thing in the world to do, but I was in no mood for some sort of Camus/Andy Griffith juxtaposition of absurdism-meets-the-myth-of-Sisyphus. Once I roll a rock up a hill, I'm done with it, whether or not it rolls back down. If it does, I figure that's where it wants to be and I move on. Plus I usually pause to admire the view from the top of the hill. That was my giddy, four AM motto: Admire the view no matter where your rock rolls.

The boys in blue didn't see it that way, but I just figured they just hadn't spent as much idle time reading useless mythology as I had.

They pursued with siren and light. I got to the Clairmont parking lot and pulled in right by the front door. They were close behind. Good, I thought. If someone was messing with Danny, let's wake everybody up and let them know the cops are here.

I was out of my car before the cops had come to a complete stop, but the passenger-side guy was already out with his pistol drawn and leveled right in my direction.

"Freeze!"

Just like on television.

"Okay," I said, and immediately went for the door.

I was inside before the kid even knew I was gone, because the car had come to an abrupt stop, bumped him, and sent him tumbling onto the pavement. Then the driver was out and waving his weapon too.

I heard him shout, "Where did he go."

"I didn't see," the other yelled back, scrambling up. "I didn't see!"

I opened the door and peeked back out. "In here, boys."

For a second they both looked like stupid Labradors—if that's not a redundancy—and then they loped toward me the same way.

I slipped back into the lobby. Danny was sitting in a chair. Lucrezia was standing behind him rubbing his head. The concierge was scowling beside them both.

I moved pretty quickly to stand on the other side of Dan so we'd make a nice balanced picture when my friends came barging in.

They hit the lobby, then stopped cold.

"Hi." Dan smiled warmly at them both.

Lucy looked hard at the rug.

"Officers," the concierge began, moving their way, "I can't tell you how glad I am you're here. This man here—the one sitting, he's been fussing in some of my rooms. And then his girlfriend hit him. I want you to take them both . . ."

"Freeze!" It was the passenger-side guy again, still practicing for a bit part in the upcoming *Adam-12* movie.

The concierge looked back at me. "Oh, for Christ sake, Tucker, you couldn't find any real cops?"

My eyes brightened.

"Flap," Danny said, his voice pitched so only I could hear it, "you need to go look in Room 312."

"Flap," Lucy said quickly, "I didn't know this guy here was a friend of yours. I didn't mean to conk him. But, damn—he's lucky I didn't kill him dead. Look."

She pointed at his feet.

Dan was wearing black-and-tan, two-toned, 1940s shoes.

42

TWO TONE

"Is it me," I asked Lucy, "or are these things coming back into style?"

"I've worn these shoes since the band days," Dan reminded me, "and you're just now asking about them?"

"I hate coincidence," I explained to him, "and the fact is that the man who rushed our girl, here, wore shoes of that ilk—as did the corpse of Ronnard Raay."

"I hate that kind of coincidence too," Danny said, getting to his feet.

But before he could comment further, the cops finally got themselves organized.

"Okay," the driver said, "everybody just freeze."

"Freeze my ass," the concierge snarled, "and quit saying that. Put them guns away. I got jumpy customers and they don't like cops. What the hell are you doing here, anyway? I didn't call you."

"They're following me, I'm afraid," I told him. "I fought the law, and the law won."

"See, Mr. Tucker," the passenger-side guy began explaining to the concierge, "ran a red light, and then fled the scene . . ."

". . . Tucker," the concierge interrupted, "you got that Huyne mad at you?"

"Not mad, exactly," I said. "Why do you ask?"

"Because him and his boys have been in and out of here about half a dozen times over the past twenty-four hours, and you're *never* here this often. So I got to connect the two."

Danny leaned my way. "The cops were here because somebody got dead in a room. They think they can put two and two together."

"Why does everybody get to do that but me?" I looked at Dan. He had no idea what I was talking about.

"Now," the driver-cop began, his hand shaking and his voice high like Barney Fife's, "let's all just . . . stay right where we are 'til . . ."

But even if the kid had a thought, he didn't get a chance to finish it.

Mug Lewis came in the door at precisely that moment, saw police with guns, and did one of the things he did best. In what seemed like a single move, he swung his arm wide, flung his hand into his coat, brought it back with his pistol in it, and backhanded each cop behind the head so hard that they didn't even make a sound before they hit the floor. It was like ballet.

In one second, the cops were off their feet, out cold on the floor of the Clairmont lobby, and Mug was tucking his weapon neatly back into his coat.

"Hello, Flap," he said quietly. "Hello, everybody. Nice night."

Danny gave a curt nod. Lucy looked at me, eyes wide.

"Hey . . . Curtis." I smiled. "How's business?"

"Just about concluded." He glanced at the concierge, who was trying his best to look like he hadn't seen anything. "I apologize for the mess. Shall I clean up?"

"Might be best," the concierge said plainly, eyes on the floor, "if you just went on upstairs and packed. I'd like it a whole lot if I didn't know where you was in about five minutes—when these boys come to."

"I see." Mug tilted his head philosophically. "I have overstayed my welcome."

"To coin a phrase," Danny said finally, staring right into Mug's eyes.

Danny Frank had a way of looking at a man that let the man know he was being looked at good. Danny could come away from such a gaze knowing the man's shoe size and what he'd had for dinner . . . last Thursday. I never saw him turn that power on a woman. Maybe he did, but it seemed more likely that he considered himself a better gentleman than that.

"I don't believe I've had the pleasure." Mug's eyes were welded to Dan's.

"This is my friend Daniel Frank," I said to Mug quickly. "Plays a serious tenor."

"Ah." Mug's demeanor brightened, but his eyes remained locked with Danny's. "An artist. I see. This explains it."

"Flap?" Lucy interjected, shrill and tired.

"Yes?" I tried not to look at her.

"I have got to talk to you!"

"Can you hang on just a minute? I want to make sure . . ."

But—as so much about the previous days had presaged—I was not to finish my sentence. Things, it seemed, were to be left dangling—all over town. Because one of the cops rolled over, drew his gun, and shot Mug Lewis in the heart.

43

HEART

Lucy screamed, just like the young people in the scary movies these days. It was so good, in fact, that instead of thinking, *Oh, my God, Mug's been hit,* I was thinking, *Gee, Lucy should look into getting voice-over work.* Which told me more about my state of mind, or perception of reality, than I really wanted to know.

Luckily, Dan moved. He kicked the gun out of the cop's hand, sapped the cop in the head again, and had Mug in his arms before Mug even crumpled.

"Jesus," Mug managed.

Dan flung back Mug's jacket and ripped the shirt before he realized that all he was doing was ruining part of Mug's ensemble. Very little lifesaving was actually required, as Dan had torn Mug's clothing only to reveal a heavy bulletproof garment underneath.

Danny looked over at me. "Vest."

"I just got the wind knocked out of me," Mug gasped. "I'll be okay. Jesus, that kid scared me, though."

"You don't like to see a bullet coming your way, no matter what," I agreed.

Lucy was still in the shock envelope.

I put my hand on her arm.

She looked at me. Her eyes were troubled. "Flap. The guy that rushed me—it's not your friend, here."

"I could have told you that." I was still holding her arm. "But why were you upstairs with him at all?"

"Can I sit down?" She took the stained, overstuffed chair. "Damn." She looked up at me. "I was on my way out when I saw this chump in the parking lot and I caught a glimpse of his shoes. I couldn't see his face. I followed him. So when he started skulking around this messy room upstairs like he was going to steal something, I thought for sure he was a bad guy. I conked him on the head. I was about to call you when the concierge, here—Buster—came steaming up at me like it's the crime of the century to bean a skunk."

"But now that you have gotten a good look at Danny, you realize he is not your man."

"Correct." She looked over at him. "Sorry."

"A logical mistake," he said, still holding Mug.

"Could we *please* all get the hell out of here?" Buster was livid. "I got unconscious, pissed-off, rookie cops messing up my floor, and when they get back up, they're surely going to blame somebody—and it will not be me, because I will be on the floor too, a victim of the same scum that whacked them."

And Buster, quite ceremoniously, laid himself down on the floor.

Danny cracked up.

Mug looked down. "Would you like me to tap you in the skull to make it official? No extra charge."

"Shut up," Buster said, eyes closed, from his ridiculous position.

"Here's what I say," I announced. "Curtis? You take off. Buster, you lie low. The rest of you, come with me." I looked at Lucy. "I always wanted to say that in a real-life situation—you see it so often in the movies."

"You do?" She got to her feet.

" 'Some of you go that way; the rest of you come with me.' I think it's in a lot of jungle movies."

"They don't really make that many jungle movies

these days, Flap." She seemed amused at my lack of cinema-currence.

"I lament the passing of the art film," I explained as I headed for the stairs, "the days of Truffaut and Bergman . . ."

". . . Godard," Danny picked up, "and Fellini."

"Shut up," she intoned, "and shut up."

She and Danny followed me upstairs while the Narcolepsy Trio stayed put on the lobby floor behind us. Mug had already vanished.

"It's this way." Dan brushed past me.

We made it to 312. The door was ajar. There was yellow police tape across the entrance. Danny poked the door and it swung a foot or so.

Inside was what real-live investigators call a crime scene: "Doesn't look like a struggle of any sort took place, Dano." That kind of thing.

"This was Ronnard Raay's room."

"Hold the phone." I let my eyes roam over the chaos. "You mean that Ronn, Jersey, and . . . Curtis *all* stayed here at the Clairmont? You'd think a high roller like Higgins would check in at the Ritz."

"Speaking of coincidence"—Dan nodded—"not to mention that Curtis bears an uncanny resemblance to a guy they used to call Mug Lewis."

"I noticed that, too," I said, avoiding Dan's eyes.

"This is the guy," Lucy began, ducking under the tape and stepping lightly into the room, "or I mean this is the room of the guy you think might have crowded me. The one I was supposed to go look at in the morgue."

"Right." I was still looking for any angle on all the coincidence. "Best not to run yourself too far in, either. It's called 'disturbing the scene.' "

"Scene of what?" She blinked in my direction.

"We believe that Ronnard Raay Higgins died in this

room," Dan explained plainly, "and was carted across the street in a plain brown wrapper."

"What's he talking about?" She looked at me.

"I didn't tell you the whole story," I said, "but mainly the guy who zoomed you was also menacing our Ms. Oglethorpe as well, and he was also in big with bad drug money—or is that in bad with big drug money—but nevertheless, and oh by the way, did I happen to mention he was Ms. Oglethorpe's husband?"

Before anyone could comment on the nuttiness of my short but brief tirade, a familiar voice startled us all.

"Miss? You'll have to step out of the room."

I turned. "Detective Huyne. What a pleasure."

"Tucker," he said patiently, "I have such a lot to say to you."

"Look," I started, "I'm here with my operative and my client investigating the possibility that the inhabitant of this room was the same man who attacked my client."

Huyne looked back and forth between Dan and Lucy before he caught my eye again and heaved a mountainous sigh. "I don't even want to know which one of these miscreants . . ."

". . . miscreants?" Lucy's hackles were on end.

". . . is your client"—Huyne ignored her—"and which is your so-called operative. All I care about is that you all get the hell out of my crime scene. And then somebody needs to explain the two semiconscious policemen downstairs."

"Lucy," I beckoned.

She stood her ground for a second, then looked at me.

I inclined my head toward the hallway.

She sipped a breath through her nostrils and then reluctantly acquiesced.

"I thought we agreed a couple of chapters back," I

said to Huyne, "that you would cut me loose a little and have those boys lay off me. They tried to arrest me for running a red light just now, you know."

"And you were supposed to call me, remember? You're lucky they didn't fling you into the trunk of their car and haul your ass to Birmingham and back. But that's neither here nor there at this point. I came to tell you something I think you'll want to know."

Lucy was just ducking her head under the tape when Huyne made the announcement he'd really come to make—the one that stopped my heart.

"I thought you'd like to hear," he said, as if he were continuing an ongoing conversation with me, "that we've arrested Ms. Oglethorpe for the murder of her husband."

44

DREAMLAND

Visiting Dalliance Oglethorpe in jail was an experience I don't think I could ever bring myself to talk about.

Sometimes, in the red labyrinth of dreams, you visit a cold gray hallway. And inside a cell where the sun's refused to shine, you see someone you love—broken, dejected, at an end. Your own suffering isn't a fraction as bad as seeing someone you love suffer. But it's only a bad dream, you keep saying to yourself. And then you wake up.

I woke up from that nightmare when I left the station house, just after the sun had risen. She was being held there until they could transfer her. We hadn't said much. But the last sentences were important.

"What with your big secret marriage out in the open and your previous investigator dead," I had said, studying the pattern of the floor in her holding cell—a visit that Huyne had arranged, which reinvented my opinion of the guy considerably, "I think I'll just take the bull by the horns and find out who killed your husband."

"Flap . . ."

". . . it doesn't really matter what you have to say on the subject at this point," I interrupted. "I'm doing it."

She knew the tone. She knew I meant it.

So instead of the ten thousand other things she might have said, she said the magic word: "Thanks."

And I was gone.

Huyne had taken care of the rookies on the floor of the Clairmont. Buster the concierge had told everyone most of the story, omitting—I wasn't certain why—the presence of "Curtis."

I was handed—and I'm not making this up—a "courtesy warning."

I said to the one cop, "What do I do with this?"

He said, "It doesn't matter. It has no official police standing. It's just a courtesy warning."

"Well," I said, "it's very courteous indeed. I'll think twice about running that red light again, I can tell you."

He said that he hoped I got the mange, and that concluded our meeting.

The day was already hot. Midsummer air around me was as still as the grave. It didn't matter. I was marble on the inside, and more tired than Sisyphus after the first century. Still, I knew what I had to do.

I didn't even bother going home. I got back into my car and got to Easy, parked in back, went straight to Dally's office, and sat in her chair. I didn't know if I thought it would help or I just wanted to sit in her chair.

I took off my shoes, loosened my tie, and waited.

You have to wait. The angel is shy and doesn't always come right away. Patience is one of my least attributes, and patience is essential. That's a lesson I've learned over and over and over again.

I sat. I watched the motes of dust float in the amber light from her desk lamp. I let my eyes unfocus. I was thinking that I'd been doing this little trick for years and I still didn't understand it. Every time I'd tried to think about it, the picture'd just gotten fuzzier. So that the more I'd done it, the less I'd understood it. But I knew you had to sit and wait, try to be a blank slate. I saw a *National Geographic* story once about an Aboriginal tribe in Australia who all thought that dreaming was the real life, and the waking hours were just what you had to do to rest up from the dream time. They seemed pretty happy.

I was just waiting.

And somewhere about the third year of my waiting, I realized I was already in dreamland.

Dreamland was very nice in the middle of the summer, what with the foliage—and the nymphs.

I was Bottom, the jackass-headed buffoon. I was lumbering through the midsummer night in my dream, watching lights blink on and off all around me. There was Huyne as Oberon. Dally as Titania. Lucy was Puck—paging Dr. Freud. Danny was Danny, a very amused audience member. Mug Lewis and poor old Jersey Jakes were Pyramus and Thisbe. And here's the good part: I thought I could solve the riddle. But that's what the jackass always thinks.

The next thing I knew, I was in a darker part of the woods, and Jersey came stumbling toward me, trying to speak, but he couldn't because there was a high-heeled shoe stuck in his chest, the heel had stabbed his heart and he was mouthing Dally's name and holding out his hand.

Then he dropped like a stone and he was dead.

Still, his hand—his left hand—was twitching and trying to write something in the dirt on the ground, but it was hard to see in the moonlight.

He was dead and he was still trying desperately to tell me something. And all around him the ground was cluttered and chaotic. Like the floor of his room at the Clairmont.

But that was a mistake, thinking like that—thinking

about something outside of the vision-state. I was shot out of the dream like a bottle rocket. I lurched forward in Dally's chair.

Damn, I thought, *you know better than to think when you're in dreamland.*

45

CHAOS THEORY

And I didn't just lurch forward. I lurched and then stood and I was headed for the door before the momentum of my expulsion from the dream subsided. By then the will to barge across the street and break the law was strong enough to carry me past the doorframe and out of the club.

I was certain I had seen something on the floor of Jersey's room that had triggered some other thing in my mind. That's what the image in my trance-state was all about. I had to go and stare at the mess long enough to see what it was. I was hoping maybe Buster was off.

No such luck.

"You back?" He was more irritated than ever, but he didn't bother to stand. "Should I just go ahead and call the cops now?"

"Can if you want to," I said, "but it'll only make Huyne madder than he already is. I've just recently left the jailhouse, where he's already up to his ears in all the suspects he can handle."

The poor guy was thinking as hard as he could, but it simply wasn't enough. He finally gave up.

"Okay, what the hell." He looked away. "What do I care?"

I was on the steps before he was finished with his sentence.

Jersey's room was also barred by the yellow police tape—I imagined it was a common enough decor accent in the hallways of that particular place.

I slipped under it and tried not to let my feet touch the floor, but gravity won out, and I stepped on something breakable right away. I crunched a glass. It had been buried under newspapers and towels.

The whole room looked like a post-disaster newspaper photo. Much worse than the few days before when I'd roused him out of it. "Wreckage of Hurricane Jakes. Details at ten." No one would ever suppose that all the carnage in that ten-by-ten could have been perpetrated by a human being. Magazines and wrecked clothes were everywhere. Take-out cartons and pizza boxes ruled. The walls were a cobwebbed pattern of dust and arcane wallpaper. The ceiling was yellowed from years of inhabitants who had ignored the no-smoking plaques. The bed was askew, the chair at the desk was turned over, the lamp by the bed was broken, and the shade at the window was torn. It looked like—and here I paraphrase Hunter Thompson—a museum exhibit: "Denizens of the Underworld—see their filthy living habits!" No one person could have created such dark chaos. A team of behavioral scientists working around the clock had concocted this environment. "Your hoodlum believes in the disoriented living space, because his whole life is psychopathically off kilter, hence our mock-up of the typical quarters of your criminal element."

I'm saying the place was a mess.

I waded into the room, trying my best not to break anything else. I let my eyes roam over the rubble.

What was it, I kept thinking, that poor old

Jersey Jakes was trying to tell me from beyond the grave?

Month-old newspapers, unopened mail, single crusted socks, a set of fingernail clippers, three coffee cups, two glass ashtrays, an antique brass letter opener, cardboard, pants, shirts, double-colored cloth shoes, ties, two hats, five beer cans, a pillowcase, and a clear plastic bear filled with honey—these were a few of my favorite things.

I gave some thought to righting the chair, having a seat, and trying my trick while I was staring at the mess. But the thought of what might come crawling from underneath the bed—that undiscovered country—gave me pause. Besides, after about a half an hour's worth of useless rumination, my whole theory—that I could have seen something there that hadn't registered consciously but was somehow stuck in my Jung-brain—seemed utterly ridiculous in general.

I decided to wander on back downstairs to see if I could discover where Mug might have gone. Strictly speaking, he was still a client. So was Lucy, for that matter. I was still waiting to hear from her after her trip to the morgue, a visit with odd little Reese, but I was certain it would only be a confirmation call: Yes, that was the guy who mashed me. Good riddance/bad rubbish. That sort of thing.

I was ducking my head back under the yellow ribbon when I crunched on the same glass I'd broken on the way in. I looked down for a second. When I did, I caught a glint of something from the single ray of morning light through the torn place in the shade. It was something important.

"Damn." I thought it called for an audible expression.

I took a step back into the room and bent over. The thing that had caught my eye was the antique letter opener.

It only took a second before I realized where I'd seen it before—and who had been holding it in her lovely hand.

46

SOMEBODY'S BLOOD

Letter opener in pocket, I flew downstairs and waved a small message to Buster on my way out of his lobby. My message was simple: I hope I never come back here again, I hope this is the last time I see you in this life.

He seemed to understand, and I felt a shared wish, a kindred mutuality on the subject.

I was back across the street in no time. Molecules seemed to be moving like a whirlwind around me, and I thought I was about to make some very unpleasant discoveries. Some *more* very unpleasant discoveries.

I had to get the letter opener tested right away, to prove that the idea ransacking my brain was erroneous—that the last time I'd seen that blade hadn't been in Dally's office, in Dally's hand, threatening Ronnard Raay. It just looked like that letter opener.

I stood outside the Clairmont for a minute trying to remember where my car was. That's how whacked I was. By the time I remembered it was behind Easy, I was already in such an agitated state that I couldn't find my keys, and they were right there in my pocket.

I was certain that the last time I'd seen the letter opener that I was concealing, wrapped in newspaper, in my breast pocket—the one that I'd just removed from a crime scene—was when Dally had been holding it in her hand the day Ronnard Raay had been in her office. I remembered then that I'd thought she was holding it like a weapon.

How it had gotten into Jersey's room I had no idea, but I really didn't want Huyne or his boys or anybody else finding it and putting that famous old two and two together.

I made it across Ponce and into my car, finally grasping the concept that my keys were where they always were.

I headed straight to the laboratory of this guy Paul, a longtime friend and occasional helper.

He was a professor at Georgia Tech. We'd known each other for ages. He'd also been sweet on Dally for the same amount of time. I thought he would help and I thought he would keep quiet about helping—as he usually did. Hence, I dispatched myself to his digs with remarkable haste. Down Ponce, left on Peachtree, right on North, past the Varsity, and onto the campus. I made it in under ten minutes.

He was bent over a Bunsen burner.

"Paul."

He jerked as if someone had shot him in the leg, eyes wildly searching the big room for the source of the voice.

"It's me, Paul. Flap."

"Jesus."

"No. Flap. But thanks for the compliment."

"What the hell are you doing here at this time of day?" Paul knew me as a denizen of the night.

"I've got trouble. You need to look at this thing I've got in my pocket and tell me everything there is to know about it. And you've got to do it quick. But before I show it to you, you also have to promise not to say anything about it to anyone ever. That's important."

"It's about Dalliance." He could see it in my face, I guess.

"Can you do this or not?" I locked eyes with him.

He blinked once, saw the steel in my gaze, and nodded. "I can do that."

I assessed his solidarity, judged it complete, reached into my coat pocket, peeled back the paper, and presented the letter opener.

He looked at the thing in my hand, then back up at me. "Gee. Just like Clue. Isn't a letter opener one of the weapons in Clue? Miss Scarlet, with a letter opener, in the library?"

I remained silent. He got the message.

He reached into his pocket, pulled on a pair of surgeon's rubber gloves, and took the thing out of my hand.

"Sit. I'll be a while." He started off, then turned. "You do want to wait?"

I nodded. "Use your phone?"

He pointed to his office and was gone.

I made my way past the tables and lab equipment to his little cubicle. It was the same kind of mess that Dally's office was: Everything looked like chaos, but Paul had a system, one only he could understand. Ask him where anything was, and he'd go right to it. Me? I barely found the phone. It was under a splayed magazine, opened to an article about a woman who had figured out how to slow down light—so slow you could almost see it travel.

I sat at Paul's desk, pulled out the crumpled check I still hadn't cashed, and dialed the number on it.

"So?" she answered.

"So did you go look at a dead body? And isn't Reese a character?"

"Flap?" Her voice changed dramatically, warmed and lightened, which did something to my stomach—or my heart. It was hard to tell which at that point.

"Yeah." I managed to make my voice sound casual, "How're you doing?"

"I'm okay." Shy. "Where are you?"

"Working. So did you go see Ronnard Raay's two-tones?"

"I did. I don't think he's the guy."

Hello? "Not the guy?"

"Well," she cleared her throat, "it's kind of hard to tell when you're looking at a cold white slab of dead guy in place of a hot, coked-up juggernaut, but, no, I don't think it was the same guy who mooched me, I don't."

"Why not?"

"Not the same kind of shoes. This stiff I just saw? He was a fancy dresser. The guy who rushed me was a thrift-store character."

"Why do you say that?"

"The guy who bothered me smelled like mothballs, don't you remember I told you. The stiff I saw at the morgue? It's not my guy."

"Look again." I wasn't willing to let it go.

"I'm not going back there to look at that dead guy again. I've seen enough dead guys."

"You have?" I was tapping my fingers on the mess on Paul's desk. "How many?"

"Counting the one you made me go see?" she asked. "One. And that's aplenty. I did like Reese, though. He was cool."

"As a cucumber."

"And he told me what all you did for him." Her voice was getting warmer. "You're really kind of a Lone Ranger type, right?"

"Lone Ranger actually had a sidekick," I answered her, "I work totally alone."

"Is that right?"

"I don't know whether it's right or not"—I sighed—
"but it's what I usually do. So you don't think Ronnard
Raay's the guy?"

"If that's the name of the meat I ogled, no."

"Damn."

"Why?"

"Well," I said, "you kind of like to have all your rotten eggs in one basket, in a way—no matter how too-
much-of-a-coincidence it would be."

"Jeez, Flap." She laughed into the phone. "You need
some sleep or something. I have no idea what you're
saying. That's nut-talk."

"What I need," I began, "is to find out who it was
that bothered you . . ."

But I didn't finish the sentence. Paul's face stopped
me. He was looming in the doorway of his own office
wearing a mask of Munch-like disbelief.

"Flap?" he said.

"Look, kiddo," I murmured into the phone, "could
I call you back?"

"Sure." She seemed confused. "You okay?"

"We'll talk." I hung up. Then I looked at Paul.
"What?"

"Before I go any further with this," he said shakily,
"you have to tell me why somebody's blood is on the
pointy end of this thing . . ." He paused and looked at the
letter opener in his hand. ". . . and Dally's fingerprints are
on the other end."

47

WHY

"It doesn't mean anything, Paul," I told him steadily, even though my own impulses were on fire. "And how did you figure all that out in such a short time?"

"You bring this thing to me in a rush." He leaned against the doorframe. "You hold it like it's a bottle full of disease. You act all mysterious, even for you. And you look worried. I put two and two together."

I let that sentence pass unheralded. "And you came up with?"

"This thing is a murder weapon. So I check. Bingo: blood. Then I look for prints. There are three sets clear and several other partials." He paused, then went on softer—and a little redder of face. "I recognized Dally's prints. I've studied them."

He was obviously in some biologist/voyeur realm that I didn't even want to know about, so I let that sentence go by too.

He let out a breath and relaxed a little. "So tell me."

"Nothing to tell," I said. "Somebody lifted that from Dally's office, so natch it's got her prints. Check the others. I suggest you just tell me all you can about them, and then forget I brought it to you."

"Brought what to me?" He smiled gamely.

"Good. Now go. I have a few more calls to make."

"All the other prints are from men I think."

My hand hovered over the phone. "You can tell that?"

"Sort of. Plus, I have an intuition."

"Go."

He went. I dialed.

"And?" The terse voice was tighter than usual.

"Danny? Your voice sounds funny."

He made no answer.

I got it. "You're not alone?"

"Why, no I'm not. Thanks for asking."

"Can you tell me who's there?"

"Remember the Bobbsey Twins?"

"Those goofs who came to beat you up?" I couldn't believe it. "The ones I had to pop?"

"Right. So I'm kind of busy."

"Are you okay?"

"As well as can be expected," he said slowly, "under the circumstances."

"Are they standing right there?"

"Yup."

"Want me to come over?"

"Not necessary. Talking is more the order of the day at this juncture."

"Nobody's trying to rearrange your biological order. They don't want to beat you up anymore."

"That's right," he told me. "I'm just trying to figure out exactly why, is all."

"Okay, so here's why I called," I said as if there were nothing else in the world going on. "One: When you called me to the Clairmont, you said the phrase 'we were wrong' and I wanted to know what you meant, because the odds of our *both* being wrong are pretty significant. And two: What was all that bizarre behavior between you and Mug Lewis—we both know that's who that was."

"Yes." His voice betrayed amusement. Dan always

enjoyed my oblique attempts at apology. "But your questions are pertinent. Alas, they will have to wait."

"I get it. You sure you don't need help?"

He moved his mouth away from the speaker. "Boys? This is Flap Tucker on the other end. You want him to come over? He misses you."

I didn't hear what the response was.

"They said they'd just as soon conclude their business with me and let you get on with your business with you."

"To coin a phrase." I grinned. "But, Dan? Three? What exactly do you think those goons want with you at this point?"

"There," he said a little louder, "is where I believe we come to the crux of the biscuit, as it were. Give me a half an hour. Where are you?"

"At Tech."

"With that guy Paul." He was wise to my patterns. "Wait there. His office is still in the same building?"

"Right. See you in a nonce."

He hung up. I kept the phone in my hand. I thought for a second it might be better if I didn't call Huyne, but eventually the vision of dead Jersey trying to write in the dirt got the better of me, and I wanted to have all the information I could have. I was hoping I could get some more from him about where he was with Jersey's demise, and what he was thinking about Ronnard Raay's. So I dialed the police station.

"Huyne." He answered in a hurry.

"Yes," I said slowly, "it's Flap Tucker. Do you have a second?"

"Not really. And not necessary. I think we've just about got things wrapped up around here where you're concerned. You and Ms. Oglethorpe."

"What?" I leaned forward. "Wrapped up good or wrapped up bad?"

"I suppose that depends on your point of view." He was still in a rush. "But the fact is, we're prepared to dismiss the charges against Ms. Oglethorpe. We have no need of you. And everything's about to be put to rest."

Stop the presses.

"You're letting Dally go?"

"That's what we sometimes do with innocent parties." He rustled some papers on his desk. "Look, I really don't have the time . . ."

". . . what's the deal, Huyne?" I tried out the overwhelming voice of strength. It was pretty impressive. "This is all happening too fast. Why are you letting her go?"

"Christ," he said, "calm down, Tucker. We're letting her go because the coroner's opinion confirms the note we found in the room of the deceased. Higgins was a suicide."

48

KAMIKAZE DRUG LORDS
OF THE SUNBELT

"I see." I brought my voice back to a calmer condition. "Suicide. Well. That explains it. What about Jersey Jakes? Who killed him, or was he a do-it-yourselfer too?"

"We believe he was murdered by an accomplice of Ronnard Raay Higgins because Higgins found out that Jakes was tailing him." Huyne's voice had taken on an edge of irony. "You notice how free I am with the information."

"I figure that's because it'll be in the papers tomorrow anyway," I opined, "but thanks for the early edition. Go on."

"Oh"—his voice got even edgier—"you want more? Okay. How about this: Higgins was the next best thing to a big crime boss in the southeastern drug world. He was a clearinghouse. Only he was in big trouble with his higher-ups . . ."

". . . whoever they would be . . ."

". . . and he needed a big bunch of cash. You don't remember a guy around town a year or so back called Mug Lewis, do you?"

Well. There was a question. I had to be very careful with my honesty around the answer.

"Yes," I said plainly, "I remember Mug Lewis."

"I thought you might." His voice was in overdrive, heavy with strange overtones. "Anyway, he was into

Higgins for, like, over seven hundred thousand. So Higgins had him killed."

"Higgins had Mug killed?"

"Correct." Huyne got quiet. "In fact, I believe you were at Mug Lewis's funeral, weren't you?"

"How you would know a thing like that only frightens me more about the whole concept of Big Brother," I said, "but yes, I was at the funeral."

"Uh-huh." Anger was creeping into the mix, though I wasn't certain why. Maybe he was just impatient with me. "So, to conclude our little info-fest, here, Higgins needed the dough because of Lewis. Higgins killed Lewis but never got the money. That's why Higgins came to Atlanta, to get cash from his wife. His wife Dalliance Oglethorpe."

"I knew which wife you meant." I tried to sound amused. "So when Dally wouldn't give him the money, he was so despondent that he killed himself?"

"Ms. Oglethorpe doesn't *have* that kind of money. And the drug lords were closing in. Higgins, as you may have determined from your own investigation, had a reputation for being something of a badass when he was in the right mood, what with cutting off of people's hands, and chunking people in the head with tire irons. He was afraid he'd get a little of his own medicine. So he took some of his own medicine—in fact, an entire gram of coke—and then he stabbed himself hard in the heart. Case closed."

Not hardly, as we used to say in my hometown.

"Pretty neat." That's all I said to Huyne. "So who brought Mr. Higgins over to Easy all wrapped up?"

"Yeah," he allowed, "that's a good one. Maybe it's your turn to share."

"I don't have any idea." But that was a lie. I had lots of ideas. "And what about the suicide weapon?"

"Okay"—Huyne sighed heavily—"you got me. Maybe the case isn't entirely closed. I'd like to know who carried the body to Ms. Oglethorpe. And why. Maybe it was the accomplice I mentioned. You're telling me you don't have any ideas about that at all? No mystic vision?"

"Nice tone of mockery," I told him. I didn't think I should bother him with the details of my little thing. "But not much in the vision department here."

"Not much." Sounded like he leaned back in his chair. "Not much. Well, see, knowing that you're Mr. Understatement, I have to ask myself why you don't seem to want to tell me what you're thinking."

"Look." My voice rose. "You can't make fun of my little thing and then, at the same time, demand to know what's going on with it."

"Demand?" His voice matched my tone. "All I said was . . ."

". . . look, Huyne." I took a breath. "Detective Huyne, that is: I don't have anything definitive to say in the matter. I did my little thing, it was a scene from *Midsummer Night's Dream*. Happy?"

"By Shakespeare?" His voice was high. "That play by Shakespeare? You are one messed-up ball of confusion."

"My point exactly," I said, "so lay off. If you don't want to hear what goes on in the troubled coffin of my brain, then don't ask."

"Troubled coffin?"

"Are you going to repeat everything I say?"

"Tucker, you can be just as weird as you want to be. That's fine by me. But don't pretend it has anything to do with finding out the truth about anything. If you want to answer a question, all you have to do is work: Think it out; put all the facts together. Period."

"I see," I brushed him off. "Well, thanks for the tip. I see how your line of inquiry has always worked out well for you in your little cubicle there at the station house, but as soon as you jam a crowbar into your belief system and let even one little sliver of light in, you'll see that there's a whole other world out there. It's a place where you can put all the facts together that you want to, and you still won't have squat in the way of answers because you discover that you're asking all the wrong questions. And that's the end of my short but brief tirade concerning my Taoist approach to things."

"What questions *should* I be asking, then?" he shot back. "Mr. Tucker."

"If you peel away the mask that you wear most of the time in this life," I said carefully, "then what does your face look like?"

"Yeah." He managed a laugh. "And what's the sound of one hand clapping. I've heard all that before . . ."

". . . you don't follow me at all," I interrupted, even softer. "I'm saying: What do you see when you see past most of what you thought there was to see?"

"Okay"—he sighed—"that's enough of that."

"You don't realize it," I said, "but I'm actually answering your question. I'm actually trying to help."

"You need to help yourself to a hot shower and a nap," he told me. "That's my advice to you."

"Actually," I nodded slowly, "that's right. You're exactly correct. A little sleep is just what I need."

"You'll see things in a different light." His voice was calmer too.

"I'm sure I will." But I knew that all the sleep in the world wouldn't smack me into his little cubicle, a place where evil drug lords from south Georgia scared Ronnard Raay Higgins so bad that he shoved a letter opener into his sternum. I knew that a hot shower wouldn't wash away the blood on one end of that murder weapon, or the fingerprints on the other.

49

SLEEP

Shakespeare said that sleep knits up the raveled sleeve of care. But he didn't have my problems. And he hadn't ever fallen asleep on Paul's desk.

When I woke up from a nap that could only be described as fitful, there was a purple-lettered mimeographed sheet of something or other stuck to the side of my face. I peeled it off. It was all about chemical compounds, and must have been thirty years old. I couldn't even remember the last time I'd seen a mimeographed anything.

I had been startled from my slumber by Paul's dramatic entrance:

"Flap! Wake up! Jesus!"

All exclamations.

I removed the sheet of paper from my face, knowing it had left purple stigmata on my cheek, and folded my hands in front of me.

"Yes, Paul?"

He sat in the chair across from the desk. "You're not going to believe it. Dalliance is married! Was married."

I tapped my thumbs together. "What makes you think that?"

"Well, I wanted to see if I could find out whose blood was . . . I ran a computer thing . . . Flap, he's got a police record." He lowered his voice to barely audible. "So does *she*."

"What are you telling me, Paul?" I didn't even want to get into a dialogue about the age of modern computer miracles.

He straightened up. "The blood belongs to some guy named Higgins that is married to Dalliance, or was. He's dead. I assume from getting stuck by this thing." He held it up in his surgeon-gloved hand. "And the only perfectly clear prints on it are hers. Dally's."

"Don't jump to conclusions, Paul." I said, a study of calm. "Like I said, the thing's been on her desk for years. Anybody could have seen it, copped it, worn gloves just like the ones you're wearing now, and jabbed it into Higgins."

"Anyone?"

"Well," I allowed, "anyone who was really mad at him."

"Yeah." He looked up from the letter opener. "What does this really mean, Flap? Christ. Dally's married."

"Was." I leaned forward. "And it doesn't mean anything. Did I ever tell you my interpretation of basic phenomenology?"

"Please don't."

"Any action or situation is nothing more than a phenomenon," I said, ignoring his halfhearted plea. "That phenomenon, that occurrence, is devoid of any valuation, any meaning, until you impart meaning to it."

"A fact doesn't *mean* anything"—he nodded— "until it's interpreted and applied. I see that."

"Right. We quote old Joe Campbell: 'What's the meaning of a flower?' It just is."

"Joe Campbell? That guy who used to be at West Georgia College and was a stringer for *Time* or *Newsweek*?"

"No," I corrected, "that's Joe Cumming—although, now that you mention it, they do look sort of alike . . ."

". . . what are we talking about?"

"I'm talking about perception." I sat back. "I don't know what the hell you're talking about."

"I'm talking about a murder weapon with Dally's fingerprints on it. You obviously stole it from some crime scene, meaning that all three of us could go to prison." He sniffed. "That's what I'm talking about."

"*What* letter opener—remember?"

"Okay." He put it down carefully on the desk between us. "Then get the hell out of here and take this with you."

I stared down at it. I tried to make it be just a letter opener, devoid of any valuation or meaning. I didn't succeed. That's the problem with a high-flung philosophy: You can't always make it work for you—and often when you need it to work the most, it fails.

So I played the glad game instead. *I'm glad,* I said to myself, *that Ronnard Raay wasn't killed by a stiletto—despite my image of a stiletto-heeled shoe stuck into Jersey's heart. I'm glad the kid, Lucy, is innocent.* Kids—everybody, in fact—ought to try to keep innocence around them as long as they can, even under the duress of experience. *I'm glad,* I concluded my little internal monologue, *that Lucy didn't kill anyone, and that the person who bothered her won't be doing it again.*

"Flap?"

I roused. "Sorry, Paul. I can tell you're nervous about this, and I don't blame you. I'll be going now. Danny Frank will be here in a while. Would you mind telling him I've gone over to Easy? I can't call him at the moment, he's busy. And you don't want me to wait."

Paul nodded.

I reached for the letter opener.

He stopped me. "Hold it." He reached across the desk and got the local news section of the paper that was strewn on one edge of his desk. He wrapped the thing in two sheets, and then handed it to me.

"I never got a chance," he said quickly, "to check on the other prints. Like I said, I think they were men's prints . . ."

". . . right." I stuffed the newspaper package into my pocket. "One set's probably mine, because I picked it up . . ."

". . . I really don't want to know any more," Paul told me, standing and holding up his hands, as if he could stop the sound of my words from going into his ears.

"Okay." I stood. Paul was a good friend. He just didn't want to know too much. Once you know too much, it's not like you can un-know it, no matter how hard you try. It's in there, in your brain, keeping you awake at night, making you distracted by its shadow in the sunlight

I knew how he felt. That was my problem—why I hadn't slept all that well. I knew too much.

50

GNOSIS / GELEAFA

Knowledge, or, from the Greek: *gnosis*—by which we mean the condition of knowing something with a familiarity gained by experience, is crap. You can accumulate facts at the rate of a thousand or even a million a day for eighty or ninety years of life, and the second you die, it all goes away. Into thin air. So what good is the accumulation of facts? Belief is so much more important than knowledge, it isn't even funny. Belief is the light that imparts meaning to any phenomenon. Belief is the filter through which we interpret our own peculiar realities. Belief is the glue that puts a soul back together whenever knowledge shatters it.

And belief, from the Old English *geleafa*, is, ladies and gentlemen: a habit of mind in which trust or confidence is placed in some person or some thing.

That person for me was Dalliance Oglethorpe. That thing was whatever was left between us. I'm certain I could have stated it better after a good night's sleep and a fine meal at, say, Le Giverny—but that was the trend of my thinking as I left the campus of Georgia Tech and headed east toward Easy.

I just wanted to see her, to talk to her, to tell her that whatever had happened, it wasn't as important as our getting back together. Nothing else mattered. When you have a passion for somebody or something, nothing else ought to matter. When you have a habit of mind, you have to exercise that habit. When you have confidence and trust in someone, you have to believe them.

So, as the nose of my car edged into the parking lot in front of Easy, I'd say I was prepared to believe just about anything.

But the fact is, Fate can be pretty unrelenting when it wants to be. Dalliance Oglethorpe was not on the premises—no one was. In fact, a quick glance at the old watch proved that it was barely past midmorning. Which only proved my theory: Early to bed and early to rise gets you exactly nowhere, don't let anybody kid you. The early bird gets the worm, all right—but I have no taste for worms, and so I think I'll just sleep late, thanks.

What happened next wasn't pretty: I had time to think. Time-to-think almost always spells disaster.

I started off thinking about all the high old times Dalliance and Ronnard used to have—and that Dally had admitted to liking them. That particular wonderful trip ended in visions of Dally hopping across the street and popping her letter opener into Ronnard's chest.

But once that calmed down, I actually began to ponder the events, and tried to arrange them in different ways, like some chess player thinking out new strategies.

I was sitting there thinking just like that, sweating in my car, when Hal's truck pulled up into the space next to mine—not quite an hour later.

"Kind of early for you, partner."

I started rolling up the windows. "Yeah, it looks like it, but the fact is, this is actually the end of a long, late night."

He looked at his watch. "I guess this would be a pretty late night if you hadn't been to bed yet. Want some coffee?"

"That awful brown water you make? Not likely. I might finish off whatever's left of my stash, though. Remember, it's not morning for me, it's just a very late night."

"You're drinking quite a bit in the daytime," Hal said, locking his truck, "for you."

"As fate would have it," I explained, getting out of my car, "there's been a whole lot more daytime to drink in—for me—lately."

"I see." He stood his ground and stared me down, leaning back against his truck with a toothpick in his mouth.

"I'm okay, Hal. But thanks for not asking."

He shoved himself away from the fender and sauntered casually toward the front door.

The day was chigger-hot, cicadas and locusts chattering up the air. The heat from the asphalt in the parking lot was already serious enough to barbecue a rack of ribs, and the light was so bright it robbed color from the grass and weeds coming up through all the ruined parts of the pavement. Clouds seemed a medieval memory, and the sky was so seared by the sun that most of the blue had been leached.

I was glad for the relative dark of the bar, and the stale coolness of the air there.

Hal was merciful, and did not turn on the radio, as was his wont. Instead, he went right to my private place to look for my sustenance.

"Flap?" he called. "I've got to open something new. All you've got right here is the Puy Blanquet—and you don't want to waste that on a midmorning gulp."

"You know what I say?" I went to the stool closest to him. "I say 'the hell I don't.' Pour me up a significant amount."

He turned, eyed me, but finally went along with my

plan. Within three short breaths, he had popped the cork, filled a larger glass, and left the rest of the bottle dangerously close to my pouring hand. Then he proceeded to his work and left me alone.

I sat, continuing my thinking rampage. Around about the end of the second glass, things were lining up pretty well. That's when someone pounded on the door. Hal had locked it behind us—maybe in an unconscious attempt to prevent any further deliveries.

"I'll get it." I threw myself off the stool and made it to the door. "Who is it?"

"Dan."

I opened. He entered.

Dan's single syllable salutation: "Hal."

Hal smiled. "Danny. Late night for you too?"

"Hm?" Dan seemed preoccupied.

"Flap was just telling me . . ."

"Do you want some coffee?" I interrupted Hal to ask Dan.

"Coffee?" He seemed momentarily puzzled by the concept. "Okay."

Hal poured without further comment.

Dan made it to the bar, took the coffee mug, and then motioned me toward a table, away from Hal and the bar. I swooped up my bottle, thinking, from his demeanor, that I might need fortification.

We sat.

"Paul was freaked." Danny sipped his coffee. "Good coffee, Hal."

Hal didn't turn. "Some people like it."

"Paul just doesn't enjoy handling weapons." I sipped my wine.

"Weapons? I guess that would explain his pique." Dan looked into his cup. "We'll have to discuss that further. But at the moment, I think you'll get a laugh out of the reason why Chuckie and Rimshot were paying me a visit."

"Yes," I admitted, "I could use a good laugh."

"They came by to apologize," he said steadily, "and to say that their business was concluded. All was well." He sipped coffee. "I told them that I thought things were far from well, and I had to know more about why they had originally wanted to bop me. So we sat and talked in my living room for a while, and here is the long and the short of it, as follows: Ronnard Raay Higgins was recently a bad man. He was in charge of a significant circle of drugs and money, and when things didn't go his way, he could be plenty mean. For example, when some crooked cop named Tommy Acree down his way in south Georgia messed with Ronnard just recently, Ronnard held Tommy's left hand down on the hood of his own hot police car, hacked off the hand with a tree surgeon's tool, slapped Tom in the face with it—the guy's own hand. Then Ronnard laughed like it was a pretty good joke of some sort, and took the hand with him as he drove away—with Rimshot and Chuckie in the car."

"Tommy Acree? That was *his* hand?" I couldn't believe it. "I know him. He and his cousin Lowe Acree . . ."

". . . there's more," Danny interrupted.

"I know. Ronn sent Dally the hand, with a wedding ring on it, to give some sort of 'remember we're still married, don't mess with me' kind of message . . ."

". . . no," Dan butted in again, "Flap. I mean, there's *more*."

I stopped my glass halfway to my lips. I saw the look on Dan's face. "Okay," I said, "I'll bite. What more is there?"

"The reason Ronnard Raay was so desperate of late," Dan told me slowly and very softly, "was because Mug Lewis was into him for a big chunk of money, but

Ronn had lost his head—went and killed Mug before Mug could pay it back."

Danny sipped his coffee then, and let the full impact of the information sink into my somewhat befuddled consciousness.

"Chuckie and Rimjob were working for Ronnard." I finally set my glass down.

"Rimshot," Dan corrected.

"Ronnard heard that you were asking questions about him," I went on, "so he sent the boys up to convince you to lay off. He didn't know who you were, but the last thing he needed was some guy nosing around. Especially when the first thing he needed was cash, and he was increasingly insistent with Dalliance concerning same. And I'm convinced he was interested in eliminating me too—although he mostly just sent me a threatening cop-gram. . . ."

"But he also had to be very sensitive, of course," Danny continued, "in light of the fact that this Tommy Acree joker—who was in the hospital in Tifton, very much alive, though unconscious from loss of blood—was on the mind of every policeman in the area. So he also didn't want someone like you or me stirring up the local constabulary."

"Actually," I clued him in, "the cops—at least the Atlanta cops—already knew Ronn had Mug killed. This is all meshing like some weird gear work in a Rube Goldberg invention."

"Nice bit of surreal imagery. I had a more Hieronymus Bosch feeling, but you know best."

"I know zip," I told him in no uncertain terms. "But the fact is, I also have news for you. The police think that Ronnard Raay Higgins killed himself."

"You don't get many suicides," Dan added calmly, "who stab themselves in the heart these days."

"No," I agreed, "you don't. But that's just what the police believe, so there you are. There's a note, they say . . ."

". . . a suicide note?" Dan closed his eyes. "One of us should have known something about that."

"And the coroner confirms that the guy stuck himself," I finished. "Though how they determine a thing like that, I wouldn't know."

"Angle of entry, force of blow," Danny told me, "stuff on the stiff's hand, that kind of thing."

"And how you would know all about that, I couldn't say. But there you are."

"Oh," he said, finishing his coffee, "I'm a cornucopia of ghoulish information. It's a hobby of mine."

"So there really are ways to tell if a guy stabbed himself." I grabbed another sip of wine.

"That's right. If the coroner says it's suicide, it very well could be."

"Hm." I reached into my breast pocket. "Then I may have done kind of a foolish thing."

He watched as I drew the package out and laid it on the table between us.

"This," I said, shoving it toward him an inch or so, "is what we were going to talk about further—in the weapons department—a moment ago." I patted it. "This, I'm now willing to believe, is the object Ronn used to kill himself. It's Dally's letter opener. It's not a murder weapon at all, as we discover. It is merely an important element of a suicide scene which I have incorrectly removed and messed with."

"You believe this because that guy Paul did his voodoo and found Ronnard Raay's guts or blood type on it." He looked down at the package with exactly the same facial expression I'm sure I had when I saw the severed hand in a similar-sized bundle.

Then he very carefully unwrapped it completely, gazed at the thing for a moment, then picked up my bottle of wine, poured an ounce or so out onto the letter opener, and turned to Hal.

"Oops. Hal." His calm was unearthly. "I spilled some of this wine. Fling me over a bar rag, would you?"

Without a word, Hal tossed a dirty towel through the air directly at Dan's head. Dan caught it with one hand. He picked up the blade end of the object in question, turned it over, sopping it in wine. Then he lifted it, shook it off, and wiped it like he was polishing a magic lamp, hoping a genie would appear. He worked at this task for at least a full minute, then wrapped it back up in some of the dry newspaper.

"There," he said finally. "Now it is not a weapon of any sort, *nor* a crime scene essential. It is simply an object that somehow got misplaced from Ms. Oglethorpe's office—an object which you will now take and put back where it rightly belongs."

51

KNOWLEDGE

I looked down at the package. "You know, I never even told you the funny thing about this particular inconsequential object."

"There's something funny about it?" He seemed curious, more so than amused.

"Yeah. I found it in Jersey's room."

He only took a second. "And *not* in the room of the person who supposedly killed himself with it. I get that. And may I say: Does that disturb the suicide concept or what?"

"Right," I agreed. "There's not much chance that Ronn stabbed himself, stumbled into Jersey's room, left the thing . . ."

". . . wrapped himself in brown paper, stumbled across the street, and then plopped himself down right over there." Dan inclined his head in the direction of the place where Ronnard's body had been dumped. "This is a little amusing, after all."

"Jakes." That's all I had to say. I was charging headlong into my reassessment of Jersey's personality—again.

"He could have killed Higgins." Dan was nodding slowly. "Then delivered the body."

"But why?" I was still thinking of how he and I had hit it off, finally, and how I'd even thought of taking him on as the occasional partner.

"Let's pretend for a second that Jakes was not

entirely on the square. What if he saw a chance to get a big bundle of money for himself."

"What if Jakes was like a double agent." I saw what Danny was getting at. "Working for Dally, working for himself—hell, maybe he even went to Higgins and said he'd been sent by Dally but he'd help Higgins for a cut of the dough. Huyne told me that the notes Dally'd been finding were written by two different people. What if one of them was Jakes?"

"See," Dan said, finishing his coffee, "it's actually easy to speak ill of the dead, as it turns out."

"I'm currently in a position," I explained, "to speak ill of my grandmother."

"I didn't know you had a grandmother. But of course the real reason you removed the item from the scene is that you thought it was possible—just like the cops did until they developed their hilarious suicide theory—that our Ms. Oglethorpe, as you sometimes refer to her, might have done something rash."

"This is all very confusing to a person like me." I leaned my weight forward on the table, eyeing what was left of the wine after Danny's twisted attempt at sterilization.

"You've been drinking a lot in the daytime," Danny said without a hint of chastisement. "Maybe it's that."

"Fifty million Frenchmen do it every day." I reached for the bottle. "And they don't seem that confused to me. As a nation."

"However much I'd like to," he began, "I won't argue that point. Because your real problem is a crisis of faith."

See, when you just blurt it out like that, it sounds kind of obvious and jejune. But that was one of Danny's specialties: shoving the obvious in my face when I was more amused with the mysterious. Or the confusing.

"Dally thinks you killed Ronn." He just kept on

offering glaring observations. "And you think she did it. The facts now seem to support either suicide, assisted by Jakes, or murder by Jakes put up to look like suicide to take the heat off."

"Or." I tilted my head. "Could still have been Dally, and Jakes is more on the up and up than we've been saying for the moment, here. She stuck him, then got Jakes to clean up the mess. She called me in a panic so I'd be her alibi when the body showed up on the floor over there. She pretended to accuse me to throw me off."

"Or." Dan stared at the spot where the body had been. "Could have been you. You stabbed him, flung the murder weapon into Jakes's room, dragged the body over here, plopped it . . ."

". . . hustled home just in time to get a call from Dally . . ."

". . . ran back down here . . ."

". . . hold it." I sat up. "Mug Lewis. He killed Jakes. Did I tell you that?"

"This is your speculation?"

"No." I pushed my glass away. Clearheaded thinking was what I needed—at least for a second. "I know he did it. I was here with Ronnard's body when Mug came busting in and then he popped Jakes. He claimed Jakes came up behind him and attacked, but there was no evidence of that—none that I could see on the body when I was at the morgue. Not that I'm a forensics expert . . ."

". . . well." Dan's fingers started moving involuntarily. When he was really thinking hard, his fingers would act like they were playing his tenor, and start to do the Charlie Parker twitch. "Mug Lewis. Jesus. He could . . . he could have killed Higgins."

"He was *in town* to kill Higgins." I sat back. "That's what he was here for."

"Damn. Mug Lewis." Dan's fingers stopped moving. "I always thought he should be called 'Brain' Lewis anyway. I never thought he was all that good-looking, but he surely is the smartest crook I ever knew."

"Not to mention the luckiest," I added. "The guys who went to kill him . . ."

". . . Chuckie and Rimshot, that's my guess now," Dan added, as if it were self-evident.

"Or whoever." I was open on the subject. "But anyway, they put the gun right up to his head and pulled the trigger and the bullet ran around under his skin and popped out the other side of his face. Didn't penetrate the skull at all."

"I've heard of that." Dan was not the least bit impressed with the Miracle of the Mug.

"You've *heard* of that?"

"Sure." He explained: "The skull is actually very hard. And if it's a small-caliber gun you've got right next to your skull, the bullet doesn't have time to pick up hurling momentum . . ."

". . . hurling momentum?"

"You heard me," he went right on. "And in fact I've heard of guys putting a pistol to the back of somebody's head, execution style, like Mug, and the bullet backing up in the chamber and blowing up in the shooter's hand."

"Get out."

"Strange but true." Dan sat back. "So I assume Mug played dead until the Hardy Boys went away—I mean, there had to be a lot of blood and all to convince them they'd done their duty—and then Mug made it someplace where he rested and thought."

"And his thinking turned to his own personal safety."

I shook my head. "He came back to town to take care of everything, he said." Light was dawning. "And he hired me to toss me off his scent . . . in much the same way we're positing that Dally might have. He deliberately wanted me to look for Jakes's connection, hoping I would find out that Jakes was burning the candle at both ends and I'd come to the conclusion that Jakes iced Ronnard. And that would take care of everything for him. And if you will recall, he told us in the lobby of the Clairmont that his business was now concluded."

"He busted in on Higgins," Danny started, "scared the hell out of him, because Mug was supposed to be a ghost. Higgins was all coked-up anyway. Mug, say, held a gun to Ronn's head, but got his hand, Ronnard's own hand—get the irony of *that*—and forced it around the knife thing, and stabbed it into Ronn's gizzard. Then he pulled it out, planted it in Jakes's room, and what's his damage? He shags the body across the street, only little Jerky Jakes is on his tail, so he has to pop Jakes too, he just doesn't know that Dally and you are so close by. He improvises getting you as his helpmeet. You buy it. He's home free."

"Wherever home would be for Mug at this point. And however improbable this scheme you've just laid out may sound."

"Do you really want to question all this much further?" Danny's fingers started twitching again. "Or would you rather just leave things well enough alone?"

"You mean," I said slowly, reaching for the bottle again, "do I really want to know the truth, or would I rather stick to a comfortable belief."

"The cops say Ronn's a suicide." He folded his arms. "Who are we?"

"We are exactly nobody." I poured. "Not that I care that much for the fact that Mug aided in screwing me up to no end." I sipped. "By the way: You never told me why you were so weird when you met him in the lobby across the street."

"That was nothing." He blinked. "I just knew he was Mug Lewis . . . not Curtis. I recognized him right away. You don't forget that kisser. I wondered why everyone else was ignoring that fact. I guess I wanted to give him the idea that at least I knew who he was."

"You knew right away?"

"I know everything," he told me. "You don't realize that?"

"Yeah, you know everything." I shook my head. "Have I ever told you my theory about knowledge in human history?"

"Please don't."

"Nobody wants to hear my line of thinking today." I took another sip. "But that doesn't seem to stop me. Human history could easily be divided into times when it was better to know, and times when it was better not to know. For example, in Greek culture, the pursuit of truth was one of the highest attainments. By the time you get to medieval Europe, everybody's dedicated to the unknowable mystery. It's better not to know."

"Your Catholic Church liked it that way." At least Dan was willing to participate. "They kept telling your serfs that only the priests could know . . ."

". . . and that the pursuit of knowledge was actually an insult to God. Correct. God knows. That's good enough for the likes of you."

"I see what you're saying." He pursed his lips. "You'd just as soon not know the whole truth in this matter. That's medieval thinking, though, and I'm not certain I can endorse it for myself."

"You think you have to know."

"So do you," he said. "You're just tired."

"But once we know . . ."

". . . we can let it go," he whispered. "I see no reason to mess anybody else up."

"What if it turns out that . . . somebody we know is, you know—wrong?"

"See?" He seemed angered by my remark. "Your problem is that you think some people are all saint and some people are all sinner. The fact is this: Everybody's a little of both."

"Icing a husband"—I smiled coldly—"is hardly a *little* of something."

"You're the worst Taoist on the planet."

"Some insult." I finished my wine. "Some esoteric, arcane insult. And I don't see what it has to do . . ."

And here's where God's Timing came in, once again. Because my sentence was interrupted when Hal called out, "Flap? Your pal Curtis is on the phone."

Dan furrowed his brow. "Curtis?"

"Now how would he know," I reminded him, "that I'd be here at this time of day?"

52

EASY MATH

"Why, hello—Curtis," I said into the phone, holding back, in my voice, the full impact of the irony I felt in my mind. "We were just talking about you."

"Yes." He sounded philosophical, and far away. Or maybe it was just a bad connection. "I'd imagine you were. Probably you and that Danny Frank wise guy."

"Exactly."

"I knew he recognized me." He was silent for a moment. "I thought about popping him, you know."

"I'm sure you thought about popping me, too. But you thought better of it. I think you came to believe that even if I figured out that it was you who killed Higgins, I wouldn't mind because it got him out of Dally's way." I thought that being blunt was called for—or maybe it was the wine talking.

"Who says I killed Higgins?" He was dead calm. "Didn't I just read in the early edition that he bopped himself?"

"There's still the little matter of Jersey Jakes."

"Yeah. I wonder who could have zotzed a cute little guy like him?" Mug's voice was loaded with something, but the connection was so bad that I could barely hear him.

"What did you ever have against Jakes?" I had to know.

"He scares little girls."

In a flash, I saw Jersey's bad outfit: gaudy shirt, cheap slacks—but the standout was his cloth shoes: they were made out of two different colors of material.

"If you don't mind me referring to your friend Ms. Oglethorpe as a little girl," Mug went on. "I don't mean any disrespect. I know she is actually a full-grown woman. But Jakes was scaring her *and* messing me up, helping out Higgins and all—so I thought it best to just . . ."

". . . stop." I said it forcefully enough to make Hal stop what he was doing and to make Dan look over. "I thought you meant Lucy."

"What?" Mug was confused.

"You've just given me too much to handle on an empty stomach and a full wineglass. Just hang on a second, okay?"

"Okay—but this is long-distance, and I don't like to waste money."

"For all I know," I said, "you could be across the street at a pay phone and just saying you were far, far away."

"That would be clever," he admitted, "but the fact is . . ."

". . . so can you just hang on a second? I've got to think."

"So think, already," Mug told me impatiently, "but can you do it fast, is all I'm asking, because I'm on a timetable, here. I called you for a reason, you know."

"Oh." That stopped my gears. "Of course you did. Why did you call?"

"I wanted to conclude our business. It's my last loose end. I wanted to let you know where the remainder of your fee—you know, your money—was."

"My fee?"

"You worked for me, right?"

"Yeah. I guess maybe I did. But the fact is, you hired me under false pretenses."

"I did?" He didn't even bother to try to sound innocent.

"You hired me to find out who you had killed. You already knew. And you already knew why. All I don't know is why you chose that particular moment."

"I see." He paused. "Well, the fact is, I did see the little rat deliver Higgins's body to Ms. Oglethorpe. In fact, that's why I was there the other night, because I'd followed Jakes across the street. I was quite upset because I thought Higgins's body ought to have stayed where it was. And I thought Jakes might spill his guts to you or to Ms. Oglethorpe—guts which I did not wish for him to spill. So I thought I should just take care of the matter then and there, you know: before things got too complicated. That's all."

"Too complicated?" I was just past the edge of no return. "Before things were too complicated, you're saying?" Heat waves were actually rising from my body.

"Take it easy," he said, trying for a soothing tone. "I realize things got a little out of hand for you in your little playhouse, there. But I had *work* to do, bud, you get me?"

"Relationships are all good and well, but when there's work to do, everything else gets pushed back. That's the American way, the American male way. Well, put me down as being primarily against it. Give me libido or give me death, that's what I say to Patrick Henry."

"When did you ever have a libido?" He seemed genuinely puzzled.

"Me? I've got enough for a small emerging country. I just don't like to sling it around."

"Well"—he laughed—"you certainly do hide your light under a bushel."

"Okay. But the point is, you helped screw up one of the world-class understandings, and I'm not that happily disposed to you at the moment."

"I screwed up exactly nothing." His voice rose and quickened. "You needed to know the kind of stuff you found out about Dalliance Oglethorpe—if that's what we're talking about. You ought to be thanking me."

"Thanking you?" I was much louder. "I ought to be finding out where you are and telling police Detective Huyne your precise location."

"Because of what? Higgins killed himself. And I don't feature that the cops will spend too much time on Jakes. What's one more dead rat in a city like Atlanta. Ever been downtown after midnight in that Central City Park?"

"Yeah," I answered, "I know all about the urban rodent problem."

"You like to think of yourself as part of the solution," he shot back, "but just as often, you get things all gummed up and people get away. You know the biggest case of yours that I ever heard about? Some nutty little guy named Lenny Cascade who killed a slew of people and got clean away. Some detective you are. Why would the cops even be interested in *what* you have to say?"

And there you had it, the real crux of the biscuit, as Danny had told me earlier: Why would Huyne even listen to me? And why should I bother telling him?

"You know . . . Curtis," I said slowly, and at half the volume I'd used a moment before, "you're absolutely right."

"I know I am." He was calming too. "I just had to make sure you could see that."

"And the fact is, you actually may have helped me to solve a small case. It's something I was handling in conjunction with the outer world—something about a masher."

"Outer world. Fine by me," he said quickly, "but as I glance at my watch, I notice I am behind my time, and I really have to fly, here. So my point is, I left you a final payment for your services. I left it at the very bar where you stand, in fact."

"How do you know I'm standing? And how did you know . . ."

". . . you sounded too mad to be sitting down," he told me quickly, before I could ask him anything else. "So if you'll just saunter into Ms. Oglethorpe's office and find a blue envelope with your name on it, I think you'll be quite happy with our parting arrangement."

Before I could get in another syllable—like especially how he had known where to find me—he hung up.

I looked over at Hal. "Do you have that caller identification thing on this phone?" I asked him.

"Star 69," he affirmed.

I punched. Here's what I heard: "We're sorry. Touch Star service cannot be used to call this number, trace this number, or enter this number on your list."

"What does that mean?" I asked Hal when I'd told him what the nice recorded lady had said.

"Could be a protected number, a long-distance number, a pay phone, a police station . . ." he started.

". . . I get it. Could really be anything."

"Yeah." He went back to work without asking me a single question, and I found myself envying his lack of curiosity.

I went back and sat with Danny, who was much more interested in my conversation on the telephone.

"Nu?"

"I'll tell you," I said patiently. "That was Curtis. You remember him."

"I do. Where was he?"

"Claimed to be in a land far, far away—but he knew I'd be here now, and I'm never here now, so I have to at least consider that something else is up. Anyway, he admitted nothing, but then he practically confessed, in my book, to killing Higgins. And he also showed no remorse about Jakes. Who, by the way, is most likely the guy who scared little Lucy over at the Clairmont Lounge the other night—that's what I think."

"Because?"

"It comes to me after something Mug just said. How much have I told you about that little deal?"

"I don't really care." He was stone-faced. "All I want to know is what are you going to do now?"

"Now?" I stared at the side of his face. "Well, I'll tell you: All I have to do is work out some simple mathematics. I have to see about putting two and two back together again."

53

TIMING REALLY IS EVERYTHING

And just to prove that He really was the greatest comedian of all, God provided another singular act of timing. Dalliance Oglethorpe walked through the door at exactly that moment.

I looked over at Danny to make sure he understood the hilarity of the situation.

"Well." He smiled and stood. "I think my work here is done." He looked at Dally. "Morning, Ms. Oglethorpe."

She saw him, smiled, nodded, but she mostly had eyes for me.

I guess Dan left then. I wouldn't know. All I could see was her face.

"You look a lot better out of jail than you do in," I said, no tone at all.

"Oh, I do, do I?"

Hal was very busy, and staring at his work with enough intent to stop a clock.

"My office?" she continued.

"I'd say so." I picked up the package Danny had wrapped, put it in my coat pocket, and followed her in.

The office was different than it had been in days, for some reason, looked more like it was supposed to look: messy, comfortable, sepia-toned. She sat behind the desk, dressed in her dark green Mother Hubbard, her hair every which way.

"Hey." Her hand shot to the desktop. "There's an envelope here for you."

"I know," I answered. "It's from Mug Lewis. Open it."

She did. There were ten Madisons and a note. She held it all out to me.

I shook my head. "Read it."

She did: "Flap, How lovely it was. Curtis."

She looked up more or less quizzically.

"It's our game," I reminded her. "The lyric game. It's a line from a song."

" 'How lovely it was'?"

" 'Thanks for the Memories,' " I clued her in.

"What does it mean, exactly?"

"It means," I told her, reaching for the note and the cash, "that he wants me to forget all about everything that's happened in the past few days and go on about my business, whatever that may be, in all the comfort and security fifty thousand dollars can buy. He's hoping that much money would make a guy forget anything."

"I see." She sat back. "And what are the odds that you can actually do that?"

"Forget what's transpired, say, between you and me lately? No odds, no bets." I shuffled the cash, looked at her, and lowered my voice to a whisper. "But I'd love to try."

"Well." That single syllable heaved out a decade's worth of worry. "Me too."

"Okay by me." I folded the money and put it in my pocket—the same one with the present. I took it out, unwrapped it, and tossed the letter opener casually onto the rest of the chaos on her desk. "This belongs to you, I think."

She locked her eyes on it and didn't look up.

After a second or two, I thought it best to break the ice. "Not to worry. I was actually just talking to this Curtis person on the phone, believe it or not, and he all but admitted to taking care of your little problem himself. In fact, it was his fault that hubby was in dutch with the bosses."

"It was Mug's fault?"

"Remember his telling us how two goons killed him because he owed money . . ."

". . . but he didn't stay dead." She remembered.

"The guy he owed money to," I went on, "was a sometime sunbelt drug lord by the name of Ronnard Raay Higgins."

"Jesus." She finally looked up. "The circle is a wheel."

"To quote the old gospel song," I agreed. "But the point is, there's no longer any doubt in my mind about who did what to whom."

"Nice sentence structure." And she smiled for the first time in what seemed like ten years.

"Thanks," I said, "I thought you'd like it. Now as to Huyne, why mess up a good gag? He's willing to think Ronn killed himself, that's okay by me too. Eventually he'll figure out that this mysterious Curtis—who was also staying at the Clairmont—killed Jakes, and he'll set somebody up to finding Curtis, who will not be found because, strictly speaking, he doesn't exist . . ."

". . . or he's already dead."

"Right, depending on how you look at it. And it looks like Jakes is the one who threatened my ersatz client . . ."

". . . the sixteen-year-old septuagenarian . . ."

". . . correct—Lucy. So that 'case' is solved too."

"Flap." She let a wild silence come between us again for a second. "What if my refusal to give Ronn a little bit of money put him in a position to end his own life? That would be my fault, wouldn't it? It would mean that I really did kill him."

"Why do you vex yourself with useless supposition," the Taoist in me said to her. "Skip that. Let's go to dinner. I'm in the money. Life returns to normal."

"Really?" She looked back down at the knife, focused on it hard. "What about this."

"I told you," I began, "I know you didn't do anything with this . . ."

". . . that's right," she interrupted quickly. Then her eyes flashed up at me in an emerald explosion. "And anyway: So what if I did?"

Some thunder you can literally feel. It rattles your chest and pops your ears. I felt it for quite a while as it resonated and then began to fade away, still echoing in the farthest places of my thought canals.

"Really?" I finally managed to say. Then I caught a gleam in her eye that I hadn't seen in years, and I thought I understood. "I see. You don't *want* things to return to normal. You don't want me to think I know all there is to know about you. You don't want me to take a lot of this—I mean what's between us—for granted." I smiled. "You want to be a woman of some mystery."

She blinked once. That's all.

As I had predicted, Huyne discovered that the mysterious Curtis might have had something to do with the death of Jersey Jakes. Huyne hauled me in a few days later and grilled me halfheartedly for around ten minutes about whether or not Curtis was my client. I told him that my client was Lucy—which he already knew was true, he'd checked with her—and that was more or less that.

Ronnard Raay's death was officially declared a suicide. I didn't know if it had been hard for Huyne to let it go at that or not. The handwriting of the fatal note did match Ronn's. Danny found out that all it said was: "Sick of it." What do you know about that? Whether or not he actually killed himself, it seemed he was at least planning something along those lines. Leave well enough alone.

Several of the other notes were clearly written by Jersey Jakes when compared to samples of Jakes's handwriting. This included the last note found on Ronnard's body in Easy. Huyne convinced himself that it was obvious: Jakes was playing both ends against the middle. Case closed—deliberately. It seemed to me that Huyne was just as anxious as I was to look the other way—forget Dally's connection with everything.

I gave Lucy one of the Madisons that Mug had given me. I just sauntered into the Lounge, ordered my orange juice, and left the bill as a tip.

She didn't know why I'd done it, and I couldn't explain. I didn't know why I'd done it either, exactly. But it got her into a better apartment and gave her a cushion to look for a new job. She ended up getting the perfect one of each: She was Reece's assistant at the morgue, and she rented the other half of Reece and Drexel's classy duplex in the Morningside area. They all rode to work together every morning—my little cadre of Waif Street Irregulars was growing. All's well that ends well.

A few days after Huyne had questioned me about Curtis, I got a call from Danny Frank. He called because he thought that I might find it amusing—in a sort of grand theatre way—that Chuckie and Rimshot had been found dead in Mysterio, Georgia, a few miles east of Invisible. They'd been shot from behind in the head, and they were both missing their left hands. Connections with the drug world were suspected.

All I suspected was that Mug Lewis's work really was finally concluded. I never did find out for certain what happened to the hands, but when I called Sonny to fill her in on the juiciest gossip she'd gotten ahold of in years, she told me that Tommy Acree had undergone experimental surgery to attach a new left hand to his arm. She didn't know whether or not it took.

After things had settled down a little, I went to town and bought a nice new gray suit with one of my remaining Madisons. So you can imagine how nice a suit it was. I showed up at Easy one Tuesday night around seven-thirty, dressed to the nines: the new suit, a crisp white shirt, a five-hundred-dollar silk tie, a haircut, and even a dab of Romeo Gigu at my neck. Hal had to look twice before he even recognized me.

"Flap?" His eyes bugged. "Jesus."

"Well," I told him, "make up your mind, which is it?"

"I'm not sure." He gave me the once-over twice. "Marcia? Get out here."

Her face appeared in the food window, and she also gave a classic double take. "For God's sake." She shook her head and looked at Hal. "Who died?"

I was pondering the answer to just that question when Dalliance Oglethorpe appeared in the doorway of her office. She was in a plum-colored gauzy thing that choked a guy's first sentence. Pearls at her neck, hair perfectly disordered, I could feel her cheek from across the room.

Hal whistled once. Marcia offered a sailor's curse. Several regulars applauded.

"Ready?" I asked her.

She locked eyes with me and nodded wordlessly.

"Dinner at eight," I told Hal as I moved across the floor toward the angel eyes. "Reckless abandon by midnight."

"In your dreams," Hal said to the back of my head, but his heart wasn't in it.

"Ms. Oglethorpe." I offered her my arm.

"Mr. Tucker." She took it.

"What the hell is going on here?" Marcia asked Hal. "They never acted like this before. Or dressed like this before, for that matter. It's like they don't even know each other."

"That's the point," Dally said, her eyes locked on mine, as we drifted out the door.

We're human, all of us. We can't help the fact that we're not perfect. One of the main things that makes us imperfect is our constant impatience with the status quo. We want change. We're restless without it. Maybe it's because we only truly understand the world by contrast. How do you know the splendor of a glorious sunrise without the terror of a moonless night? How do you come to love the quenching of a downpour without the drought beforehand? How can you truly appreciate the angel's kiss without first being convinced that you'll never touch her lips again? Contrast of opposites. That's why God divided the day from the night, the land from the water, the man from the woman—so that they'd know each other when they came back together, and show a little appreciation. So the sunrise that knits the night and day together *can* be glorious, so that the ocean will always want the shore's dry land—so that the man will never get used to seeing the woman without saying to himself, "My God, who *is* that amazing person?"

This is why we like mystery: the contrast of knowing and not knowing, questions and answers, doubt and discovery. In the marriage of these opposites, we know God's best plan. And what is God's best plan? I'll tell you. In my book it starts: "Dinner at eight, reckless abandon by midnight."

ABOUT THE AUTHOR

Phillip DePoy is the acclaimed author of four previous Flap Tucker mysteries: *Easy; Too Easy; Easy as One, Two, Three; Dancing Made Easy*, and an essay and photo collection, *Messages from Beyond*. He has published short fiction, poetry, and criticism in *Story, Southern Poetry Review, Xanadu, Yankee*, and other magazines, and is an established presence in theater, music, and folklore in the Southeast. He lives in Atlanta, Georgia.